# ARRESTED HEARTS

Visit us at www.boldstrokesbooks.com

# By the Author

Songs Unfinished

Arrested Hearts

# ARRESTED HEARTS

*by*
Holly Stratimore

2016

# ARRESTED HEARTS

ISBN 13: 978-1-62639-809-2

THIS TRADE PAPERBACK ORIGINAL IS PUBLISHED BY
BOLD STROKES BOOKS, INC.
P.O. BOX 249
VALLEY FALLS, NY 12185

FIRST EDITION: DECEMBER 2016

CREDITS
EDITORS: VICTORIA VILLASENOR AND CINDY CRESAP
PRODUCTION DESIGN: SUSAN RAMUNDO
COVER DESIGN BY MELODY POND

# Acknowledgments

When I signed my first Bold Strokes Books contract, I had no idea just how much my life was about to change. My preconception of a writer's life was of a very solitary existence. Although it's true that I need time alone to write, I've learned that I am never alone in the process. I am now a member of a very close-knit community that is, in every sense of the word, a family. We love and support each other, we share our struggles, we read each other's books and blogs, we interact on social media, we work tables together at Pride festivals and other author events, and we pitch each other's books—even more so than our own sometimes. I now have people in my life that I care about as true friends, even though I have yet to meet some of them in person. We all know the power of the written word, and through them, our connections are strong.

It would be impossible to name everyone who has touched my life since the publication of *Songs Unfinished*, but there are a few who deserve special thanks. Cathy Frizzell, thank you for taking me under your wing, and for being a friend and mentor to me. You are one of the most talented people I've ever met, and what a bonus to find out we're both guitar players! I look forward to jamming with you in Provincetown every year now. (Sending me pun jokes on my Facebook page doesn't hurt, either, but I will always be the Punster Master!) Jean Copeland, I love being your sidekick at the BSB Pride tables. Even though you knocked me out of a GCLS award category, I could not be happier that you WON with your awesome debut. (I'm not jealous at all. Really, I'm not! I'll still put my books next to yours on the table.) My love and thanks to the rest of the BSB "New England Gang": Sophia Kell Hagin, Jennifer Lavoie, Fiona Riley, Emily Smith, and TJ Thomas, as well as our adopted New Yorkers, Aurora Rey and Maggie Cummings. Thanks to the numerous authors who continue to inspire me.

Lorraine, I can't even begin to say how much your friendship means to me. No matter where our lives have taken us, I've always known that I could count on you. Teri, it's so awesome that we've reconnected and discovered that we both have a passion for writing. Who knew those crazy stories I wrote in high school would lead to this! I guess English class wasn't so TEAR-able after all!

Thanks to Radclyffe, Sandy Lowe, and the entire Bold Strokes Books team for everything you do for the LGBT literary world. I am so proud and honored to be part of your amazing organization.

A great big thanks to all the readers. It's been a blast connecting with you and you'll never know how much I appreciate your support. You're the ones who make it all worth it.

Victoria, more than anyone, you can appreciate how far I've come as a writer. I am beyond grateful for your guidance, your passion for what you do, your patience and invaluable advice, the extraordinary time and effort you put into every page, and most of all, your heart. You are truly a gift. Thank you, again, for taking this journey with me. I couldn't have done it without you.

Cindy, thanks for going through this manuscript with your eagle eye and sharing some valuable writing lessons along the way. Sarah, thanks for your amazing proofreading talents and for taking time to share your feedback.

To my family, whose love has carried me through every day of my life. Special thanks to my "other mom," Jane. I know Mom is smiling on us all, giving us strength, and inspiring us to be kind.

Penny, my love, what would I do without you? I am so fortunate to be sharing my life with you. Thank you for all you do, every day, to make my life better than I imagined possible. A huge thanks for the book cover idea—you better believe you've captured my heart, baby! I love you to the moon and back.

# Dedication

To the brave women and men who willingly put their lives on the line every day as law enforcement officers.

Although *Arrested Hearts* takes place in a very real town, my depiction of its police force is purely fictional. Any creative liberties I've taken are for the sake of the characters and the story. Any errors are solely my responsibility. I have the utmost respect for the Portsmouth Police Department, and I love this wonderful community. Thank you for your commitment to keeping us safe.

Special thanks to my father, who served for many years as a part-time police officer when I was a kid. I cherish the example you set as a model citizen and an even better person. I love you, Dad.

# CHAPTER ONE

Randi's head swam as she forced her eyes open, only to flinch at the stranger in bed beside her. She carefully slid out from beneath the covers. *Please don't wake up.* She scrambled into her clothes and crept down the stairs, grateful not only that none of them creaked, but also that she could remember where the front door was.

It was still dark when she stepped outside. The warm breeze felt good against her skin, a welcome surprise in late April before dawn. She had the day off and needed to get back to work on the car. She put in the new transmission last time. Today she was replacing the alternator and some hoses. Stevie would have been proud. She wished he could be there when she fired it up for the first time.

She showered as soon as she got home and wolfed down a bowl of sugary cereal. She poured coffee in an oversized travel mug, added a generous spoonful of sugar, grabbed some CDs, and headed downstairs. She glanced across the finished basement at the home gym she would be using later in the day. *Yeah, right. Who are you kidding?* A rigorous workout was probably what she needed last night. She cringed as the soreness in her thighs reminded her of the alternative exercise she'd chosen. *Wrong choice. Again.*

She shook her head. Right now, she had to get going on that alternator. Once in the garage, she looked her over: a classic '69 flaming red Chevy Camaro, destined to reclaim its glory as a top-of-the-line muscle car by the time she got done with it. It still needed a lot of work, but shit, when all was said and done, she was going to be beautiful.

Randi put on her favorite disc, Passion Play's self-titled debut album. They were friends of Randi's. Actually, she couldn't honestly say she was friends with the whole band, though she did know them all. She'd met Nikki Razer, the lead singer, about four years ago, when she pulled Nikki over for speeding. Randi hadn't been able to shake Nikki like the other women who paid their tickets by sleeping with her. She and Nikki were too much alike, she guessed—satisfied with being friends and occasional sex buddies. It was safer that way. They both knew the pain of having a thing for a woman who was in love with someone else.

She hadn't seen Nikki much since the album came out almost two years ago. Passion Play had gone on tour, opening for a hot young singer named Sierra Sparks right after they got their recording contract. Now their second album was out, and they were headlining their own shows across the US.

Randi slid open a drawer of the red double-decker tool chest. She looked at the row of combination wrenches, neatly arranged in order by size, and selected two of them—she already knew which sizes she would need. She organized the tools on a rolling cart that held several rags, heavy-duty plastic cups she used for the removed hardware, cans of WD-40 and 3-IN-ONE oil, and a grease-stained, faded blue, cotton ball cap. She slicked her hair behind her ears and tugged the cap onto her head. Her faded jeans had a hole in one knee, and their frayed hems bunched at the tops of her rawhide work boots. So what if she looked like a grease monkey? She was comfortable. It beat wearing the uniform she didn't deserve to wear. She removed a pack of Marlboros from the sleeve of her black pocket T-shirt and tossed it onto a wood top workbench next to the tool chest.

After pressing play on the boom box, she turned her attention to her task. She visualized Shawn, the gorgeous guitar player in the band, on stage wildly strumming her guitar. The vision damn well *didn't* include Shawn's girlfriend and fellow guitarist, Jaymi. *God, she's smokin' when she performs.* As she ducked under the hood of the car, she fantasized about Shawn's rusty brown bed-head hair that she kept cut above her collar, and her bangs that always seemed to grow out of control.

She imagined brushing Shawn's hair off her face so she could get a better look at her hazel eyes, which were full of angst and desire when she sang. If that weren't enough, there was that compact, butch body that gleamed with sweat when she lost herself in a song.

She tugged her jeans away from her suddenly aching clit and sighed. *Guess I'll hit the club tonight after all.*

# CHAPTER TWO

At thirty-three, Randi had figured she'd be done with the club scene by now. She knew there were healthier ways to spend a Thursday night, but today, she couldn't stand the thought of staying in. At least here there was a chance she'd forget about her problems for a while. Or get laid.

She adjusted her brown leather jacket and made her way to the bar.

"Evening, Randi. Your usual?" Sherrie popped the cap on a Heineken. "What's got you all black and blue, sweet thang?"

Sherrie's reference to her outfit—black jeans and a cobalt blue collared shirt over a solid black tee, made her smile.

She slid a generous tip in Sherrie's direction. "You, baby."

"Me? I haven't laid a hand on you."

"My point exactly." Randi chuckled. "What time do you get off tonight?"

"That depends." Sherrie gestured for her to come closer.

"On what?" Randi took a pull off her drink and leaned forward on the bar.

Sherrie bent over to mirror the pose. "On how quickly you can seduce me."

She drank in Sherrie's amazing brown eyes that were as dark as her skin, and a kinky do she ached to run her fingers through. She lightly stroked Sherrie's silky cheek. "Oh, how you tease…"

They straightened up in unison and Sherrie winked as she backed away. They played this game all the time, but nothing ever came of it.

Randi would sleep with her in a heartbeat, but she respected Sherrie's self-imposed vow to never date the club's clientele. Everyone hit on the bartenders, and she often wondered where Sherrie met people she *could* potentially date.

Randi scanned the crowd for familiar faces and saw Megan MacGregor. Megan was an EMT, so their professions intersected frequently. She'd just seen Megan yesterday when they both responded to a motor vehicle accident. A drunk driver had slammed into a utility pole. The front passenger hadn't been wearing her seat belt and had suffered a serious head injury.

Megan was a petite—but well-muscled—bundle of energy, who rarely came off the dance floor. At the moment, though, she was sitting alone at a corner table. Tiny multicolored lights bounced off her solemn face.

Randi slid into the booth next to her and tilted her head sympathetically. "This is the last place you should be if you're nursing a heartache, ya know."

Megan looked at her with moist, puppy dog brown eyes and forced a smile. "How is it you haven't made detective yet? You read people like a friggin' open book."

"I'm not that ambitious. Besides, I'm still on the waiting list for K-9 training." She brushed back a lock of Megan's dark chocolate hair. "You wanna talk about it?"

Megan let out a huff and slouched back in the booth. She rolled her beer between her palms. "I lost that patient yesterday. She flat-lined before we could get to the hospital."

That explained it. Randi shivered at the memory of the scene and consciously pushed away her emotions. That meant she'd be spending time in court for a case of vehicular manslaughter. The driver, of course, walked away from the wreck with minor cuts and bruises. In cuffs, but walked away. Asshole.

She wrapped an arm around Megan's shoulder. She signaled a server with her free hand and ordered them each another beer. With only three years under her belt, Megan still hadn't mastered the art of disassociating emotionally from her job. She wondered how someone with such a big heart handled it. And why she was still single.

After finishing the beer, Megan loosened up and agreed to a dance. Megan usually pulled her hair back in a ponytail while working, but tonight, she wore it down. Randi watched her work up a sweat, and after three or four songs, she was actually smiling and flipping her hair wildly with the beat. Randi smiled at the transformation, envying her free spirit. *God, she's beautiful.*

Megan grabbed her hand and twirled her around, then grabbed Randi's belt loops and pulled her close, locking eyes with her the entire time. She enjoyed letting Megan lead. The song changed to a slow one, and Megan interlaced her fingers behind Randi's neck. Randi leaned forward and tightened her hold around Megan's waist. Their breasts pressed together. Megan's breath was hot in her ear, sending a tingle through her core, which grew more urgent when she nibbled the lobe.

"Come home with me," Megan whispered, before tracing a pattern of kisses down her neck, and then across her jawline. When Megan's mouth reached her chin, Randi swiftly dipped her head and caught her lips. Megan moaned and kissed her back, hard, claiming her tongue with hers. They didn't wait for the song to end. She followed Megan home. *She's a damn fine alternative to spending the night wanting what I can't have.*

## CHAPTER THREE

"So Jule, you in or out?"

Julianna Chapin stared blankly at her friend Kathy, who was nudging her. She could barely hear Kathy's voice over the thundering club music. As usual, the club was packed on a Friday night. She hitched herself up slightly in the wooden corner bench.

"I'm sorry, what?"

"We're making bets on whether those two leave together." Kathy pointed toward the dance floor. "Loser buys the next round."

Jule didn't bother looking. "Who cares?"

"Geez, you're no fun anymore."

"Kathy, leave her alone," said Brenda. "Besides, if she loses, we'll all be drinking Pepsi."

"It's Dr Pepper." Jule grew more annoyed by the minute.

"Whatever," said Kathy, leaning back and crossing her thick arms. Kathy was a five ten big-boned woman with a bleach-streaked buzz cut and a biting attitude. She was formidable to strangers, but Jule knew she was all show. She glared at Jule. "You have to snap outta this sometime, Jule. You're getting to be a real drag."

The fourth member of the party, Toni, held up her hands. "Jesus, Kathy. Don't be an asshole! You know what she's been through."

Jule sat in silence, looking from one friend to another. They'd been doing this for years—going out for drinks after work every Friday night. They all worked at Northeast Scientific, an assembly plant down the street from the club, so they spent a great deal of time together. They rarely engaged in any meaningful conversations, though. Most of their talk revolved around two things: bitching about work or trying to get laid.

Jule sighed heavily. "I'm done with this."

Toni said, "Done with what?"

Jule scootched out from behind the table and stood up. "This!" she repeated, gesturing with her arms. "Wasting time here, doing *this*. I'm going home."

"What?" Kathy protested. "You can't go home. You're the designated driver."

"Sherrie can call you a cab," said Jule. "For God sakes, you guys, look at you! Look at us! *This* is a drag. We're wasting our lives. I can't do this anymore. I need more."

"So what're you saying, we're not good enough for you now because *you've* stopped drinking?" Now Toni looked irritated. "What's next, biblical quotes about how sinful we are?"

"Will you two shut up!" said Brenda. "Listen, Jule, we all know losing Casey was hard on you—"

"Losing her? *Losing her?* It's not like she broke up with me or left me for another woman. I didn't *lose* her, Brenda. She died. She dropped dead of a heart attack right in front of me! She was thirty-two years old—same age as us." She couldn't help it—tears welled up in her eyes. "I don't want to be next. Don't you understand? I don't want to live this way anymore. I want...more." She shrugged into her denim jacket. "I'll see you around."

She turned and left, not bothering to respond to their continued entreaties.

She'd only been on the road for ten minutes when she looked with disgust into her rearview and saw blue lights. She hastily swiped tears off her cheeks and steered onto the shoulder.

"Just my luck," she sighed, watching the figure approach. "A friggin' female cop. I'm so screwed."

"Good evening, miss."

Jule handed over her license and registration before being asked. The officer looked them over. "Do you know why I stopped you?"

"Well, I know I wasn't speeding." She bit her lip. She hadn't meant to sound sarcastic, but it felt like her nerves were exposed, raw and tight. *This is so not what I need right now.*

"No. I pulled you over because of your bumper sticker."

Jule glared at her, now even more annoyed. *Great. Just great. A homophobic female cop.* "Since when are rainbow stickers against the law, Officer..." Jule squinted to read the name badge. "Hartwell?"

The cop chuckled. "I'd have to pull myself over if that was the case."

*Okay, so I hope that's good for me.* There was something familiar about her, but Jule couldn't place where she'd seen her before.

"Actually, Ms. Chapin, I was referring to the other sticker. Is it true? Is your German shepherd really smarter than an honor student?"

Her jaw dropped open in disbelief. "That's why you stopped me? To ask me about my dog?" It was bad enough she'd pulled her over for no reason, but the officer's disarming smile was making her stomach do funky things. It pissed her off. "Don't you have any real criminals to catch?"

The officer leaned on the door and looked directly at her. Jule almost gasped at the intensity of her deep brown eyes. "Actually, you were weaving a bit. Have you been drinking tonight, Julianna?"

"Ugh. Please don't call me that. It's Jule, and no, I haven't been drinking."

"You mind stepping out of the car, *Jule*?"

"Are you serious? I had two Dr Peppers. That's it."

"Mmm, Dr Pepper. That's strong stuff." Officer Hartwell opened the door. "So you won't mind walking a straight line and proving me wrong?" She grinned as Jule swung out of the truck.

"Fine."

"Just go down to that sign there and turn around."

"Fine."

"And if that's all you do that's straight, that's cool with me."

Jule spun around with another retort on the tip of her tongue.

The officer twirled her index finger as instruction for Jule to turn back around. "Uh-uh-uh. No stopping and starting. That's cheating."

Jule relented. When she reached the sign and reversed direction, she saw that Officer Hartwell wasn't watching her at all, but was inspecting the interior of her truck with a Maglite. She cringed at the thought of what the cop was viewing. Fast food bags and wrappers. Empty Dunkin' Donuts coffee cups. Half a pack of Camels.

A half-empty bottle of, yes, Dr Pepper, in the console. When she completed her walk, the officer held up a tiny zipped plastic bag in front of her face.

"On your way to a party?"

"What the?" Jule stared at the bag of pot. *Damn it, Casey!*

"Looks like there's enough here to catch you a nasty fine."

"It's not mine."

Officer Hartwell smiled. She seemed to be having difficulty maintaining a serious demeanor. "This *is* your truck, isn't it? And unless there's someone buried under your collection of trash, you appear to be alone, which makes a pretty good case for possession charges against *you.*"

"I'm telling you, I didn't know it was there. It belonged to my girlfriend."

"So, perhaps we should call her and confirm that. I'm sure she wouldn't want you taking the heat for her carelessness."

"No! You can't…call her."

"I understand why you want to protect—"

"You can't call her. She's…she can't be reached."

The officer tilted her head sympathetically. "I'm sorry. I didn't mean to be insensitive. She broke your heart, didn't she?"

"Look, just do what you gotta do, all right? You need to arrest me?" She turned her back to her, faced the truck, and put her wrists together behind her back. "Go ahead and cuff me. Let's get this over with."

Jule waited for the feel of cold metal handcuffs, but instead felt the officer's hot breath in her ear, causing her to inhale sharply.

"You know, there's a more pleasant way of handling this."

She grasped one of Jule's hands, spun her around, and backed her against the truck. With their bodies pressed together and lips almost touching, Officer Hartwell said, "I could follow you back to your place."

Jule's ragged breath rendered her speechless, caught off guard by the proposal. Her head swam. Officer Hartwell's powerful physique was exhilarating, but it was the look in her eyes that had Jule considering saying yes. So filled with need and desire it was almost heartbreaking. Not to mention the woman was beautiful—

as in, makes-me-weak-in-the-knees-and-drool-all-over myself, and please-don't-wake-me-from-this-dream beautiful.

The erotic haze subsided and, from some repressed chasm within her, she retrieved her principles. She looked directly into her eyes. "I'd rather be arrested."

The cop's head jerked back ever so slightly, and Jule immediately regretted her words. The officer looked hurt. She tried not to care. The woman deserved it, using her position that way. Jule wasn't about to lower herself to sexual favors like some cheap whore. The officer quickly recovered though, and backed off.

"I'm not going to arrest you." She slipped the evidence into her hip pocket. "If I say I never saw this, then you say I never made a pass at you. Fair enough?"

Jule shrugged. "Fair enough." She released a lungful of air in relief. "Can I go now?"

"Yes."

She climbed into her truck and closed the door.

Officer Hartwell leaned in through the window and said, "Shame on whoever hurt you tonight."

She opened her mouth to say something but quickly realized the officer had shocked her into silence again. In her side view mirror, she watched Officer Hartwell return to her vehicle. The cruiser burned rubber as it maneuvered around her and disappeared into the night.

Jule couldn't determine what made her more furious—the audacity of the police officer's behavior, or the temptation to accept her invitation.

❖

As soon as Jule stepped inside her century-old New Englander, her black-faced German shepherd, Sirius, greeted her. It was hard to believe the 80-pound beast used to curl up on her lap. Two years ago, she had adopted him when he was eight weeks old, after he'd been rescued from an abusive home. His mother had been so malnourished and ill that she couldn't be saved. Only five of the eight puppies survived, and Sirius was one of them.

"Hey, buddy!" She took his head between her hands and scrubbed the thick fur. "Ready to go out?" He trotted to the back door, sat, and waited for Jule's next instruction. She had installed a doggie door for him, but whether he had to go or not, a walk together when she came home was their routine, no matter what the hour.

She wandered the fenced-in yard with him and reflected on the evening's events. Being the only sober person in a party of drunks was an enlightening experience. Had she acted that idiotic when she was drinking, too? *What a bunch of losers we are.* Losers. *Great way to think of your friends. Or yourself.*

There had to be more to life than wiring medical equipment for forty hours a week and spending the other waking hours consuming fried food and alcohol. It wasn't that Kathy, Toni, or Brenda were bad people, but tonight Jule had felt like an outsider. How well did they really know each other? How well had she and Casey really known each other?

She hugged herself and looked up into the clear April sky. She took in a deep breath of crisp cool air and closed her eyes. Casey's face came to mind. She'd been blond-haired and blue-eyed, with a killer smile. She'd been so wild and full of life. Other than her hot temper, Casey had been a lot of fun. She'd hated doctors and scoffed at every health fad that came along. The beautiful, lively image morphed into the woman dying in her arms. *I don't want to be next.*

"Come on, Sirius. Time to go in."

Sirius eagerly followed her to the kitchen. She tossed him a couple of biscuits, and then he lay down on a blanket in the corner of the room. She dragged the garbage bin to the fridge, and after she had filled it with frozen dinners, chicken nuggets, and other assorted processed foods, she moved on to the cupboards and did the same with the potato chips, boxed sides, and so on. She hesitated fleetingly, thinking she really should be donating this stuff, but why clog other people's arteries? She was doing them a favor by disposing of it.

"Things are going to change around here, Sirius." She tied off a bag and started filling another one. "For one, I'm going to finish all these projects on the house." She hefted the two bags and carried them out to the detached garage. She returned with a cardboard box and gave Sirius a quick scratch behind the ears. "And I'm going to learn to cook. Hell, I may even become a vegetarian. Don't give me that look—I'll still broil you a steak every weekend." She loaded the box with every ounce of alcohol and soft drink she had. That, too, went into the garage.

"Looks like I'm going grocery shopping in the morning."

Things were going to change, all right. No more fast food. No more drunken weekends. No more wasted time. Her health mattered. Her life mattered.

Most of all, her heart mattered. *I deserve to be happy.*

## CHAPTER FOUR

Randi rolled over and groaned at the insistent ringing of her phone. Only one person called her this early in the morning, especially on a weekend. The caller ID confirmed her assumption. She resisted the temptation to let it go to voice mail and fumbled for the receiver.

"Hello, Mother."

"Morning, sweetie. Did I wake you?"

"It's okay. I have to get up anyway." She swung her legs over the side of the bed, sat up, and ran her fingers through her hair. She straightened out her twisted tank and then did the same to her boxers when she stood. Reruns of old nightmares had her tossing and turning all night. *I'd be better off sleeping naked.*

"I wanted to catch you early in case you had to work today."

"I'm off this weekend." She walked down the hall into the kitchen. She wedged the handset between her ear and shoulder and lit a cigarette.

"Oh, good."

Randi pictured her mother chewing her lip—a habit that replaced smoking a few years ago. She did it more often when she struggled for something to say.

"I'm going to visit your father today."

*I knew it.*

"I was hoping you would come with me."

"I can't."

"You just said you're off—"

"I have plans."

"Something more important than your father? When's the last time you saw him? Or called him?"

Randi took a deep drag and dropped onto a kitchen chair. She flicked ashes into an ashtray. Scrubbing her eye with the heel of her hand, she strained to keep her cool.

"Miranda? You still there?"

"Yeah. I'm here." Only her mother got away with calling her Miranda, but it still made her wince. *Named after "Miranda Rights." What a joke. If they'd only known the kind of cop I'd become.*

"Sweetheart." The irritation in her mother's tone subsided. "Sweetheart, you need to talk about it—"

"I don't want to talk about it. It's not going to change anything. It hasn't before, and it won't now."

"I'm not talking about changing things. I'm talking about *dealing* with things. It will help you to talk about it, just like it helped me."

She nearly knocked her chair over as she stood. "You mean lock me up in a nuthouse like they did to you? No way." She paced a worn path from the table to the counter and back again.

"Don't call it that, Miranda. It's a hospital. I'd be dead if those people hadn't helped me."

"Mom, don't say stuff like that."

"Well, it's true. They saved my life."

Randi snuffed out her cigarette.

"Look, honey, what's important is that it doesn't matter who you talk to, as long as you talk about it. You must have friends you confide in?"

Who? Nikki? Her fuck buddy who was always out of town living her dream as a rock star? *Like she wants me dragging her down.* Shawn? Same as Nikki, minus the fuck buddy part. Megan, someone she barely knew outside crime scenes and tangled sheets? *No way. Why spoil her innocence?* Sherrie? *Nope. She listens to enough of people's problems tending bar.*

"Yeah. All right. I'll talk to my friends. Okay?"

"Good."

Randi pulled the carafe from the coffeemaker, placed it in the sink, and turned on the faucet. "So how's Aunt Sandy?" she asked, referring to her mother's sister, and housemate.

Her mom didn't miss a beat, despite the sudden subject change. After another ten minutes of chitchat about their present lives, Randi hung up, poured a strong cup of black coffee, and lit another Marlboro Red. There had been no other mention of visiting her father, or of his upcoming parole hearing in June. Her mother knew not to push the subject.

When she finished her coffee and smoke, she hopped in the shower. Dismissing the conversation with her mother, she let her thoughts wander to the woman she had pulled over last night. *Damn, she was feisty.* When Randi stopped people, she typically got one of two attitudes: nervous and apologetic, or indignant. This one was neither. This one was all confidence and knew damn well she had no reason to stop her. She chuckled. She really *had* pulled her over because of the bumper sticker about her dog. The rainbow decal didn't hurt either.

*She must think I'm an ass. She probably knew I made her get out and walk just so I could check her out.* Jule Chapin. *Shit.* She even remembered her name. The look in her eyes just about broke Randi's heart when she first saw her. She'd been crying, her eyes were still slightly red and puffy, and clearly the reason the SUV was weaving a little. Her eyes were pale golden brown. Her hair was chestnut, with streaks of gold and fell to shoulder length. Even in old jeans, work boots, and an oversized sweatshirt, she was a head turner.

Randi headed to the garage with a handful of CDs, thinking she would probably wind up at the club again tonight, seeking release. *Thinking about yet another woman I can't have. What the fuck is wrong with me?*

## CHAPTER FIVE

Jule stared at the empty space beside her and hoped to see an indentation in the pillow that would indicate Casey's presence, something to suggest her premature death was just a horrific dream. Casey had enjoyed making them pancakes on Sunday mornings. If she wasn't too hung over, that is.

There wouldn't be pancakes today.

They had been together for almost a year when Casey moved in, and they'd had so many plans for this house. It was an old fixer-upper Jule bought cheap. It wasn't much to look at from the outside, but other than keeping up with mowing the lawn, they had focused their initial efforts on the interior. People could say what they wanted about blue-collar workers, but Jule made damn good money at her factory job. The economy had forced two layoffs in the past six years, but Jule had survived them and stuck it out. Thankfully, business was picking up again. With over a decade invested in the company, she had a growing 401k and a sizable nest egg in her savings account. She knew there weren't many single women her age who could say they owned their own home, and she took pride in all she'd managed to build on her own.

She made herself comfortable on the back porch. Sirius roamed the yard while she sipped her morning brew and smoked a cigarette. She flipped open a notebook.

Yesterday, after she had restocked her refrigerator and cupboards with exclusively fresh, organic, and natural foods, she had gone from room to room with the notepad and made a separate page for each room of the house. She was disgusted with the results. Thick dust. Dirty carpets. Un-swept floors. Windows fogged with cigarette smoke. Her mother would have a fit.

Every room had at least one project that either she or Casey had started and never finished. They were always more interested in partying. She hadn't worked on the house at all since Casey's passing eight months ago.

When she had finished going through the house, she continued on to the garage and then spent over an hour removing trash and vacuuming out her GMC Jimmy. A wave of shame had swept over her when she thought of the impression it must have given Officer Hartwell.

Heat rose in her cheeks as she remembered the feel of that hard body pressed against her own. She shook her head and shoved any thoughts of the hot cop out of her mind. She needed to learn to be present, to be in the moment. She'd let things go in her life, but damn it, she needed to give herself a break. She'd taken time to grieve. No one would fault her for her recent lack of motivation.

She spent the rest of the day on routine housework, figuring it was best to get that out of the way before she resumed work on renovations. Going through a rebellious phase during her time with Casey had been liberating in many ways, but now it felt good to be putting her life back in order. She wanted to find meaning and value in her life again. She was done wasting time.

"You ready to go in, Sirius?" She extinguished her cigarette, thinking that giving up this nasty habit was priority one.

She went upstairs to the master bathroom and undressed. She scrutinized her naked body in front of the mirror and was repulsed. Without even stepping on a scale, she guessed she was about twenty pounds overweight. What happened to the taut abdomen she used to have? What happened to the toned arms and legs? Her skin was pale. Her hair needed trimming. Her shoulders slumped into an unhealthy posture developed from years of working hunched over a bench. She turned and looked at her backside. Since when did her ass and thighs jiggle like that? Since when did her butt cheeks resemble cottage cheese? No wonder the last time she'd bought jeans she had gone up two waist sizes.

She scowled at her reflection. *Why in God's name would that gorgeous cop want to sleep with me?*

She started another list on things to change with herself.

After showering, she fired up her computer, opened her notebook to a blank page, and began a list of local gyms and rates. She called her health insurance company and signed up for a quit smoking program. Then she headed to her chosen gym, where she paid for a year's membership and scheduled appointments with a trainer and a nutritionist. She went next door and signed up for a yoga class. She then made stops at the drug store for nicotine patches and vitamins, the bookstore to buy books on nutrition, and the salon for a haircut. She was home by one. She ate a salad topped with tuna for lunch and went back to work on the house. Her body and mind buzzed with excitement, as if she'd just awakened from hibernation and wouldn't need to sleep again for a month. She was off to a good start. She needed to keep up the momentum.

She scrubbed floors and woodwork, scraped off peeling paint, sanded the banister, and filled boxes with scrap wood, rusty nails, and junk. The strong scent of sawdust assaulted her senses, triggering a memory of helping her father refinish an old dresser. She must have been around ten. She smiled, thinking of how grateful she was for the work ethic he'd instilled in her. How strange, that details of her childhood that had seemed so insignificant loomed large in her mind now. She'd never given much thought to how her parents' influence might have shaped her own life.

Maybe they weren't so nerdy after all. Come hell or high water, she was going to follow her parents' example of stability and routine. If that meant putting a little distance between herself and her barfly friends—or anyone else who might be a bad influence for that matter—so be it.

She wondered how they'd feel about that. *I guess I'll find out who my true friends are, won't I?*

## CHAPTER SIX

R andi was on second shift again this week, and she was grateful last night's shift was uneventful, unlike tonight's chaos. She was already at the second of two car accidents, though there were no serious injuries, and her mood brightened when Megan's unit showed up at the second. They were too busy to interact on a personal level, but they discreetly exchanged smiles and winks. They hadn't gotten together since that one night, but there hadn't been any awkwardness. It was clear neither of them wanted anything serious, and it was good they were on the same page.

Between accidents, Randi had to go to a grocery store and question two teenage girls who were caught shoplifting. As much as she hated being a cop, there were times when she was grateful for the opportunity to give teens a nudge in the right direction.

"One of you girls want to tell me what happened?"

They studied their hands in their laps. Middle class kids, Randi guessed. Too young to get jobs for spending money. Desperate to fit in. Probably not allowed to wear makeup yet, which was why they were trying to steal it today. Randi cleared her throat to get their attention. They stole nervous glances at each other, and then shyly looked at her. Carly, the pudgy curly-headed blonde, broke first.

"It's all Tiffany's fault! She dared me to do it!"

Her friend gasped. "I did not! You liar!" The skinny girl turned to Randi with wide eyes. "She's lying! I didn't dare her to do anything. I just told her she'd look better with some makeup, I didn't know she was going to *steal* it!" She looked at her friend. "You're just jealous 'cause I'm skinny and pretty—"

"Hey!" Randi interrupted. "I thought you two were friends?"

They averted their eyes again and mumbled, "We are."

"Well, I don't know about you, but where I come from, friends don't rat each other out. And I'll tell you something else; it'll get you killed in prison." That got their attention. Randi could tell the one called Carly was about to cry. "Let me ask you both something. What do you want to be after you graduate?" This question always threw them.

Carly wiped the back of her hand across her eyes and then looked at Randi questioningly, as if she wasn't sure she was genuinely interested.

"A veterinarian. Or a dog trainer. I love animals."

Randi smiled. The answer didn't surprise her. Carly was wearing Snoopy earrings, plastic cat-shaped barrettes, and a pink scoop-neck top covered in pictures of puppies. "I love animals, too. What about you, Tiffany?"

"I don't know." She shrugged.

Randi leaned forward on her thighs and folded her hands. "Come on, you must have some idea. If you could do anything, anything at all, what would it be?"

"Well, I like clothes. I like to draw, too. So…I don't know, maybe I could be a fashion designer."

Randi smiled. "Now you're talking. Listen, ladies, the point is that neither one of you said you wanted a life of crime. But that's *exactly* what you're starting out with if you do this again. If the store presses charges, you'll have a juvenile record and a bad reputation that will really screw things up for you. Say you want to make a little money while you're still in school, or you want to buy a car when you turn sixteen, so you decide to look for a job. Who's going to hire you? It might blow your chances of getting into college, too.

"Now, I'm sure that if you apologize to the store manager, I can convince her not to press charges. The worst that might happen is that she might ban you from the store. You're only what, fourteen? Fifteen? Be a shame to throw away your futures over fifteen bucks' worth of cosmetics. Don't you agree?"

They both nodded.

"Good." Randi stood. "I'm going to go talk to the manager and your parents and let them know that everything's cool, and that this won't happen again. Can you look me in the eye and promise me that?"

"Yes, ma'am."

Randi reached for the doorknob. "And one more thing. You're not fat, and you are *both* pretty enough without makeup. Don't let anyone tell you otherwise—*especially* each other, you hear me? There are enough bullies and shitty messages out there that make girls feel bad about themselves. Don't do it to each other. Friends need to stick together." She grinned, and for the first time, they both smiled. *Sometimes I like my job.*

That was the good part of the day. With an hour left of her shift, she responded to a report of possible domestic violence.

She entered the cul-de-sac and pulled into the driveway of a large house in a cookie-cutter development. She hated the assumption that only poor people were in abusive relationships. It was her experience that an asshole was an asshole, no matter what they had in the bank.

She put her ear to the door. She heard a woman screaming and then a muffled male voice shouted, "Shut up, bitch!" She heard a slap and someone landed hard on the floor.

She had to knock twice before she heard a man ask who it was. When she answered, the door opened just wide enough for her to introduce herself. A thirty-something, clean-cut white man filled the small gap between the door and doorframe. He was in a white dress shirt and dark dress pants, but they both had the crumpled look of the end of the day. He forced a smile, the fake kind big bosses like to use when they're about to spew some bull, but no one dares contradict them because they're in a position of authority.

"What can I do for you, Officer?" His tone could rot teeth.

*Pompous ass.* "Gerald Peterson?"

"Yes?"

"We received a report of a disturbance. Do you mind if I come in?"

"You've got the wrong house. There's no disturbance here." He started to push the door shut, but Randi had braced her foot against it.

"After what I just heard, I'm sure I've got the right house. Your choice: either you let me in now, or we can do this the hard way and I get two more officers down here."

He made no motion to let her in, which didn't sit well with her. He pasted another phony smile on his face and nodded. "I know what this is about. My wife fell—tripped on the stairs, actually. She screamed a bit when she bumped her head. I'm sure that's what the neighbors heard. She's fine, really."

"Then in that case, you won't mind if I check on her, make sure she's all right? I'm fully trained in emergency first aid."

His smile faded and he seemed to struggle to hide his agitation. "That won't be necessary. I told you, she's fine, and she's resting now. I'd rather not disturb her."

As she stared at him long and hard, she heard a woman's distressed voice, saying something unintelligible. He turned his head to speak and she rammed her shoulder against the door. He stumbled backward and shouted something about knowing his rights as the door flew open.

The shattered shards of a lamp were scattered on the floor, next to the broken remains of a drinking glass, and a swivel recliner tilted on its side. There was no stairwell she could see. She heard a whimper from behind the chair and then she saw her, crumpled face down on the floor. There were fresh bloodstains spattered and smeared all around her. She drew her gun and aimed it at the man.

"Don't move or I'll blow your fuckin' head off." She noticed blood on his knuckles. Without taking her eyes off him, she squatted next to the woman, placed her free hand on her shoulder, and whispered, "Did he do this?"

"Yes."

It was all she needed, though she didn't even need that, technically. Randi snatched the two-way radio off her belt and called for backup and an ambulance.

"You're under arrest, sir. Get your hands on your head."

He smirked and didn't move. "My lawyer will serve your head on a platter."

Randi secured her weapon in its holster and stepped toward him. "Place your hands on your head. I'm not going to ask you again."

"Go to hell, dyke bitch."

Randi smiled. She spun him around and pushed him against the wall. When he twisted back around and shoved her, she slammed him to the floor. She made sure his face was sufficiently acquainted with the hardwood before she cranked both arms behind his back and slapped on the cuffs. Her muscles burned with forced restraint. She wanted so badly to rough him up and give him a taste of his own medicine.

Instead, she reveled in satisfaction as his smug expression disappeared. *Not such a big man now, are you?*

❖

Randi finished her reports and formalities at the station and fled to her car, still fuming after the situation with the wife-beater. She lit a cigarette and sped out into the night. It was after midnight and the moon was almost full, illuminating the streets through a crystal clear sky. She navigated her Miata through downtown Portsmouth and onto Route 1A South—the scenic route alongside the ocean.

It was spring now, but Randi wasn't feeling cheery. She was pissed off at the injustices of the world around her. She cranked up the stereo and forced down the accelerator, hugging the curves as fast as she could go without rolling over. She had responded to so many fatal accidents along this route, she'd lost count. It had more twists and turns than a tangled set of Christmas tree lights. She wasn't afraid of becoming one of those statistics herself. Maybe because a part of her believed she deserved it if it happened. Sometimes she imagined it—floating above her mangled car, watching her fellow officers from the Portsmouth PD as they pulled her body from the wreckage, just seconds before a spark found the leaking gas line and threatened to cremate her body at the scene.

The road finally straightened out. Ocean Boulevard in Hampton Beach was a ghost town, especially this late on a Sunday night. She made the loop to reverse direction and parked by the concrete barrier that separated the pavement from the sand. She got out of the car and put on her leather jacket. She shivered and wished she had thought to stop for a coffee. Instead, she lit another cigarette and descended the cement steps to the beach. Taking a diagonal path toward the water, she walked until she'd finished her smoke and then extinguished it in the sand. She placed the butt in the back pocket of her jeans—she respected the planet and refused to add to the pollution.

There was little breeze, but the waves still looked rough. They sparkled as they ebbed and dipped, making a black and white checkerboard of water and moonbeams. The scene mesmerized her for about half an hour until she was able to clear the wife-beater's face from her mind. Soon, she was wishing she had her camera with her to indulge her lifelong interest in photography.

But she didn't deserve to pursue that dream anymore. She gave that up when Stevie died. She owed it to him to become a cop, since he never had the chance to be one. *It's all he ever wanted.* She still subscribed to photography magazines—she could at least live vicariously through the works of others, without cheating Stevie out of his dream. It didn't hurt to keep up with the latest technology and techniques. She still had the Minolta 35mm SLR camera her parents had given her for her twelfth birthday, along with several long lenses, filters, and other paraphernalia she had accumulated over the years. She didn't have the desire to replace it with a fancy, pricey digital camera. There was something about keeping her mind sharp by doing everything manually. She felt it opened more creativity if she had complete control over every aspect of the craft, instead of having a built-in computer doing it for her. There weren't many creative outlets she enjoyed, but that one never got old.

She could have easily shot an entire roll tonight. She walked along the water's edge for a good half-mile and turned around. She was getting cold, and her ears began to ache from the wind. Too bad Passion Play was still out on the road. She could use a night with Nikki tonight. The club closed at twelve on weeknights, so that was out. It was too late to call Megan, and it wouldn't be fair to use her that way. She was too good a person, even if she'd seemed to enjoy their arrangement just as much.

She finally crawled back into the car and headed to Dunkin' Donuts for a decaf—it would be hard enough to fall asleep tonight. Good thing she had a few joints at home, courtesy of Jule Chapin. Ah, now that was a pleasant picture. Too bad Jule had a girlfriend. *And too bad she turned you down flat. "I would rather be arrested."* She grinned. Just over a week later and she could still picture the look on Jule's face. What a spitfire. *A spitfire with beautiful eyes and a cute ass.* She'd rather have the real thing, but imagining Jule Chapin's hands on her would be enough to get herself off tonight.

## CHAPTER SEVEN

Jule lay flat on her back. Her arms rested comfortably at her sides with her palms up. Her legs were dead weight and equally relaxed. She focused on her breathing—inhaling deeply through her nostrils and exhaling slowly out her mouth. She listened intently to the soothing voice of the yoga instructor as she guided the class through the relaxation. This exercise was supposed to clear the mind, but Jule wasn't having much luck. Instead, she replayed the various exchanges with her friends at work during the previous week.

On Monday, she'd wanted to growl at anyone who said boo to her. Patch or no patch, kicking the habit of smoking with her friends during breaks was kicking her butt. She dug deep for an alternative and went for a brisk walk instead, bouncing a tennis ball along the way. The brief burst of exercise exhilarated her and boosted her willpower. It also cleared her head—something she needed for her upcoming interview at the end of the week. She wanted that promotion. Hell, she deserved it, too.

Tuesday, she left work early to go to a doctor's appointment for a physical exam. She had to look up the name of the primary care physician she had selected seven years ago, and when she called, she'd had to admit that this would be her first time seeing her. Fortunately, not only was Dr. Claudia Lewis very personable, but Jule felt comfortable enough to reveal that she was a lesbian when questioned if she used contraceptives or had ever been pregnant. Dr. Lewis did a thorough exam and ordered a full blood panel. As suspected, she was indeed slightly overweight, though not nearly as much as she thought she was. Jule left feeling good about herself, with a handful of pamphlets and advice on ways to improve her health and reduce her risk of acquiring numerous diseases.

The next day, Jule sat down for lunch with Kathy, Toni, and Brenda. Kathy was the first to comment on her cuisine.

"What the hell are you eating?"

"A veggie burger, salad, and organic bagel crisps."

Toni peered at the food. "So, if that's a veggie burger, what do you need the salad for?"

"You can't eat too many vegetables. I've been reading about how to become a vegetarian."

Kathy snorted. "Yeah, right. The day you give up steaks on the grill is the day I give up drinkin' Buds!"

"Well then, I suggest you start cutting down, because I've already made out a vegetarian shopping list for when I go to the grocery store after my yoga class on Saturday."

Kathy and Toni started laughing. When they saw that she was serious, they looked at her incredulously.

"Oh, for Christ's sake, Jule," said Toni. "Going to the gym and jogging aren't enough? Now you're doing yoga, too?"

Brenda shot Toni and Kathy a glare. "I think it's great. It's probably a great way to get your mind off Casey, right? Better than drinking away your troubles."

Jule shook her head. "This isn't about Casey. Well, I guess that's what started it all, but this is about *me*. I don't like the way I feel. I don't like the way I look. I don't like the way I *live*. So I'm doing something about it. Don't you get that?"

Similar conversations took place every day during lunch hour the rest of the week. Brenda was the only one who seemed to understand, and Jule was gradually feeling more alienated and frustrated with defending her decisions. They were especially offended when Jule refused to accompany them to the bar on Friday.

"Wake up, sleepyhead."

A honey-smooth voice startled Jule back to the present, and her heart raced slightly at the knowledge she'd been so distracted in a room full of strangers.

"Class is over."

Jule opened her eyes to see a beautiful spiky-haired blond woman kneeling at her side. She offered a hand and Jule was impressed with the strong, yet gentle grip that pulled her into a seated position.

"Thanks."

"The first class is always the toughest," the woman said with a crooked smile. "But once you get comfortable with the basics of keeping your arms and feet and hips properly aligned, the poses won't be so overwhelming."

Jule rolled up her mat and tucked it under one arm as she stood. "I hope so. I felt a little lost today."

"Well, you've certainly got the relaxation part under control."

Jule sighed and shook her head. "Not really. My mind was racing the whole time."

The woman chuckled softly. "That comes in time, too. I'm Laurel, by the way. Laurel Bentley."

Jule extended her hand and was again warmed by the woman's soft, confident touch. "Jule Chapin."

"I've been doing yoga for a few years now," Laurel said as they walked out together. "If you want, I'll do class beside you so I can give you some pointers." Brilliant blue eyes sparkled with the offer, and a hint of something more.

"Yeah, thanks. I'd like that." Jule gave her a small smile. *God, she's hot.* And if she wasn't mistaken—interested. *Am I?* Jule's bodily response left no doubt. She hadn't thought about dating since Casey's death. Maybe this was a sign that she was ready.

Then again, maybe getting involved with someone right now wasn't such a good idea. All these lifestyle changes needed her full attention. She'd been neglecting herself for too long already.

Laurel said, "If you need any help with relaxing, I own the massage therapy business right there between the yoga studio and the gym. First session is on the house."

*Hmm. Now that could be fun.* "Okay. I'll keep that in mind."

"There's too much stress in this world. I say why not do something about it?" She winked and added, "I'll see you soon, Jule."

She watched Laurel walk to her car. Her movements were fluid and graceful, and Jule was almost caught checking out her toned limbs, her tight ass in black spandex shorts, and her slender, tanned shoulders beneath her teal tank.

*A casual date here and there wouldn't hurt, would it?*

## Chapter Eight

Traffic detail sucked. Randi tried to think of it as job security, since there was always roadwork going on during the spring and summer. It was also proof that the state was spending tax dollars on something worthwhile. After all, everybody hated potholes, and winter always produced plenty of them.

It was three fifteen on a Friday afternoon, and the construction crew was wrapping up their day. As they removed the last few cones and equipment, Randi directed traffic through the single lane when she recognized a black SUV at the end of the line. She stepped in front of the truck with her hand up. Jule Chapin slowed to a stop just short of hitting her. Randi approached the driver's side with a smile.

"We meet again, Ms. Chapin. Off to the bar for a Dr Pepper?"

"No. You stopping me to sexually harass me again?"

"Harass you? That's a little harsh." Jule looked away and inched her truck forward. "Whoa, I didn't say you could go yet."

Jule let out an exasperated breath. "Don't tell me you want to search my truck for pot again. There isn't any. And if you don't mind, I'm late meeting someone at the gym."

"The gym, huh? Let me guess, Avyanna?"

"Yes. Not that it's any of your business."

"The 'center for powerful and beautiful women'!" Randi raised her arms into a body builder's pose, flexing her biceps and grinning, hoping to get one in return. "How appropriate." She dropped her arms and gave Jule a wink. "Then by all means, don't let me hold you up." She stepped back and motioned her forward.

What she wouldn't give to jump into Jule's truck and go with her. Maybe Jule could use a spotter. *Or help showering afterward.*

❖

Jule veered into the parking lot of Avyanna and slammed on the brakes. She wasn't meeting anyone, but it was a good excuse to get Officer Hartwell to back off and let her go. She sat for a minute trying to motivate herself. She didn't feel like working out. She felt like a strong drink and a cigarette, two things she hadn't had in two weeks. Nearly a month into her new lifestyle, and her self-discipline had been threatened, but unshaken. She would be seeing Laurel in yoga class in the morning, and showing up hung over and reeking of cigarette smoke would probably kill any chance of a date. And she definitely wanted a date. Didn't she?

Officer Hartwell's sexy grin popped into her mind, and she grimaced. Damn, that woman bugged her. She shoved out of the truck, grabbed her gym bag from the backseat, and slammed the door. After changing, she spent ten minutes going through a stretch routine and then found an available treadmill. She settled her water bottle in the holder and headphones on her ears, then she selected her favorite album, *Passion Play*, on her iPod, and began to run. She had seen Passion Play perform locally before they hit it big. She and her friends had debates over who was the hottest member. Brenda liked Jaymi Del Harmon, the lead guitarist who sometimes sang lead. Toni liked Shawn Davies, the other guitar player, whom everyone knew was Jaymi's girlfriend. Kathy liked the bass player, Kay Burnes. Jule lusted over the black-haired babe magnet, lead singer Nikki Razer. Nikki was tall, sleek, charismatic, and oozed sensuality on stage in tight jeans and leather. The drummer was a straight guy, so they didn't pay much attention to him.

Five minutes into her run, she increased the speed and added intermittent inclines. Nikki Razer's voice crooned in her ears, her smooth alto growing to an emotional crescendo in one of the band's harder rocking tunes. She pictured Nikki on stage and soon acknowledged that if she didn't replace the image quickly, she would be in no shape to run. Subconsciously, the face morphed into that of Officer Hartwell. *That's not going to help.* She wished she knew the cop's first name. It would be easier than thinking of her as Officer Hartwell all the time. *Wait a minute. Why am I thinking about her at all?* The woman was smug. She was cocky as hell. She was unrelentingly flirtatious. The faint smoky odor of her uniform tipped off that she smoked. She probably drank, too. She was exactly the kind of party girl Jule needed to avoid. She was also unethical. Offering sex to get out of an arrest? She should file a complaint. No, she couldn't do that, not after she found marijuana in her truck.

After wrapping up her workout and showering, she stepped outside. Laurel's salon was two doors down. She scanned the parking lot for Laurel's car. Yep, she was still at work. It wouldn't hurt to stop in and say hello, would it?

Tiny bells jingled as she pushed open the glass door. Incense and mellow New Age music greeted her. The lighting was purposely dim. Thick canvas prints depicting serene landscapes and seascapes decorated the sage green walls, along with a few wooden plaques with inspirational quotes. There was no one at the front desk.

She waited a few beats, and just as she was about to lose her nerve, Laurel entered from a hallway with an exiting client. She lit up when she saw Jule.

"Jule! How good to see you." She waited for the other client to leave and added, "Are you here for business or pleasure?"

Jule felt her face grow warm. "In this line of work, aren't they one and the same?"

Laurel linked her arm through hers. "Would you like to find out firsthand? First massage is complimentary."

Jule was sure that if she submitted to a massage right now, Laurel could probably feel her heart pounding no matter what part of her body she placed her hands. She'd probably have to get naked... *Not sure I'm ready for that just yet.*

Laurel seemed to sense her apprehension. "How about we start with a simple chair massage?" She led her into a room with a strange leather-padded contraption shaped like the letter Z tipped forward. "You settle into it like this, rest your arms and legs in these supports, and your face goes in this cushioned hole." She demonstrated the position and then gestured for Jule to do the same.

Fully clothed with Laurel's hands on her? Yeah, she could handle this for now. Then as she got into better shape, maybe she'd have the guts to have a nude massage. She filled out the necessary forms, signed a waiver, and climbed on.

"Focus on the music and let yourself just sink into the chair. I want you to completely relax your body and mind."

Jule wasn't sure how that was going to happen, when all she could think about was the sensuous tone of Laurel's voice and the anticipation of her touch.

Laurel began with slow circles at the base of her skull. She worked her way down her neck, gradually increasing the pressure. Her fingertips were soft, not calloused like her own, and the movement practically lulled her to sleep. When Laurel reached her shoulders, she worked them with both hands and Jule was in heaven.

"You're really tight in here. Did you have a bad day?"

"It was okay." Okay? It was better than okay. She just left work with the news that she'd gotten the promotion. She was feeling great until Officer Hartwell had irritated the hell out of her an hour ago.

"Something wrong? You just tensed up."

"Hmm? Oh, nothing. Just normal work stress, I guess." It wasn't a complete lie. Brenda had been supportive as usual, but Kathy and Toni had been pushing her buttons all week. She thought they'd be proud of her, but instead they seemed to resent her moving up in the company. She made an effort to focus on something else—anything but her supposed friends or that damned cop.

"Well, you're not at work now, so let it go. Relax, okay? Let me work those kinks out of you." Laurel dug into her shoulder blades. "You know, if people paid more attention to what they ate and put a little more effort into taking care of themselves, the world would be a much better place."

That was a bit of a stretch, but following the "your body is a temple" philosophy wasn't a bad idea. Even if Laurel did sound a little snobby with that superior tone, maybe taking pride in oneself was a good way to stay on track. *If Casey had cared more about her health, she'd probably still be alive.*

And at least Laurel wasn't like that cocky cop. Pressing their bodies together against the car, propositioning her with that knowing grin and witty charm. *As if she knew I wouldn't be able to resist her.* She relaxed and drifted off.

Hartwell's hands were on her hips. Her thumbs dug deeply into her lower back, rocking Jule's groin into the chair with a steady rhythm, triggering a pleasurable response in her core. No, wait. *Laurel's* hands were on her hips. Jule wasn't on the side of the road with the cop—she was in Laurel's massage chair.

She heard Laurel step back and ask, "Better?"

Jule blinked and for a moment couldn't move. Her shoulder and back muscles were definitely more relaxed, but the flesh between her legs was about to explode. She forced her head up. "Um, yeah. Better."

*Holy shit. What just happened?*

Laurel helped Jule out of the chair. Her smile was radiant, and Jule was struck by how attractive she was. Maybe this was the woman she should be fantasizing about, not that gorgeous cop. *Right?* Right. She was on a mission to transform her attitudes about life and take control of her physical health. But her libido? She obviously needed to work harder to control that. Especially when it came to thoughts of Officer Hartwell.

# Chapter Nine

R andi was putting the finishing touches on her look before she headed out to the club, when the doorbell rang. *Strange.* It was eight o'clock on a Friday night. She wasn't expecting anyone. She had invited Megan to go with her, but she was on second shift this weekend, so it couldn't be her. It obviously wasn't her mother—she rarely showed up without calling first, and she wouldn't be out this late anyway.

She ignored her thrumming chest and pulled open the nightstand drawer. With her gun firmly in hand, she drew back a curtain and peeked out the window. She laughed, set down the weapon, and flung open the door.

"Nikki!"

She was engulfed in a tight hug that caused her to stumble backward a step. Nikki Razer kicked the door closed behind her and urgently pressed her lips into Randi's neck.

"Going somewhere?" Nikki claimed her lips before she could answer.

"Oh, yeah. Wherever you take me, Nik."

Nikki practically dragged her to the bedroom and gave her a shove, causing Randi to fall backward onto the bed. Nikki peeled off her shirt and unfastened her jeans.

Randi fingered the buttons of her own shirt.

"Oh no you don't. You'll spoil my fun." Nikki pounced on her and took over the removal of her clothing, lavishing her body with her lips every step of the way. Nikki was the only woman Randi ever allowed to dominate her in such a way. Her body screamed for satisfaction that no other woman had been able to give. Nikki continued to torture her with her lips and tongue as she undressed her, until they both were naked. Nikki slid her body over her, brushed their breasts together, and then pressed her thigh into her rhythmically as they kissed hungrily. Just when she couldn't take anymore and was about to beg, Nikki pulled away, and moved to the drenched folds between her legs.

Randi gasped at the first touch. Nikki's tongue and lips worked expertly, knowingly, exploring and teasing her as they had countless times before. *God, it's good to go to bed with someone who knows how to please me.* Nikki's tongue slipped inside her.

"Ah fuck! Oh, Nikki, that's it. Oh God, I'm gonna come."

Nikki's long, slender finger joined her tongue. Randi screamed, her voice hoarse and her body convulsing as Nikki slowed her strokes and gradually withdrew. Nikki collapsed into her arms, her velvet skin moist, her short black hair soft against her shoulder.

"Can you tell I've missed you?" Nikki whispered into her ear, sending another shiver through her body.

"Missed me? You just about killed me."

"Not a bad way to go, if you ask me."

She pushed up and rolled over on top of Nikki. "I didn't ask."

"How about a little trip to heaven with your ol' pal?"

She sat up, straddled Nikki's body, and ground herself into her center. Nikki moaned. "How about I read you your rights?"

"How about you strip search me?"

She took Nikki by the wrists and locked her arms down above her head. "Good thinking. You may have concealed weapons. I may have to handcuff you, too."

"Promises, promises."

She closed her eyes. Handcuffs. She would've loved to have handcuffed Jule. Not for an arrest, but right here, right now, to her bed. Pleasing her over and over until she couldn't take anymore. She couldn't stop thinking about her, which was absurd, given the number of times they'd met. She pressed into Nikki's wetness. She rode her relentlessly until Nikki began to tremor. Nikki reached for her hands and Randi pulled Nikki's body into her as their wet, swollen centers pounded together until they both climaxed.

"Holy fucking shit, Randi." Nikki went limp and fell back.

Randi followed, landing by her side before pulling a sheet over them.

Nikki said, "How is it you're still single when you're such a goddess in bed?"

Randi propped herself up and reached for a cigarette off her nightstand. "You're either full of shit or you haven't been getting any on the road."

"How about I'm full of shit, and I *have* been getting some. But no one can get me off the way you do."

Randi slid out of bed and slipped on her shirt. She walked to the window and shoved it open. *Where are you tonight, Jule? Are you with your girlfriend? Is she making love to you? Does she satisfy you?* She tried desperately to shove the thoughts aside. She lit up and took a long drag, blowing the smoke outside. She knew the smoke bothered Nikki, who needed to protect her lungs for her singing career.

"You always were a considerate smoker."

Randi shrugged and stared out the window.

"Randi, you okay?"

"Yeah."

"Can I ask you something?"

Randi shrugged again. "Sure."

Nikki sat up and pulled her knees to her chest. She wrapped the sheet around herself. "Do you ever want more than this?"

Randi's eyebrows shot up. "You mean...?"

Nikki shook her head. "No, I don't mean us. Shit, that didn't come out right. I mean, do you think women like us could ever fall in love? You know, and have what Jaymi and Shawn have?"

She extinguished her cigarette into an ashtray on the windowsill and sat on the foot of the bed. "Are you still pining over Jaymi?"

"No."

"It's gotta be hard, though, seeing her and Shawn together all the time. We could team up to break them up, you know. I'll go after Shawn again and you can make your move on Jaymi." She grinned to show she was kidding. *Like I'd ever do that to Shawn. She deserves Jaymi. Not a loser like me.*

"No offense, my friend, but you haven't got a prayer with Shawn, and I wouldn't do that to Jaymi. I'm just glad to see her happy."

She scooted up next to Nikki. "Even if it's not with you?"

"Yeah. It's weird, but after living with them almost nonstop out on the road, you'd think it would have driven me nuts. It's been just the opposite. I love Jaymi—I always will—but it's different now. I've accepted their relationship. I've accepted that Jaymi and I will never be more than just friends, and I'm okay with that now. I'm honestly happy for her. I'm happy for both of them."

"And now you want that for yourself."

"Well, yeah. Don't you?"

She swung her leg over Nikki and sat on her lap. "What I want," she said, bringing her breast within an inch of Nikki's lips, "is to make you come again." She leaned closer until Nikki had no choice but to suck in her nipple. "Oh, Nikki. Yeah."

Nikki spread her fingers over her back, nudging her forward. Nikki indulged the other nipple and then moved up to nibble her ear.

"I guess this will hold me over till then."

Randi slid her hand between Nikki's thighs. "Me too."

Jule was cozy on the couch watching *Fried Green Tomatoes* for the hundredth time when the phone rang Friday night. She recognized the cell phone number on the caller ID.

"Hey, Brenda. What's up?"

"You have to get down here to the club!" Brenda hollered over the music. "You'll never guess who's here!"

"Brenda, it's friggin' ten o'clock. I'm not falling for that line that Suzanne Westenhoefer just walked in the door just so you can get a ride home out of me—"

"No, not Suzanne. Nikki Razer. You believe it? Nikki Razer is *here*. She's with some hot brunette, but who cares. You should be out celebrating your promotion anyway. Get your ass down here!"

"Well, if she's with someone, she won't give a shit about me."

"You don't believe me, do you?"

"Nope." Jule heard crowd noise and a shuffling sound. She then heard Brenda talking to someone before another voice came on the line.

"Jule? It's Sherrie. Brenda's not pulling your leg. Nikki just came up to the bar and ordered two beers. I can introduce you, if you want. We used to bartend together at the club in Haverhill way back when." She swung her legs off the couch and nearly tripped on her afghan. "I'm on my way."

Within thirty minutes, she was paying her cover and entering the club in her best outfit—indigo blue jeans with a black blazer over a white collared cotton shirt, unbuttoned enough to show off a hint of cleavage. She hoped she looked good. She hoped no one noticed she was having trouble breathing in the pants that used to fasten with a lot less effort. *A few more weeks at the gym and they'll fit again.* She caught Sherrie's attention at the bar and ordered a virgin strawberry daiquiri before her friends surrounded her.

"So, you gonna go talk to her?" asked Brenda.

Toni said, "My thought is that she has to come off the dance floor eventually. You can catch her when she comes back up for a drink."

Jule took a sip and rolled her eyes. "Calm down, you guys. She must get bugged all the time by fans. I think we should respect her privacy."

Kathy was taken aback. "Well then, why you'd come down here?"

"I don't know. Just to be around her, I guess."

"What did you plan to do when you got here, then? Just sit back and gawk at her from a distance?" asked Toni.

Sherrie, overhearing the exchange, interjected. "Don't be nervous, Jule. She enjoys meeting fans." Sherrie looked over Jule's shoulder and smiled. "Here they come now. Hey, Randi! Nikki!"

Jule's blood ran hot and her legs threatened to crumble beneath her. She was about to be face to face with Nikki Razer. *Okay, be cool, be cool. She may be a rock star, but she's still a human being.* She slowly turned and then froze. Standing next to her celebrity crush was Officer Hartwell. *So that's her name. Randi. I like it.* She had never seen the officer in civilian clothes, and damn if she didn't fill them out well. She looked sexy and casual in tight blue jeans, sneakers, and a short-sleeve red pullover. Her dark brown hair fell to her shoulders. She looked at Jule with mesmerizing deep brown eyes and smiled.

"It's good to see you again, Ms. Chapin." Randi grinned. "Or should I call you Dr Pepper?"

Her throat went dry. "Hi. Yeah, nice to see you too, Officer Hartwell."

"*Officer* Hartwell?" Nikki said, chuckling. She lightly punched Randi in the arm. "You sure do scare up the public's respect around here, don't you?"

Jule swallowed hard as she looked at Nikki.

"Hi," said Nikki with a smile. She was even more gorgeous in person—slick jet-black hair and large dark eyes. She wore tight jeans, a black leather jacket with matching boots, a low-cut top, and silver and turquoise jewelry. Standing next to Randi, however, someone who didn't know them would be hard-pressed to determine which one was the rock star.

"Jule, this is my friend Nikki Razer," said Randi. "She sings in a band. You may have heard of them—Passion Play?"

"Yes, I know." Jule vigorously shook Nikki's hand. "Big fan, Miss Razer. Great band. Both albums—have both. Love them." Her ears grew hot. *Shut up, you idiot. You sound like Tonto.*

"Thanks, Jule. That's always great to hear. Call me Nikki, okay?"

"And when the uniform's off, it's Randi. Deal?"

That's why Randi had looked familiar. She'd seen her here, at the club—without the uniform, but she hadn't been in the emotional space to notice her. "Yeah. Okay."

Someone cleared her throat loudly behind her. "Oh, my friends wanted to meet you, too, Nikki." Jule introduced Nikki and Randi to Brenda, Toni, and Kathy. Nikki then politely excused herself with a promise to return with 8x10 photos autographed by the whole band—one for each of them. Apparently, she kept a stash of them handy for such occasions.

Jule watched Nikki walk away as her friends rattled on about this being their lucky day. Jule looked past Brenda and caught Randi's eye. She stood alone just a few feet away, leaning against a wall with her hands in her pockets. Jule smiled at her. Randi gave her a small nod and returned the smile. The smile was genuine, but in her eyes, Jule saw something else. Sadness? Apprehension?

"Excuse me," said Jule as she slid off the bar stool.

"Where are you going?" Brenda asked. "Nikki'll be back with our pictures any minute."

Jule held Randi's gaze. "I trust you with mine."

She wasn't sure what she was going to do when she got to Randi. She just knew she wanted to be near her. To find out what she was like when she wasn't working. She wanted to dance with her. Well, on second thought, Randi was here with another woman. A famous rock star, no less. Hitting on Nikki's date? Not such a great idea.

She had two steps to go and nearly lost her nerve. Randi still hadn't looked away, so she couldn't exactly change direction now or she'd look like a jerk.

Jule closed the gap. "Hi."

"Hi." Randi straightened and shoved her hands deeper into her jeans pockets, as if she was resisting the temptation to put them elsewhere.

*On me would be nice.* "I see you got a night off."

"Yeah. I go back on second shift tomorrow, so I figured I'd let off some steam tonight." Randi finally broke eye contact and looked over Jule's shoulder.

Jule turned and saw her friends suddenly look away, trying hard to look as if they hadn't been watching. Except for Brenda. She gave Jule a questioning look and was then distracted when Nikki came back and distributed their pictures. Randi smiled at Nikki and shook her head.

Nikki walked over and said, "Hey, if you two want to dance, go right ahead." She leaned into Jule and wiggled her eyebrows. "I've got no claim on her, so be my guest."

Jule had no time to respond before Nikki grabbed each of them by the elbow, escorted them to the dance floor, and disappeared. They stood facing each other and each gave a nervous laugh.

Randi shrugged and held out her hands. "Well?"

Jule took her hands and Randi pulled her closer. They moved to the music, easily falling in step with each other. The next song was a slow one. Jule's heart pounded, sending a pulse downward instantly when Randi spun them around and then slid her arm around Jule's waist. Their bodies came together, this time without the stiff cop uniform impeding their connection.

She wanted desperately to rest her head on Randi's shoulder. She wondered if Randi's heart was beating with the same intensity. She wanted to feel it against her chest. She tugged Randi closer, unable to ignore the craving.

Randi leaned in and brushed against Jule's cheek. Jule shivered at the touch and almost spontaneously combusted when Randi spoke into her ear. "You feel so good, but if we keep this up, I'm bound to get you into trouble."

*Trouble? What kind of trouble?* If it was the same kind of trouble Jule was imagining, she was all for it.

The song ended and segued into the fast, driving beat of Madonna. Randi followed its cue and backed away. Jule inwardly cursed the deejay as Randi led them back toward the bar. Randi breathed heavily as she searched the room.

"Randi? Are you okay?"

"Yeah. Just need some air." Randi stepped away. "Thanks for the dance, Jule."

Jule's heart dropped as Randi grabbed Nikki's arm and made a beeline for the door. *What just happened?*

❖

"What gives?" Nikki asked as Randi lit a cigarette.

Randi leaned back against the building. She raised a leg and planted her foot against the wall. "Nothing." She took a deep drag and waited for it to calm her nerves.

"Spill it, Randi. What's the scoop with you and Jule?"

"There's no scoop. I pulled her over once, that's all."

"Ah." Nikki nodded. "So instead of giving her a ticket, you slept with her and never called again, didn't you?"

She sighed. "I didn't sleep with her."

Nikki laughed. "Why not? She's cute."

"Cute? She's gorgeous."

"So?"

"So what?"

"So what's with the attitude?" Nikki tilted her head and raised her eyebrows. "Oh, I see what happened. She said no, didn't she?" Nikki nudged her shoulder. "Wow. That must be a first."

"Fuck you, Nikki. She has a girlfriend."

"Really? Where? She introduced those women as friends. She danced with you, didn't she? You two were getting awfully cozy out there."

"Which is exactly why I needed to get away from her. You know I don't mess with people's girlfriends."

"True, you don't. Still, something doesn't add up. She's into you. Didn't you notice that she couldn't take her eyes off you?"

"Yeah, right. Like I can draw attention away from the rock star."

"It wouldn't be the first time you stole my thunder. You *are* a babe, you know."

She snuffed out the cigarette on the concrete wall and pushed off. "Yeah, well, even if she doesn't have a girlfriend, she deserves better than me." She started to walk away.

Nikki grabbed her elbow and stopped her. "Hey, why do you always do that?"

"Do what?"

"Put yourself down. Why are you so hell-bent on being alone?"

"Look, just because you're at a place now where you want something serious doesn't mean I am." She resumed her trek toward the parking lot.

Nikki fell in step beside her. "I'm not saying you have to get married. And you didn't answer my question."

"Come on, Nik. You know I'm not relationship material."

Nikki unlocked the passenger door of her red Mustang and Randi slumped into the seat. Nikki got in behind the wheel and brushed Randi's cheek.

"And how do you know that if you've never tried being in one?"

"I just know, all right?"

Nikki reached for the key in the ignition and slowly turned to look at her again. "In that case, you wouldn't mind if *I* ask her out, would you?"

Randi glared at her.

Nikki grinned and revved the engine. "That's what I thought."

## Chapter Ten

This week's yoga class was less intimidating than the first one. Jule spent the whole hour trying to focus on her body and clear her head, but replays of her encounter with Randi and Nikki niggled at her. She couldn't believe what a babbling fool she'd been in front of Nikki.

Deciding that Nikki was probably used to fans being nervous around her, she finally let the guided relaxation take effect. For a few minutes, anyway. There was still the image of Randi last night—sexy as hell and even more charming in off-duty mode. She tried to suppress the hurt that bubbled up unexpectedly. *She ditched me as soon as she saw a chance to escape. She probably only danced with me because Nikki threw us together.* Attraction or not, Jule didn't need someone toying with her feelings. She had enough on her plate these days.

The class ended and a shadow drifted across her as she rolled up her mat. She looked up and saw Laurel standing beside her. *A stable business owner who's smart and health conscious and gorgeous and not out clubbing.* Stability and light. That's what her life needed. *Not sexy sensuality and...* She forced herself to focus.

"Too bad we weren't able to be next to each other this time," Laurel said. Several tendrils of blond hair curled against the edges of Laurel's face and along her slender neck, damp with sweat.

"Yeah, I know. I was late getting here." She didn't offer the reasons—that she had been out late last night making a fool of herself, and then went home and drank two glasses of wine because she couldn't sleep. Getting up this morning was a bitch.

They walked out together, making small talk.

"Jule," Laurel said before they separated to go to their vehicles, "would you like to go out to dinner with me tonight?"

Jule hesitated only for a moment. "I'd love to."

"Great." Laurel let out a small breath, as if she was relieved at Jule's answer. "What do you like to eat?"

"How about I drive and you choose the restaurant—since you probably know better than me where to get a good vegetarian meal."

"I know a great place right downtown." She gave Jule her address. "What time?"

"How about I pick you up at seven?"

"Perfect."

❖

Jule pulled into Laurel's driveway and didn't even have to get out of her truck—Laurel ran out of the townhouse and hopped in.

"Am I late?" asked Jule.

"No, you're right on time, but when I called for reservations they said they were booked solid for seven thirty, but they could squeeze us in if we got there by seven fifteen. It's not far. We should make it if we hurry."

"Oh, okay."

Jule jammed her truck into reverse and backed it out into the street. She caught headlights in her rearview and swiftly took off, squealing tires as she did so. Laurel lurched backward and let out a surprised yelp.

"Sorry," said Jule sheepishly.

"That car nearly hit us!"

"Sorry."

"I should have called and asked if you could come earlier."

"I'll try to be more careful."

Laurel finally smiled, which eased the tension. She told Jule to change lanes to make a turn, and then gave her the name and address of the restaurant. Jule glanced at the digital clock on her dash. 7:10.

"Why don't I drop you off at the restaurant so you can get our table while I park the truck?"

"Good idea."

At 7:12, Jule pulled over and let her out. Careful not to burn rubber again, she eased back onto the street, took a left, and drove one block to the parking garage. She was about to sprint for the stairwell but stopped herself. It was horribly warm and muggy in the garage. The rank odor of car exhaust was nauseating. She reminded herself there was no need to hurry now. Laurel was there on time, holding their reservation. She didn't want to show up for their date all sweaty. Her nerves could do that well enough on their own, thank you.

She descended four flights and stepped outside. She breathed in the pleasantly fresh sea air. She hadn't been out on a first date in a very long time. Laurel was unlike anyone else she'd dated. She seemed so sophisticated and together. Laurel was probably way out of her league, but what the hell? It was only dinner. Considering the changes Jule was making in her life, she figured it couldn't hurt. It was all about making healthy choices now. At least Laurel wasn't out at the club like Randi. *Damn it. I'm out with Laurel. Laurel. Not Randi.*

Laurel was still in the foyer, and greeted her with a smile, but then her eyes grew wide.

"Oh no," Laurel said. "We have a problem."

"Are we too late?"

"No, we'll have a table. But they won't seat us now."

"Why not?"

"There's a dress code, Jule. You're wearing jeans."

Jule had spent an hour agonizing over what to wear and had chosen black jeans, polished black leather shoes, a purple pinstriped dress shirt, and her black blazer. She'd thought she looked pretty sharp.

"Are you serious? These are practically new."

"It doesn't matter. They won't let you in."

Jule made a move toward the concierge. "Well, let me just ask him. Maybe he'll make an exception."

Laurel caught her by the elbow and walked her away from the waiting crowd. "They don't make exceptions," she said under her breath. "Trust me—I've eaten here before."

"I'm sorry. I wish you'd told me that this morning."

Jule's face grew hot. For the first time tonight, she noticed what Laurel was wearing—a white silk blouse and matching slacks with heals. Her skin looked a darker tan than it had yesterday. Or was it the bright outfit making it look that way? Perhaps Laurel had gone next door to the tanning beds after Jule left. "Why don't we just go somewhere else?"

"After all the fuss I made to convince them to schedule our reservation? This is so embarrassing."

Jule couldn't believe they'd refuse to serve someone over a freakin' pair of pants. Even worse was Laurel's reaction. The embarrassment was Laurel's, not hers. *It's not like I'm wearing sweats.* She noticed a scantily clad woman seated in the waiting area. *They'd have a problem with me, but it's okay for that woman to wear a dress that barely covers her ass?*

Laurel must have seen something in Jule's expression, for her mood seemed to soften. The host called her name. She gave Jule's hand a gentle squeeze and said, "Hold on." She informed the man they were leaving and then led Jule outside.

They walked away from the entrance and stepped to the side of the brick walkway beneath the awning of a neighboring business. Jule had the sudden urge to light a cigarette. There was something nostalgic and soothing about standing still, overlooking the streets of an old town, watching people stroll by. Everyone was enjoying a well-deserved evening out, the temperatures finally close to tolerable after enduring what always seemed like an endless winter. Couples out on dates. Women of all ages sharing ladies' night out. Young men heading to the sports bars for a brew. It felt odd to be among them. Now she had a hankering for a thick, juicy steak with a side of loaded mashed potatoes and an ice-cold beer.

If Casey were here, that's exactly what they'd be doing. She wondered if Randi enjoyed hanging out in a place that had no dress code. Places where the clientele had no qualms about cheering at the TV when the Bruins scored. Where people pigged out on fried stuffed mushrooms, mozzarella sticks, and loaded pizza, and washed it all down with a draft beer. *I want something different than that, though, right? Isn't that why I wanted to date Laurel in the first place?*

"So, Jule. Where to now?"

"What? Oh, right. How about the Gas Light?" she answered impulsively.

"Oh God, not that place. I went there once and it was so loud we couldn't hear each other talk. And I'm not really in the mood for pizza."

Jule didn't bother telling her they served more than just pizza. If she didn't like the Gas Light, then the Rusty Hammer or the Portsmouth Brewery were definitely out. Then she remembered Laurel mentioning that she liked seafood. Her mouth watered at the thought of mowing through a plate of fried clam strips. *Casey's favorite.*

"I know," said Jule. "What about the Seafarer? Classy place, but I know there's no strict dress code."

"Good choice. The Seafarer it is, then."

They walked quietly and Jule looked straight ahead. She was thinking of Casey again. If she looked at Laurel now, she would probably start crying. She hated feeling so out of place, and wished she were home, curled up on the couch. She was relieved when they arrived at the restaurant within a few minutes and, despite it being crowded, they were seated immediately. The server took their drink orders and left them to peruse the menus. Jule found what she wanted right away: a half-and-half fried combo of clam strips and baby shrimp, with garlic-mashed potatoes, coleslaw, and a side of onion rings. *Screw the diet.* She had been good for three weeks and had already lost a few pounds. One meal like this wasn't going to kill her. Her stomach rumbled. She hadn't eaten a thing since her lunch of yogurt and the recommended serving size of Triscuits seven hours ago.

"Mmm, the broiled salmon looks delicious," said Laurel. "A nine-ounce filet? Are they crazy? I'll have to take half of it home for lunch tomorrow. Let's see what they have to go with it. Garden salad with light dressing and rice pilaf sounds good. Can you believe all the fried crap on this menu? It's no wonder our country is leading the world in obesity and heart disease."

Jule inwardly winced at the heart disease comment. *Casey.* The server returned with her iced tea and Laurel's Perrier on ice with a twist of lemon, and Jule went into a panic, reviewing the broiled and baked entrees as Laurel placed her order. She settled for the broiled sea scallops, thinking how bland they would taste after gearing up for her original meal, and mimicked Laurel's sides of salad and rice. She refrained from adding sugar to her tea and took a sip, trying to hide her distaste at its bitterness by asking Laurel a question about her job.

"Oh, I don't want to talk about work. I wanted to ask you about your truck."

"What about it?"

"You must spend a fortune on gas."

"It's not bad, actually, for an SUV. I know it's not much to look at, but as long as I change the oil every three thousand miles and keep it tuned up, I can usually get twenty-three miles a gallon, and it runs like a charm. I do all the maintenance myself," Jule said proudly. "And I'm damn glad I have four-wheel drive in the winter, I tell ya."

"Hmm. I suppose that's one thing to consider. But have you read about what those kinds of vehicles do to the ozone? You might want to check into trading it in for a hybrid. I bought my Prius last year and I just love it. I can go over a month without stopping for gas."

Jule worked her expression into an impressed look and nodded. Their food arrived, saving her the trouble of answering Laurel's question. She looked at her dish and tried to tell her brain that she didn't really want fried clams after all, and dug in. *Not bad.* She added pepper and forced herself to eat slowly, even though she was starving. Nevertheless, she did indulge herself on the bread, even though Laurel wouldn't touch it. She reminded herself that it would take time to adjust to this healthier lifestyle. Besides, she was out with a beautiful woman who had her shit together. *The way I want to have my shit together. I wonder if Randi has her shit together?* She nodded at some comment Laurel made, but was busy recalling her dance with Randi. What a turn-on.

How was she supposed to enjoy herself with Laurel when she couldn't stop thinking about how good Randi felt in her arms?

# CHAPTER ELEVEN

*Sooo bored. Bored, bored, bored.* So bored, Randi began daydreaming. Not a good thing when you're out on patrol on a Saturday night. Even if the subject of her fantasies was the gorgeous woman in her arms on the dance floor last night.

Randi was jolted back to the present when she turned down an empty street. A van was moving at a crawl, as though the driver was watching someone. As Randi's cruiser got closer, it suddenly sped up. Randi hit the gas hard, but her peripheral vision caught movement to her left. There was someone curled up in a fetal position on the shoulder of the road. Randi screeched to a halt and leapt out of the car. Her heart sank. She knew this girl. And in her gut, she knew—before she knelt by her side, before she checked for stab or bullet wounds, before she took her into her arms, and before she even asked her—that she had probably been raped.

"Off'er...Har'well?"

"Yes, Carly, it's me. I'm gonna get you to the hospital, okay?" Randi tenderly brushed the matted hair off her eyes. The insecure would-be shoplifter Randi had spoken to just a couple of weeks ago was barely conscious. Her right eye was swollen shut, the plump cheek below it already turning purple. Her lip was bleeding. Visible marks around her throat indicated his means of keeping her quiet.

Randi called for an ambulance and gave the dispatcher a description of the vehicle along with the partial license plate number she'd seen. She then performed a series of first aid checks to ensure Carly wasn't in any imminent danger. When she was sure it was okay to move her, she lifted Carly into her arms and laid her on the backseat of her cruiser.

"Carly? Do you know who did this to you?" Feebly, Carly shook her head. "That's okay. I'm going to find out and I promise you, he's going to pay for it. Okay? Okay. You just hold on, all right? The ambulance will be here shortly. You're gonna be okay, you hear me?"

While waiting for the ambulance, Carly managed to utter enough fragmented sentences for Randi to put together her story. She had walked a quarter-mile from her house to a nearby convenience store. She wanted to surprise her mother and pick up a gallon of milk so she wouldn't have to stop on her way home from work. That was six hours ago. She never made it to the store.

Randi made one last circuit around Market Square and headed back through town. Her shift was almost over. She just had to file her reports at the station, then she could head home to sink into her couch and lose herself in a *Cagney and Lacey* DVD marathon. Her mood brightened when she came up behind a familiar SUV. *I shouldn't. I have no reason to pull her over—other than I want to see her again.* She flipped on her blues.

Her light-heartedness dissipated when she walked up to the truck and saw that Jule wasn't alone. A smartly dressed blond woman was in the passenger seat, looking terribly embarrassed. She looked familiar. *So...this must be the elusive girlfriend.* Jule had an odd expression on her face, a kind of mixture between annoyance and pleasure.

"Good evening, Jule."

"Hello."

"You know her?" the passenger asked Jule.

"We've sort of met before."

"I don't need to search your vehicle again tonight, do I?" Randi asked Jule in a teasing tone, but the other woman answered.

"Search for what? You have no reason."

Randi remembered her now. Powder blue Prius. Super uptight. Randi had stopped her for going too slow. That's right—*too slow.* Any slower and she could have caused a major pileup. As far as Randi was concerned, that was almost as dangerous as speeding.

"You mean Jule didn't tell you that your carelessness almost got her arrested for possession of an illegal substance a few weeks ago?"

"Excuse me? My carelessness? For your information, Officer, I've never even been in this truck until tonight. Jule, what's she talking about? Illegal substance?"

Jule's head swiveled from one woman to the other a couple of times before she finally gave Randi an exasperated glare.

*Oh shit. Guess I opened a can of worms.* "You know what," said Randi, "I'm confusing you with someone else. My mistake." She looked directly at Jule and said, "Sorry about that." She straightened up. "You're free to go."

She lumbered back to her cruiser and dropped into the seat, one foot still planted on the ground, her head down. She looked up when a car door slammed and she saw Jule walking toward her.

"You mind telling me why you pulled me over?" Jule stood next to her, her left arm draped over the top of the door, her right hand on her hip. Cocky as hell. And dressed to kill.

Randi had to look away. *She looks even hotter than she did last night.*

Jule wasn't giving up. "Well? Are you giving me a ticket, or were you looking to get laid again? That would've been more appropriate last night, don't you think? Or do you need to put on that uniform to have any guts?"

*No one talks to a cop like that. Put on your cop face.* She couldn't. She kept seeing Carly's bruised face. The limpness of her body when she picked her up. The shattered innocence. The way her eyes had lit up two weeks ago when she talked about a career working with animals. Randi looked into Jule's eyes. They were full of fire, waiting for an answer.

"Have you ever looked into the eyes of a fourteen-year-old girl who's just been raped?" Randi's voice was barely above a whisper, but Jule's head jerked back as if she'd been slapped. Her mouth opened as if she were about to say something, but couldn't find the words. "That's what I was doing earlier tonight. Trying to comfort her. Telling her she was going to be okay, when I know damn well she'll never be okay ever again."

"I…that's horrible."

"You know what she said to me? She said, 'I thought only skinny girls got raped.' Can you believe that?"

Jule didn't answer.

"Anyway, I stopped you because..." Randi shrugged. "I just wanted to say hi. That's all. Just wanted to see a friendly face, I guess." She pulled her foot inside and closed the door. She started the engine, and when Jule stepped back, she added, "Sorry I bothered you."

She drove off, but kept an eye on Jule in her rearview, until she got back into her truck. *Screw watching TV tonight.* She was going for a drive.

❖

"What was that all about?" demanded Laurel when they got back out on the road.

"Nothing."

"She wanted to search your truck for drugs, and you call that nothing?" Laurel pointed suddenly. "Take a left here."

"You heard her. She said she mistook me for someone else."

"I find that hard to believe, since you two obviously know each other. She knew your name. People don't run up to a police car, chasing a cop who just pulled them over either. What did you say to her?"

"It doesn't matter. Let's just forget it, okay?" Laurel again told her she needed to turn. Jule knew the way, but nothing looked familiar anymore.

They rode in silence for a minute or two, and then Laurel said, "She pulled me over once. She gave me a ticket for driving too far *under* the speed limit. Have you ever heard of such a thing?"

"She gave you a ticket? You mean she didn't offer—" She stopped herself. She knew the answer. Randi must have known Laurel would have filed a complaint.

"Offer what?"

"Nothing. Forget it. Here we are." She pulled into Laurel's driveway.

"Thank God. This night was a disaster."

Jule shuddered. She thought about the night Randi had had. Laurel thought *their* night was a disaster? Why? *Because I embarrassed her by wearing jeans, and then I got stopped by a cop who wanted to say hi because she was distraught over a rape victim?*

"You're right. It was."

"I'm sorry. I didn't mean it like that. You know what I mean. It wasn't all bad. Dinner was nice."

Jule shifted sideways in her seat. "Laurel? I think we might be better off as just friends."

Laurel's eyes widened slightly with surprise. "Well..." She stiffened, as if regaining her composure. "That's direct."

"I'm sorry."

"No. It's okay. I guess it's better than playing mind games. I think you're being rather hasty, is all. We've only gone out once. Are you sure you don't want to give this a little more time?"

Jule gently shook her head. "I'm sure. I'm sorry—I think you're smart, and you're beautiful, but...I just don't think this is gonna work out."

She drove off and fought back tears that had nothing to do with her lousy date with Laurel. She was hurting for Randi, even though she barely knew her. A few chance encounters and one dance, which had ended much too soon. Would there ever be another? Would Randi even want to see her again after the way she'd just treated her?

She doubted it. And she wouldn't blame her at all.

## CHAPTER TWELVE

Randi fought the urge to put her fist through the wall and quickly filled out her reports. She changed out of her uniform and headed south. She traveled down a long, hilly road lined with trees. The houses in this part of Portsmouth were spaced far enough apart to provide privacy and quiet. Shrubs or trees separated the lots that were at least a third of an acre in size.

She slowed and veered off onto the shoulder at the near corner of the lot. The mailbox was twenty feet ahead and disappeared into blackness as she shut off the lights and cut the engine. It was the same old battered aluminum mailbox, but the name on it had changed. She stared at a split-level house with pale gray clapboard siding and faded trim that was the color of dried blood. Even in the dark, it looked the same as it always did. She wondered if the people who lived there now had kids. She wondered if those kids played cops and robbers in that yard like she and Stevie did. She wondered if it looked the same inside.

She dropped her forehead onto the steering wheel, hugging it and curling into herself. From nowhere, Nikki's words reverberated in her head. *"Don't you want more than this?"* For the first time in her life, Randi wondered what it would be like to have someone to go home to every night. Someone who offered a shoulder to cry on. Someone she would *allow* herself to cry on. Someone to hold her when she needed comfort.

She wondered if that's what Jule Chapin had with her girlfriend.

She was suddenly aware of heat swelling up through her body. Her breathing quickened, and she felt her face flush. She lowered the window all the way down. She brushed back her sweaty bangs and swiped wetness from her eyes and cheeks.

She turned back onto the road. Fifteen minutes later, she was across from Jule Chapin's house. *What the hell is wrong with me?* It was almost two. She and her girlfriend were probably in bed screwing each other right now. While this pathetic excuse for a cop, or human being for that matter, was lurking across the street.

She let out an exasperated sigh and jumped slightly when a car blew by and honked its horn. She pulled into the driveway with the intention of turning around right away, but stopped. There was no Prius, just the black SUV. The house was dark except for a pale light that shone through a small first floor window. She caught a glimpse of a movement and a shadow against a kitchen cupboard.

It was Jule. She could tell by the way her long hair cascaded down her back as she reached into a cupboard and then turned. She remembered the feel of it against her fingers when they'd danced. So soft. Why hadn't Randi made a move on her? She'd done it plenty of times before with plenty of women. Why not Jule?

Because she'd thought Jule had a girlfriend, that's why. Tonight confirmed that. Or did it? Jule was alone again. Something didn't make sense.

*Or maybe your ego is bruised because she's not interested in you.* Yeah, maybe that was it. She put the car in reverse. She'd never needed anyone before, and didn't need anyone now.

"I think I'll stick to hanging out with you, Sirius," Jule said.

He cocked his head and gave her an impatient look, anxious for her to toss a tennis ball. "Laurel turned out to be totally wrong for me," she continued when Sirius returned and dropped the ball at her feet. "And I can't stop thinking about that obnoxious cop."

Except Randi was far from obnoxious tonight. She was almost... vulnerable. Who wouldn't be if they dealt with ugly crimes for a living? That might explain tonight, but what kind of cop tries to pick up women after pulling them over? *What kind of person does that?*

They went inside and she picked up the dog's water bowl and emptied it into the sink. As she was refilling it with fresh, a horn sounded and a light outside caught her attention. There was a car at the end of her driveway. And it wasn't moving. The glare from the headlights made it impossible to recognize the car.

"Maybe we should investigate, huh, Sirius?" They stepped out onto the porch, but the car backed out into the street and took off. "Huh. That was strange." She gave Sirius a pat on the head. "Oh, well. You ready for bed, buddy?"

She crawled into bed a few minutes later. She was exhausted but restless. Sirius settled onto his sheepskin bed on the floor beside her, content and cozy. She knew she'd done the right thing breaking it off with Laurel. Before tonight, she'd hoped for at least a friendship with her. She thought Laurel could teach her a thing or two about a healthy lifestyle. She shuddered at how judgmental she'd turned out to be. *Lesson learned: a healthy body doesn't guarantee a healthy mind.*

And there was the matter of the cop. Randi did things to her that she hadn't felt since…Casey. If she were being completely honest with herself, even Casey hadn't had this strong an effect on her. Each time they'd encountered each other, Randi had done or said something totally unexpected, leaving Jule feeling unbalanced, yet intrigued.

The look on Randi's face tonight when she spoke of the teenaged rape victim broke Jule's heart. Beneath that tough, womanizer exterior was a sensitive, sweet, and caring human being. Jule didn't have to know her to see it. She had the feeling it wasn't a side of herself Randi normally exposed to others. *So why show it to me?* If it hadn't thrown her for such a loop, and if Laurel hadn't been waiting in the truck, she might have been tempted to…to what?

She rose slightly and fluffed her pillow before rolling onto her side. She had wanted to give Randi a hug. Hold her. Comfort her somehow. *Was that what she was looking for from me when she pulled me over, only to find out I wasn't alone? Did she find comfort in the arms of someone else?*

Jule's restlessness kicked up a notch with that thought. She hung her arm over the side of the bed and scratched Sirius's head. He made a soft sound and jerked slightly, as her touch must have awoken him. She patted the bed.

"You want up?" He twisted to look at her, clearly questioning the request, since she didn't usually allow him on the bed. "It's okay, buddy. Come on up." She patted the bed again. "Up!" He hopped up and over her and happily settled himself into the empty space beside her. "Good boy." She gave him a bear hug and finally drifted off with her arm around his massive body.

He wasn't Randi, but he'd have to do for now.

## Chapter Thirteen

"Thanks for coming over to help me today," said Jule as Brenda wiped her ancient high-topped sneakers on the welcome mat the next morning.

Brenda was dressed for painting—faded blue jeans with holes in the knees and frayed hems, and a black concert tee that was so worn you could barely make out the picture of Bruce Springsteen. She wore a denim blue baseball cap backward over her dirty blond shoulder-length curls. Her pale blue eyes lit up her lightly freckled face.

"No problem. What're we working on?" Brenda hung her jacket on the coat tree in the corner of the foyer.

"I finished the walls, so if we can get the trim done today, that room will be finished."

Brenda followed her upstairs to an empty room. Clear plastic tarps covered the hardwood floor. There were two cans of paint and an assortment of accessories arranged neatly on a collapsible aluminum workbench in the center of the room. A six-foot ladder was set up in one corner.

"So what's this room going to be?" asked Brenda as she positioned herself on the floor and started on the bottom trim. Jule climbed the ladder to work on the crown molding.

"The study."

"*The study*," she repeated, with a dramatic flair. "It sounds so sophisticated. I suspect that Mrs. Peacock killed him, with the lead pipe...*in the study*. What's the room next door going to be—the billiard room? The library?"

Jule chuckled. "You know, it would make more sense to call this room a library, since I'm going to put my book collection in here. I thought it would make a good reading room, since I get a lot of sunlight in here most of the day to keep it toasty warm."

"Good idea."

"That wall will have built-in bookcases, and I'm going to build a couple of freestanding ones this summer. I picked up a great chair and ottoman when I went antiquing with my sister."

"I'm so jealous. I wish I could afford my own home. I like my apartment, but sometimes the neighbors drive me crazy. Hauling laundry up and down the stairs sucks. I'd give anything to have my own washer and dryer."

They worked in silence for a while, concentrating on their tasks. Jule set up a boom box in the hall and tuned in to a classic rock station. She set the volume high enough to keep them motivated, but low enough to allow conversation. Sirius was outdoors so he wouldn't be tempted to join them.

"You're doing a good job, ya know," Brenda said after they had been painting for about an hour.

"Well, this is the third room I've painted this spring. I think I've got the hang of it by now."

"No, I mean at work."

Jule finished her brushstroke and turned to look at her. "You think so?"

"Definitely. Don't let Toni and Kathy get to you. They're just seeing how far they can push you. They think they can get away with giving you a hard time since we're all friends."

"Yeah, well, they're causing me a lot of grief with Mr. Roberts."

"I told them yesterday to cut the shit. They got all indignant on me, but I flat out told them they didn't act that way with Ron when he was inspecting, so they should show you the same respect. *More* respect, in fact. You're learning a new job. You don't need any added pressure from them."

"I appreciate that."

"No sweat."

"So you think I made the right decision taking this position?"

"Oh yeah. You deserved it, Jule. You were a perfect choice for that job and I'm proud of you."

Jule cracked a smile. "Thanks."

"Give 'em time to adjust. I'm sure things will settle down once we all get used to the change." Brenda put one last stroke on the trim she was painting and wiped her brow with the back of her hand.

"I hope so. You ready for a break? I could use a cup of coffee."

"Sounds good."

They made themselves comfortable in the kitchen of the century-old New Englander, which oozed of country charm, but needed some updating. Jule talked about her plans to refinish the cabinets with a brighter stain, remodel the master bath, upgrade to energy saver appliances, and buy new curtains after she painted the walls.

"I'm determined to get most of this done this year. One room at a time. Right now, it's just a matter of fresh paint and some TLC. Then I can focus on the big stuff next year when I get my tax refund."

Brenda took a bite of banana bread and washed it down with a slurp of coffee. "Casey would've liked what you're doing with the place."

Jule fiddled with her napkin. "I hope so."

"Of course, even if she were here, you'd be stuck doing all the work, ya know."

Jule shook her head and let out a sigh. "No shit."

"Listen to us, dissing her when she's no longer here to defend herself. We're going to hell for sure."

"Nah. It's the truth. I've done more by myself in a couple of weeks than when she was alive and we had been here for four months. You're right. She'd still be in bed right now sleeping off a hangover."

The two fell silent for several minutes while they finished their bread and coffee. It stung to talk about Casey, but it was therapeutic at the same time. She felt better every time she did. And it felt good to talk about her flaws, too. She wasn't perfect, although Jule had nearly convinced herself otherwise.

"I miss her, Jule."

"I know. Me too. You know what's weird, though? This is going to sound awful, but in some ways, my life has improved without her."

"You think so?"

"Definitely. I'm working out. I'm eating better and taking care of my health. I had the guts to go for that promotion, and look what happened. A new job and a raise. I'm even more determined to fix up this place now that I know I can afford it. Sure I miss her, but I'm happy."

Brenda rested a hand on Jule's forearm. "I think her death has helped us put things into perspective."

"That's an understatement."

"I don't know about Kathy and Toni, but I know it has for me. I know you've been making some changes, too. I'm really proud of how well you've bounced back."

"Sometimes I think of how things were before Casey died. I had gone through life just existing. I settled for what was familiar. I'm busting my ass to take care of myself now, but it's not always easy. There are still times when I want to say the hell with it and have a drink or a smoke."

Brenda got up and refilled their cups, adding just the right amount of cream and sugar to each. She knew how Jule liked her coffee, and Jule took comfort in that familiarity. Old friends were good to have.

"I think it's just a matter of replacing old habits with new ones," Brenda said as she returned to the table. "Once that happens, you won't know the difference, 'cause you've adapted. Just like this new job, ya know? I'm thinking about checking out that yoga class of yours."

"Really? You wanna be a yoga geek with me?"

Brenda shrugged and grinned. "Why not? Maybe I should go to the gym, too." She patted her stomach. "Get this old bod back into shape."

Jule let Sirius out again and they headed back to work.

"Speaking of yoga class, what's the scoop on you and Laurel?"

Jule filled her in on the trying date they'd had, and of the encounter with Randi that had left her even more confused.

"Maybe I'm just not ready to start dating again."

"Maybe. I wanna tell you something, Jule, and don't take this the wrong way, but if Casey had lived, I don't think you two would've lasted." Brenda shot her a tentative look.

Jule couldn't argue with her. She'd been living alone with her thoughts for almost a year now, and she'd often come to the same conclusion.

When Jule didn't reply, Brenda continued. "I liked Casey. We all did. She was sweet, and a blast to hang out with, but she was just so irresponsible. Not like you at all. You've always been the good girl, you know? When you started dating Casey, it was like you needed to get something out of your system."

Jule sighed. "Maybe I wanted to see what it was like to be a badass for a change. I couldn't have kept that up long-term. It's not who I am."

"It's like with us—maybe you would've been better off as friends."

"Yeah, I think you're right. Doesn't mean I didn't love her."

"Of course not. You still love me, right?"

Jule smiled and put a dab of paint on the tip of Brenda's nose. "Nope. Not at all."

Brenda dipped a finger in a paint can and returned the favor on each of Jule's cheeks. "Yeah, I hate your guts, too."

Neither of them wiped off the paint as they laughed and refocused on the job at hand. After a few minutes, Jule asked, "Do *you* think I'm ready to date again?"

"You're the only one who can answer that question. You're letting go, Jule. You're finding closure and moving on. It's okay to do that, you know. As far as dating, if you meet the right person, you'll know."

Jule felt her insides flip as Randi came to mind. Her killer smile. Her raw sensuality. Her muscular frame slumped in the seat of her police car. The compassion in her eyes when she mentioned the rape victim.

*The fact that she pulled me over just because she wanted to say hi. She saw me as a source of comfort. Why? She doesn't even know me. Now I can't stop thinking about her.*

"Jule?" Brenda was standing next to the ladder and waving. "Hey, where'd you go?"

"If there's one thing I learned in all this, Bren, it's that life is too short to spend it with the wrong person. I need to figure out what kind of person that is. I don't want to lose my identity in a relationship again."

"After the skid marks Randi left bolting out of the club the other night with Nikki, and then the date from hell with Laurel, I think you're right. Too many crazy women out there."

"We also have softball starting in a few days. I can concentrate on that."

"Wednesday night. I can't wait!"

"It's all good, Brenda. It's all good."

❖

Jule leaned forward with her hands on her knees and shot a quick glance to her right at the shortstop, Megan. She peered in at the batter. The game was tied in the bottom half of the last inning.

The hitter drove a hard line drive in Jule's direction. She leapt and snagged it out of the air, robbing the batter of a base hit. *Damn, that felt good!* Nothing revived her spirits more than softball in the spring. The early evening sunlight peeked through the surrounding trees. A light breeze cooled the sweat on her neck.

The next batter dropped a clean single into left field. Jule and Megan positioned themselves at double-play depth as the batter approached the plate. Out of the corner of her eye, she noticed Megan tip her hat at someone. Randi was standing behind the fence along the third base line. She was in full uniform, hands on her hips, her feet spread wide in an authoritative stance.

Randi nodded to Megan and then seemed to recognize Jule. Even from this distance, she could see a smile break out on Randi's face. Jule reflexively returned the smile.

Megan shouted something and Jule turned her way just as she heard the crack of the bat. *Shit.* Jule thrust her glove down, but it was too late. The ball skidded between her legs into right center. The runner blew by her, rounded second, and headed to third. Jule took the cutoff throw, spun, and airmailed the ball over the third baseman's head. *Fuck!* The runner zoomed home with the winning run.

Jule hung her head and braced her hands on her knees as the other team celebrated the walk-off win. Megan gave her a supportive shake on the shoulder as she walked by.

"Hey, don't sweat it. It's just a game."

It wasn't just the game. She couldn't believe she had just humiliated herself in front of Randi.

She stood alone as the rest of her team headed to the dugout. She looked toward the fence. Randi was gone. Disappointed, but also relieved, she joined her team on the school's steps for a brief pep talk from the center fielder, who was also the team manager. She declined offers to go out for their traditional drinks and appetizers with Brenda, who had pitched, and Toni and Kathy, who had come to watch. After her bonehead play, she just wanted to go home and chill. She really hated making mistakes, and letting other people down always messed with her head.

She shuffled to her SUV, swung open the rear gate, and tossed her gear inside.

"Great play."

Jule turned around to find Randi leaning over the roof of her cruiser, wearing a beaming smile.

"Oh, yeah. Stellar. Just call me Bill Buckner."

"I was talking about the line drive you caught. And we forgave Buckner in '04, remember?"

Jule nodded, looked at the ground, and suppressed a grin. *I never thought I had a thing for women in uniform, but holy shit is she hot.*

"Anyway, I know your team's going out for drinks, so I won't hold you up."

"I thought robbers held people up, not cops."

Randi grinned. "Are you always such a wiseass?"

"Better than being a dumbass, don't you think?"

"Good point."

Jule held her gaze for a long moment. Randi's eyes were warm, inviting, and intense all at the same time. She could easily lose herself in those eyes. She had a sudden urge to slide Randi's police cap off her head and run her fingers through her sleek dark hair. *Get a grip. You're supposed to be resisting the temptation to date right now, remember?*

"Actually, I'm heading home."

"Ah. Need to let the dog out, huh?"

"Yeah." Jule's heart stirred. *She's thinking of my dog. How sweet. She's not making this easy.*

"Okay. Well, I suppose I should get back to work. You have a good night."

"You too." Randi straightened and was about to dip back into the cruiser when Jule said urgently, "Randi?"

"Yeah?"

"I'm sorry for the way I acted the other night when you pulled me over."

Randi shrugged. "Don't worry about it."

"Our next game's Friday night at seven thirty." *Good going there, bonehead. You might as well have asked her out. Way to hold strong to your resolve.*

"Good to know." Randi touched her cap in salute. "I'll try not to distract you next time." She flashed a dazzling smile and left.

*Fat chance, Officer. Fat chance.*

Jule sped home with the windows wide open, the wind in her hair giving her a rush. She laughed out loud when Pat Benatar's song "All Fired Up" came on the radio. *Now* that's *a deejay who knows what I need!* She cranked up the volume and sent another message out into the universe: *Please come to Friday's game, Randi. God help me, I want to see you again.*

## CHAPTER FOURTEEN

"You wanted to see me, sir?" Randi asked her commanding officer, as she poked her head in the door of his office on Thursday. Even seated, Lieutenant Timothy Baldwin looked huge. Six foot four and still muscular for a man in his early sixties, his only physical flaw was the gut he had grown since taking the desk job last year.

"Sit down, Hartwell," he said, motioning her to a seat as she entered the cluttered confines of his workspace.

"I'm fine standing, Lieutenant."

His eyes reflected a touch of annoyance, but he didn't push the matter. He slid a file folder toward her on the desk and tapped it with his fingertips. "You want to fill me in on what's missing in this report?"

Randi leaned forward, squinting to read the name on the folder. Gerald Peterson. The white-collar wife-beater she arrested a couple of weeks ago. *Shit.* "I'm pretty sure all my i's are dotted and my t's are crossed, sir."

"Really? Is that what you want me to relay to Captain Downes? You think he just chewed my ass out because of proofreading errors?"

"Sir, I—"

"Save it, Hartwell. You don't recall threatening Peterson's life and then assaulting him? Because apparently, those details failed to make it into your report."

"He resisted arrest."

"That's not what he told his attorney. And now he's suing the department for police brutality."

Randi felt the blood rush upward through her neck and burn her cheeks. "Did you see what he did to his wife?"

Baldwin shot up out of his chair. "That's not the point!" He ran a hand over a head of graying brown hair. "I'm not saying the bastard didn't deserve it, but damn it, you can't keep doing this!" He took a deep breath, trying to calm himself. He pulled open a drawer and fumbled a Tums into his mouth. When he spoke again, his voice was softer. "Randi, sit down."

Randi didn't move a muscle. She had known this man most of her life. He graduated from the academy with her father. They were partners for years. She knew he tried hard to treat her as just another officer, but when he used her first name, she knew he had slipped into his pseudo-uncle mode. She waited until the silence that stretched between them was too uncomfortable to bear. She sat down.

"Look. We all know you have a short fuse when it comes to men who hit women. After what happened to Stevie, well...it's understandable. But you have got to find a way to keep your emotions under control, or one of these days, you're going to get yourself into some serious trouble. And being a cop's kid isn't going to mean squat in a courtroom."

"The prick's guilty, isn't he? What about Mrs. Peterson's statement?"

"That's irrelevant. The condition of his face is pretty good evidence, Randi. They're not disputing his wife's deposition. In fact, she filed a restraining order against him."

Randi snorted. "Well, that changes everything. She'll be perfectly safe now, since the last two she had worked so well."

"Randi—"

"Just tell me, am I suspended or not?"

"No. Until they sort all this out, the department's placing you on desk duty. Effective immediately."

"Lucky me."

Baldwin pounded his fist on the desk. "You're not a vigilante, damn it! You're an officer of the law!" He slumped back in his chair, expelling a breath and shaking his head.

She leaned forward on the desk and spoke calmly. "And I can't be both, isn't that right?" As she reached for the door, she turned to face him. "Maybe I'm more like my father than you care to admit, Lieutenant."

"You're *too* much like your father. Jesus, Randi, don't you get it? That's what scares me."

She slammed out of his office and clocked out for the day, incredibly glad it was the end of her shift and she had a couple of days off. Randi didn't care about being off patrol. Part of her was relieved. She hated the damn job. What bugged her was that creeps like Peterson were out on bail, Carly's rapist was still at large, and as long as she was stuck behind a desk, she was powerless to do anything about either.

After mowing and weed whacking the yard, Randi spent the better part of the day Friday working on the Camaro. It seemed foolish at times, to be investing so much money and effort into restoring a piece of machinery. It ripped her heart to shreds to even look at it. But she wanted desperately to finish what Stevie started. It'd be a shame if she didn't fulfill at least one of his dreams. She damn sure wasn't living up to the cop part. She didn't deserve to answer to "officer" or wear the badge. Stevie, though, he would've done the family proud. *Sorry, bro, but what'd you expect from this misfit who'd rather roam the woods with a camera than walk a beat with a gun?*

But that wasn't her life. She was an embarrassment to his stolen legacy. She was a bad cop on desk duty when she should be dead. It wasn't that she wanted to die. It was that most of the time, she couldn't stand living.

These thoughts wandered through her head as she lay on the creeper under the chassis. Working on the car usually calmed her, even though it made her think of Stevie. Today, she found herself thinking of something else. *Someone* else.

Jule Chapin popped into her mind more and more frequently these days. Seeing her again Wednesday night had left her shaken. Jule had hinted at an invitation to tonight's game. *Where's the girlfriend?* She wasn't at the field Wednesday, and she hadn't been at the club last weekend. They'd run into each other how many times now? And she'd only seen them together once.

It dawned on her that the garage was silent. The CD had finished playing a while ago, and she had no idea how long she'd been lying there motionless and daydreaming. She finished installing two tailpipe support brackets and shoved out from beneath the car. After a long, hot shower, she threw on jeans and sneakers, a dark gray T-shirt that advertised Mike's Clam Shack, and her leather jacket.

She headed to the ball field. She smiled for the first time all day. If there was anyone who could swing her mood back in the right direction, it was Jule.

❖

Jule was fortunate to play on a team that focused more on having fun than on serious competition. No one mentioned the errors she'd made on Wednesday, and she'd eventually let go of it herself. It was recreational slow-pitch softball, after all. She stretched and ran a lap around the perimeter of the field, and enjoyed friendly banter with her teammates as they took their warm-up tosses. Though she knew she shouldn't get her hopes up, she caught herself scoping the horizon for a police car every chance she got. She wasn't sure how she was going to get through the game. She was going to be distracted whether Randi showed up or not.

As she came to bat in the bottom of the first, she spotted Randi, sitting alone on the bleachers beyond center field. Spectators rarely watched the games from there, choosing instead to sit on the baseline bleachers so they could interact with the players and have a better view. Randi was by herself and avoiding the crowd. Why? Didn't she have friends to hang out with? At least she wasn't with Nikki. *I'm happy that the gorgeous rocker I've been drooling over for two years isn't here? What is this woman doing to me?*

Jule walked toward home plate and went through the motions of her warm-up routine. She stepped into the batter's box and readied herself for the pitch. Ball one. She stepped out and adjusted her batting gloves. *She's not in uniform, so she's not working.* Why that made her more nervous, she wasn't sure. She dug in and took a cut at the next pitch, fouling it off. If she wasn't working, then maybe after the game she was free to—

"Strike two!"

*Damn it, pay attention! Free to do what? Go out with me? I'm not exactly dressed for a date.* She backed out of the box again and remembered to draw upon her yoga lesson of focused breathing. What was she thinking, telling Randi about tonight's game? The fiasco with Laurel last weekend was proof she wasn't ready to date. But, God. One dance and now Randi's presence here and... *Make up your mind, Jule. You wanted to see Randi; she's here, now you're second-guessing yourself. Sheez.*

"Let's go, batter," urged the umpire.

She took a deep breath and focused on the game, on the ball, on the feel of the bat in her hands. She smoked the next pitch into a gap in left center and slid safely into second base with a double. The exhilaration she felt surprised her. Not only was she relieved that she managed such a solid hit, but physically she noticed everything felt different since she'd quit smoking and had begun working out. When she'd last played in the league, three years ago, she was gasping for air, and her legs felt as if she was running in quicksand. Her healthier lifestyle was starting to pay off. She had already dropped five pounds and knew if she kept doing what she was doing, she'd be down to her ideal weight in no time.

She took a moment to revel in how good she felt. She didn't dare look back at Randi—base running errors could be just as damaging as defensive errors. Unfortunately, the chatter between the shortstop and second baseman distracted her instead.

"Hey, Gina, check it out," said the shortstop, Pat. "Look who's here. It's Officer Heartthrob."

Gina waited until after the pitch to see who Pat was gesturing to before answering. "Officer Heartbreaker is more like it." Another pitch.

"What're you bitchin' about? You got out of a speeding ticket *and* you got to sleep with her. Talk about a sweet deal. She's fucking hot."

Jule's teammate hit a routine fly to center field for the first out. Jule's gaze followed the flight of the ball and captured a titillating glimpse of Randi. She was on the next to the top bench, leaning back on her elbows with her legs stretched out in front of her, crossed at the ankles. She was wearing sunglasses and had taken off her jacket. She was the sexiest thing Jule had seen in a long time.

The conversation continued, bit by bit, in between every pitch. There was mention of seeing Randi with Nikki Razer and wondering if they were an item. Jule was praying one of her teammates would get a hit so she wouldn't have to hear any more. *I wasn't anything special, just another stop in the chain.* The flicker of interest turned into deflated disappointment.

"I've seen her at the club goin' at it with your shortstop." Gina directed this comment at Jule. *Megan, too?* Jule said nothing and acted indifferent.

"No shit." Pat laughed. "The girl gets around."

Jule was itching to say something to them. *So she likes to date, so what?* She didn't know Randi well enough to defend her, yet that's exactly what she wanted to do. At the same time, she was getting angry—or was it jealous? *What a fool to believe that Randi had hit on me because I was different.* How many similar offers had she made to other women she stopped? How many had accepted and slept with her? *I knew she was bad news. When will I stop being so stupid?*

Randi stretched her legs out in front of her. The early evening sunlight peeked through the surrounding trees, highlighting the golden streaks in Jule's hair, which she had slicked back beneath her cap. Every time she jogged out to take her position at second base, Randi could see her face glow with a childlike excitement. *God, she's beautiful.* She tipped her head back and closed her eyes, breathing in the sweet aromas of fresh cut grass and blooming lilacs, and savoring the long-anticipated warmth of spring. A slight breeze teased her hair. She smiled at the joyful sounds of the players, the cracks of the bats, and the smack of the ball hitting the gloves.

As much as she loved the game, she hadn't played since she was a kid, when she and Stevie used to spend endless summer days playing pickup games with other kids in the neighborhood. Her desire to play died with Stevie. Then they'd moved to Aunt Sandy's and put the house on the market. The neighborhood kids shied away from her at school. She heard them whispering in the halls. The few friends she had didn't know what to say to her, and eventually they stopped talking to her altogether. What do you say to a kid with a dead brother, a father who's a murderer, and mother who's a basket case? When summer vacation came along, Randi spent most of her time in her room listening to music and reading photography magazines or Stevie's detective novels. On other days, she went for walks in the woods with her camera.

She shook off the old memories and focused on the game.

Jule was two-for-three so far and had played solid defense. Randi was impressed. She felt drawn to Jule like a magnet. Even now, as she watched her at the plate, she couldn't take her eyes off her. Jule had a cute little wiggle as she geared up for a pitch. *I bet she doesn't know she does that.* She played her position in the field with precision, handling every ball hit to her by sticking to the fundamentals. Nothing fancy, but with an ease, confidence, and dependability that Randi was sure her teammates appreciated. She played hard and gave a hundred percent on every play.

Randi wasn't sure what she was going to say to her after the game. As far as she could see, there was still no sign of Miss Prius. Perhaps the whole story of the pot belonging to her girlfriend was a farce. Maybe there was no girlfriend. Even if that were the case, she couldn't get involved with Jule. She'd never offered a woman more than a one-night stand. Would that be enough for Jule? *Would it be enough for me?* Was Nikki right? Was it time to try out this relationship thing? She sighed. It probably wasn't wise to have such musings. They barely knew each other. If Jule knew about her past, about her family...her gut filled with acid at the thought of telling her. *Would Jule be willing to take a chance on me?* She shook her head and turned her attention back to the game.

It was now the fifth inning and the sun had gone down, along with the temperature. Randi was getting stiff and a bit chilled, so she headed to the car to stretch and grab a sweatshirt. She had just pulled the sweatshirt over her head when she saw it. A dark-colored panel van was moving slowly along the lot between the school and the field. She had to see the license plate to be sure. She quickly jumped into the Miata and took off. *That's it.* The van headed down the drive toward the main street. She punched 911 into her cell phone and told the dispatcher she was in pursuit of a child rapist.

The van moved out into traffic on Middle Street. Randi was four cars back and knew she had to be careful not to tip off that she was following him. She still had the dispatcher on the line, set on speakerphone, and relayed his location. A familiar voice took over as she saw the van turn at a light.

"Hartwell, what the hell are you doing?"

"Lieutenant, I've got him in sight. He's heading west on Islington."

"It's not safe. And you're off duty!"

"Then you better get someone on his tail, or I'm taking him down myself."

"Damn it, Hartwell! Keep him in sight, but don't you dare do anything stupid until we've got our guys in there."

The vehicles ahead of her stopped at a red light. A steady line of cars entered the intersection. With no blue lights aboard her vehicle to overtake the traffic, Randi was stuck. "Shit!"

"What?"

"I'm stuck at a goddamn red light!" When the traffic finally cleared, she checked her rearview mirror. No one behind her. "Screw this," she muttered. She swiftly backed up, cranked the wheel, pulled around the car in front of her, and floored it. A car coming from the opposite direction laid on the horn, narrowly missing her. She squealed tires as she turned sharply down the street where she had last seen the van, but it was nowhere in sight.

"Hartwell! What the hell's going on!"

"I'm losing him! Where the hell's my backup?" She drove on, looking frantically down every cross street. This part of town was a crowded residential area populated with townhouses and multi-family apartment buildings. Baldwin replied that Officer Fisk was in the area, but hadn't seen the van. All other available officers were dealing with a barroom brawl farther south on Route 1.

Men and their freakin' machismo. *Let 'em fight it out and kill each other off. Who gives a shit when this piece of crap is ruining kids' lives?*

She sped through the tiny town, passing motorists who honked and flipped her the bird. She screeched into another turn and then saw blue lights behind her. *It's about fuckin' time!* She sped up, as did the cruiser, but then his voice boomed over the bullhorn and ordered her to pull over. She jammed on her brakes. She flew out and pummeled the hood of the police car.

Officer Fisk jumped out. "Hartwell? What the—?"

"You idiot!" She ran her hands through her hair. She was about to release a barrage of profanity on him when they spotted the figure slumped on the sidewalk about thirty feet up the street. Randi reached her first.

She took one look at the teenager and knew they were dealing with the same rapist that had victimized Carly. She crouched beside her while Officer Fisk called for an ambulance.

The girl opened her eyes and looked at her. Randi shoved her emotions aside in a much-practiced fashion. The bruises on the girl's face and neck were already visible. She had a wide scrape along one cheek from the pavement when he had thrown her out of the van. Her hair was caked in blood. Randi tenderly brushed bangs off her forehead and away from her face.

"I'm Officer Hartwell. But call me Randi, okay?" The girl nodded, then winced. "We're going to take good care of you, I promise."

"Okay."

"I'll keep you safe now. The medics are on their way, okay?"

Twenty minutes later, the EMTs strapped her onto a stretcher. Just before they hoisted her into the ambulance, Randi made her a promise. She was going to catch the bastard.

And he was going to pay dearly for what he had done to her. And to Carly. *And to me.* Another chance to spend time with Jule shot to hell. She'd have cherished even five minutes with her after the game. Instead, she had to go to the fucking station and fill out reports. She really, really hated her job some days.

## CHAPTER FIFTEEN

Jule looked out her kitchen window. This time, she knew whose car it was when she saw it pull into her driveway. Initially, she was pissed. She had spent the entire game trying in vain to dismiss the talk about Randi, hoping that the two players on the opposing team were exaggerating. When she couldn't take it anymore, she had asked Megan if she knew her.

A mischievous smile had broken out on Megan's face. *"Oh yeah,"* she drawled. *"I know her quite well."* She cocked an eyebrow. *"If you know what I mean."*

*"So, you've dated her."*

*"I wouldn't exactly call it that. Let's just say when one of us has a bad day, we take care of each other."*

In other words, Randi sleeps around to avoid dealing with her feelings. Great. *Is that what she wants with me?* She didn't know if that was a good thing or a bad thing. On the one hand, she was flattered—Randi was gorgeous and intriguing. On the other hand, she hated the thought that Randi was only interested in sex and nothing else. For some reason, her gut told her there was more to Randi. It was time to satisfy her curiosity.

Jule called Sirius and they stepped outside.

Sirius started barking and Jule held him back by the collar. Randi slowly inched the car forward, but he continued to voice his objections. It wasn't a very long driveway, maybe forty feet, but it seemed to take forever. Just as she pulled even with her truck, she saw Randi smile nervously. Sirius obeyed her command to be quiet, but as soon as she let go of his collar, he bolted for her driver-side door and started up again.

"Sirius! No!" Jule pulled him back and scolded him again. She stiffened her arm and pointed at him. "Sit!" He dropped his hindquarters onto the ground about six feet away, but kept his ears on high alert. He held Jule's gaze and seemed to calm when she told him to stay.

Randi powered down the window and greeted her. "Hi."

"Is this what you call undercover surveillance?"

Randi grinned. "I guess you could call it that." Sirius let out a single bark. "Your dog's very protective."

"Especially when a strange car pulls into my driveway in the middle of the night. You scared the shit outta me."

"You couldn't have been that scared. You opened the door and came outside. I could've been a mass murderer."

"You're not, are you?"

Randi chuckled. "What do you think?"

Jule cocked her head to one side and grasped her chin. "Well, no, but I'm starting to think you're stalking me, Officer. You pull me over for no reason. You show up at my games. You keep turning around in my driveway."

Randi blew out a breath and shuddered. "Please, you've got to drop this 'officer' shit."

"Okay. I'm sorry. So, Randi, what *are* you doing here?"

Randi's smile faded. "Guess I wanted to say sorry for missing the rest of your game."

"You missed a good one."

"Something came up. Police business."

"I guess that's a good excuse." Jule looked at her with concern. "Something bad?"

"The rapist. He uh…"

Jule recognized the solemn look on Randi's face and knew why she'd gone silent. "Oh no. Again? Another teenager?"

"Yeah."

"I don't know how you handle it. I'd be crying my eyes out every night. Then I'd want to hang the bastard by the balls and beat the living shit out of him."

"Join the club."

Jule shifted her weight and shoved her hands into her pockets. "I'd have trouble sleeping, too, if I had to deal with that kind of stuff every day." Their eyes met again. "That's why you go out for a drive, isn't it?"

Randi tipped her head back against the seat. "Yeah. Couldn't sleep, so I went for a drive."

Jule smiled. "And you just happened to drive to *my* house?"

Randi's lip curled up. "I was just going to turn around in your driveway, that's all. Then you came outside. I couldn't just take off. You'd *really* think I was a stalker."

"Maybe you just wanted to say hi." Jule gave her what she hoped was a flirtatious little smile.

"Maybe."

"You wanna come in?"

"Are you serious?"

Sirius suddenly whined and looked anxiously at Randi. His tail thumped the ground.

"No, I'm Jule. *This* is Sirius."

"You lost me."

"Sirius is my dog's name. And if you'd get out of the car, I can formerly introduce you so he won't bark at you anymore."

"I'm not so sure about that. If you named your dog Serious, he obviously has no sense of humor. How do I know he won't attack me?"

Jule laughed. *God, she's adorable. Please say you'll come in.*

"What?"

"He's named after Sirius Black. You know, from the Harry Potter books? You take his black face, the character's last name, and how he transfigured into a dog, well…it just fit."

"Oh. Gotcha. So instead of ripping my arm off, I have to worry that he might put a spell on me?"

Jule had to smile. "Good thing I'm not a big fan of *A Farewell to Arms* by Hemingway."

"Lucky for me."

"Just get out of the car and come in, will you? I promise he won't attack you."

❖

"You'll have to excuse the mess. I've been doing some remodeling."

Randi stood in the foyer, took in her surroundings, and wondered what "mess" Jule was alluding to. There were four neatly stacked paint cans in a corner and a small foldable aluminum table next to them, aligned with an assortment of paintbrushes and supplies. There was a blue tarp folded into a perfect square on the floor.

"If you think this is a mess, I'd better not let you see my place."

Jule came up next to her and looked around. "I've been working on the upstairs, too, but it's worse up there. I'd give you a tour, but I'm afraid you'll cite me for unsafe conditions."

Randi jumped slightly when she felt a wet nose nuzzle her hand. She automatically petted Sirius's head and began scratching behind his ears.

Jule smiled. "He likes you."

"I think tossing the tennis ball helped."

"It's more than that. I trust a dog's instincts. If he likes someone, I know I'm probably safe. So, you want a drink or something?"

"Let me guess. Dr Pepper?"

"Nope. No soda. I gave it up."

"Okay. How 'bout a beer?"

"Mm, sorry, don't have any beer either. I know. I'll make you some herbal tea. You've had a rough night. It'll soothe your nerves."

"I'm not much of tea drinker, but I'm not in a position to be choosy now, am I?"

"You want to go out for a drink instead?"

She knew Jule didn't mean the question to sound flirtatious, but Randi was suddenly grateful Jule didn't have any alcohol on hand. Her defenses were already down. She could barely keep her eyes off her. Jule was dressed in faded blue jeans and an untucked smoky blue T-shirt, a look that Randi found damn sexy. Her hair was damp. A light breeze from an open window captured her clean scent—a mix of shampoo and a musky vanilla lotion or body mist.

"Randi?" Jule's eyes were warm with kindness.

Something stirred inside her—a feeling, a wanting she'd never had before. It was exhilarating and enticing. *And scary as hell. Maybe I shouldn't have come here.* "Tea is fine."

"Okay then, tea it is. Make yourself at home, okay?"

Randi wandered into the living room, grateful for the moment alone to rein in her hormones. The furniture was old but inviting. There were hardwood floors throughout the house, and the room was rich in earth tones and warmed by a large area rug. The bay window, a trademark of traditional New Englander style houses, faced the small front yard. She looked out the window and noticed that Jule would have had a perfect view of her turning into the driveway. There wasn't much on the walls, other than a few generic scenic pictures.

A giant stone corner fireplace drew her interest. The mantle was loaded with photos. Judging by the strong resemblances, Randi guessed that most of them were of family. A big family. She swallowed hard and shook off a jealous pang.

Another photo that caught her eye was of Jule and a cute blond woman. They were arm in arm and laughing—and were obviously much more than friends. It wasn't the woman Jule was with last weekend. *What's your story, Jule? Hung up on an ex? Rebounding with Miss Prius? Cheating with Miss Prius?*

She sank into the couch and suddenly felt exhausted. *What is going on with me? I'm not even trying to seduce her.* Sirius sat on the floor against her leg and stared at her with a begging look in his eyes, which subsided as soon as she smiled at him and caressed his head. Without warning, he scooted down and rolled onto his back.

"You want a belly rub?" He replied with a soft whine, and she complied.

"Oh my God. I've never seen him do that before with someone he just met. You have a way with dogs, don't you?" Jule sat next to her and placed two cups of tea on the table in front of them.

"I'd love to have a dog."

"Why don't you?"

"My work schedule isn't exactly routine. It wouldn't be fair to him."

"You'd be great with a K-9 unit."

Randi let out a small grunt. "Yeah, tell them that. I've been trying to get into one for years." She took a sip of her tea. "Hey, this isn't bad. I'm not sure what I was expecting—more of a medicinal flavor or something, I guess."

"I find it helps me sleep. And...well, you said you couldn't sleep." Jule curled up cross-legged on the other end of the couch. "So why can't you get into a K-9 unit?"

"I haven't exactly lived up to the precinct's expectations. It's okay. I get my dog fix every so often helping out at the animal shelter."

"You volunteer at a shelter? That's kind of you, Randi."

Randi shrugged. She took another drink and set her cup on the table, and then reclined with her legs stretched out in front of her. "I like your place."

"Thanks. It's old, but I think that gives it character."

Randi nodded and surveyed the room. She couldn't think of anything more to say.

"So what made you decide to become a cop?"

"I liked the uniforms."

"Seriously, come on. Tell me."

"You know, it's late. I think that tea is working. I should go before I'm too tired to drive."

"No! Stay." Jule bit her lip and blushed. "I mean, I wouldn't want you to fall asleep at the wheel. The guest room is finished, so you could test it out for me, let me know if it's comfy and all that."

Randi raised an eyebrow. "What about your girlfriend?"

"Girlfriend? Oh, right. Laurel's not my—"

"I'm not talking about her." Randi motioned toward the fireplace. "I'm talking about the woman with you in that picture."

A wave of sadness washed over Jule's face. She didn't answer and looked down at her hands.

"Is that who you're trying to get over?"

A slight shudder in Jule's shoulders prompted Randi to place her fingers under Jule's chin and lift her head. Jule's eyes were moist.

"It's not what you think. I'm not rebounding with Laurel."

Randi waited for her to continue.

"That's Casey. She *was* my girlfriend. She died last summer."

Randi flinched slightly at the revelation. "Oh, geez. I'm so sorry." Randi swiveled, folding one knee up on the couch so she could face her. "How'd it happen?"

"Heart attack."

"Damn. How old?"

Jule wiped her eyes. "Thirty-two."

"Christ." Randi had to look away. The pain in Jule's eyes was too much. She wondered if people could see that kind of helplessness in her own eyes. It was clear that Jule didn't want to elaborate on the subject, and now Randi was sorry she had mentioned it.

"Well, we're a fine pair, aren't we?" Jule smiled and stood. She picked up the teacups and headed toward the kitchen.

The sound of a distant owl seemed to echo off the awkward silence in the room. Jule put the cups in the dishwasher and then braced herself against the counter. She took a few minutes to collect herself, needing a moment to settle the anxiety and guilt that swept over her at the mention of Casey. Calmer, she returned to the living room. Randi's arms were folded over her stomach and her eyes were closed. She seemed to be dozing. There was tranquility in her face that erased the intense, guarded expression visible even when she looked like she was having a good time.

She resisted the urge to caress her cheek and feel the softness of her skin. Jule shook her head and turned away. She lifted the quilted throw from the neighboring easy chair and gently covered her. She wasn't sure how far away Randi actually lived, but at the moment, it didn't matter. Jule wanted her to stay, though she refused to analyze why.

Randi looked weary when she opened her eyes and smiled slightly. "You may not believe this," she whispered, "but I didn't come by here to seduce you."

Jule knelt beside Sirius—who had stretched out on the floor against Randi's legs—and began untying Randi's sneakers. She slipped off each one. "I'm not sure why, but I *do* believe you. Although I don't know if I should take that as an insult or a compliment."

Randi pulled her legs up, adjusted a throw pillow under her head, and settled into the couch on her side. Her eyelids drooped. "I guess that depends on what you were looking for when you invited me in."

"I was looking for the chance to get to know you."

Randi closed her eyes and mumbled, "Nobody knows me."

Jule fell back on her heels and put a hand to her heart. Those three words struck her as the saddest thing she'd ever heard. She gazed at the stranger on her couch, and whispered, "*I* want to know you."

"Hmm?"

"Good night, Randi."

"G'night."

She tiptoed upstairs in a daze with Sirius at her heels. She walked into her room and crawled into bed, hugging herself as she closed her eyes. She could almost feel Randi curled up under the covers beside her, wrapped within her arms as they slept. She took in a deep breath and let it out slowly, willing her heartbeat to slow down. The urge to hold Randi and comfort her was overwhelming. It wasn't even about sex. Although she imagined it would be amazing…but there was something more going on here. She was sure of it.

What she didn't know, was what she was going to do about it.

## CHAPTER SIXTEEN

R andi awoke to the sounds of movement in a kitchen. She
lay motionless with her eyes closed, loathe to rise from
the comforts of the broken-in couch and the soft caress of the spring
breeze floating across her body. She couldn't remember the last time
she had slept so soundly. She knew instantly where she was, though
she didn't feel as if she were in a stranger's house—she didn't have
the usual urge to bolt before the break of dawn.

*Maybe that's because I'm not waking up to a stranger beside me.*
She finally opened her eyes. Now she was nervous and thinking about
awkward conversation on the morning after…after what?

The aroma of coffee filled the air. *Coffee. Good.* She needed
it to clear her head. She sat up, shook out her hair, and found the
bathroom. She made her way through the foyer and passed a flight of
stairs that were directly opposite the front door. Straight ahead was
an open archway that led to a small galley kitchen and a connecting
dining room to its right. At the back of the dining room, a pair of
doors led to a back porch. *Spacious, but cozy. I like it.*

She went to the kitchen, filled a cup from the carafe, and
added two scoops of sugar. She found fat-free half-and-half in the
fridge among an assortment of juices, milk, more fresh vegetables
than she had ever seen in her life, and other foods in packages she
didn't recognize. Hummus. Egg substitute. *What the hell is tofurky?*
Curious, she opened the freezer. Veggie burgers. Organic pizza.
Spinach ravioli. Haddock and cod fillets. Several sealed baggies of
chicken breasts. No red meats.

The windowed cupboards were original and in need of refinishing. This was the only room she had seen so far without hardwood flooring. Instead, it was covered in a dingy vinyl that used to be white. Cuts and black shoe marks scarred its surface. It was peeling up in the corners and along the edges beneath the overhang of the cabinets. The ancient white appliances had seen better days. Jule had her work cut out for her.

*Where is Jule?* Randi saw her jacket draped over a dining room chair. She fished a cigarette out of the pocket and placed it behind her ear like a pencil, then shoved her lighter into the hip pocket of her jeans. She followed the path of sunlight to the back doors. She swung open one door and stepped out onto the porch. She saw Sirius sniffing the ground around the perimeter of a wood fence.

Jule was in the yard nearby, bent over, stretching fingers to her running shoes. She was dressed in loose black nylon shorts with red piping and a white mesh tank. Her bronze skin looked smooth and healthy against the brightness of her shirt. The sun further intensified the gold and brown streaks in the hair she had pulled into a ponytail. At the sound of Randi's lighter, she straightened and turned to face her.

She greeted Randi with a brilliant smile. "Good morning."

"Morning."

"I see you found the coffee. How'd you sleep?"

"Like a baby."

Jule walked toward her and pointed to Randi's cigarette. "Those things'll make you look old, ya know," Jule said.

"I don't plan on getting old." Randi regretted her words immediately. "I'm sorry. That didn't come out right." She crushed out the cigarette on her shoe and tucked it into a pocket. "I meant that in the sense that I plan on staying young at heart," she lied, hoping to revive the smile she had seen moments before.

"Yeah, well, you can be young at heart all you want. It doesn't count for shit if you don't take care of yourself." If Jule hadn't spoken with a smile on her face, Randi might have been offended. Jule clasped her hands together and reached her arms over her head. She leaned first to one side then the other in a full body stretch. "You're welcome to hang out till I get back and I'll make us breakfast."

"Where you going?"

"Running."

Randi's jaw tightened, once she managed to focus on the words instead of the body in front of her. "Running? No, I can't let you do that."

Jule put her hands on her hips. "You can't *let* me? You spend one night on my couch and now you're my keeper?"

"That's not what I meant." Randi softened her tone, but was adamant. "There's a serial rapist on the loose, Jule."

"It's broad daylight. I jog this route three times a week and I've never had a problem. Besides, I'm not a kid. I thought he was after teenagers."

Randi's mind raced. The rapist had nabbed both victims before sundown, but Jule was right. She didn't fit the profile. As irrational as it was, Randi still felt the need to protect her.

"Okay, you've got a point. Why don't you at least bring Sirius with you?"

"He's not a good jogger. He gets distracted too easily and breaks my stride." Jule moved a step closer. Her clean scent was inviting. Her gorgeous golden brown eyes were full of mischief. "If you're so worried about me, Officer, why don't you come with me?"

Randi felt her face flush. *I can think of a better way to help you burn calories this morning.* "Me?"

"You took an oath to serve and protect, didn't you? I know you're off duty, but—"

"Fine. I'll go. You got something I can wear?"

A half-mile later, Randi was struggling to keep up. Perhaps she could slow Jule down a little with conversation.

"Why don't you go to the gym and run on a treadmill? At least until we catch this guy?"

"No way. When the weather's this nice, I'd rather be outside with nature and in the fresh air." Jule stole a quick glance at her and picked up speed. "And this way, I'm not adding more pollution and I save gas."

Randi was a bit uncomfortable in Jule's shorts, which kept slipping below her hips. Randi was a couple of inches taller than Jule, so she didn't mind the oversized T-shirt quite as much. She pictured the food she had seen in Jule's refrigerator earlier and wondered what she planned to make them for breakfast. Her stomach gurgled. They turned off the town street and onto a rural road. Jule was getting ahead of her, and Randi swore she was doing it on purpose. She mustered up a burst of energy and caught up.

"How…far…we going, anyway?" Randi asked, realizing now that trying to run and talk was making her short of breath.

"Five miles."

"Five miles!"

"Yep. This is the one-mile point here."

"You're crazy."

"I thought cops had to pass a physical every year. Shouldn't you be in better shape?"

Randi surged forward. Her willpower seemed to be her only source of energy. She couldn't tell Jule that she had failed portions of her physical and they let it slide because they had promised her father they would take care of her. Even if she didn't take care of herself.

They ran in silence until they hit the halfway mark. Finally, Jule seemed to take pity on Randi's labored breathing and slowed to a stop.

"You sound like I did a month ago—before I quit smoking."

Randi pulled up beside her and bent over, bracing her hands on her knees. "You smoked?"

"Yep. Can't tell you how much better I feel since I've been smoke-free."

Randi straightened and her breathing steadied. She wiped sweat from her brow with the back of her forearm.

"I have some nicotine patches left if you want them. I don't need them anymore."

"What makes you think I want to quit?"

Jule crossed the street and reversed direction. "You'll have to quit if you want to keep up with me three times a week." She didn't wait for Randi to cross before resuming her run.

Randi charged across diagonally after her and said, "What makes you think I'm going to run with you three times a week?"

Jule turned and smiled at her while jogging backwards. "I get the feeling your protective nature will be enough to motivate you."

"You're a pain in the ass, you know that?"

Jule laughed and then slowed down. "Let's walk the rest of the way."

"Don't slow down on my account. I can keep up."

"I'd rather walk. It gives the body a chance to cool down and relax the muscles so they don't cramp. Especially for you, since you're not used to running."

"Now look who's being protective." Randi was grateful but didn't want Jule to know that.

"Don't think I didn't notice you scouring the woods and every car that went by since we left the house. And so what if I'm protective of you, too. Why does that bother you?"

"It doesn't bother me." Randi tried to sound nonchalant, but she knew Jule wasn't buying it.

Not paying attention, Randi stumbled and lost her balance. Jule reached out to catch her and still had her arm around her as they tumbled into the gravel and thicket off the side of the road. Jule fell onto her back and Randi landed on top of her.

Jule looked up into her eyes and said, "Still think I'm a pain in the ass?"

Randi lowered her head. Holding Jule's gaze, she began to close the gap between them. Their lips were only inches apart. "Yes. I do."

Neither of them moved. She could feel Jule's chest heaving, from the stress of what had just happened, or the anticipation of what might happen next, she didn't know. What she did know was that there was an unbearable ache filling her body. She wanted her. She wanted her for reasons she couldn't explain. She had always wanted women, but for only one reason. She got her release and that was it. This wanting was unfamiliar and it scared her to death.

Randi braced her palms to the ground, pushed herself up, and stood. She offered Jule a hand and Randi pulled her to her feet.

"Thank you," said Jule as she brushed herself off.

"No, thank you. Are you all right?"

Jule looked herself over. "A few scrapes maybe, but I'll be okay. You?"

"I'll feel better after a shower and some breakfast."

"You got it. What's so funny?"

She pulled a leaf from Jule's hair and showed it to her. Laughing, she then took out another. And another.

Jule grabbed a leaf out of Randi's hand and glared at it. "I'm *leaving*," she stated, looking indignant. She spun around and started walking home.

Randi groaned at the pun before joining her.

"You don't really have to make me breakfast," Randi said when they got back to Jule's house. She pictured the weird food she'd seen in Jule's refrigerator earlier. She was drenched in sweat. She had no change of clothes and was disgusted at the thought of redressing in the clothes she had slept in last night. Worse, she had no idea where this was leading. "I should get going."

"Not so fast, buster." Jule pointed at her with a spatula. "You insisted on going jogging with me for protection, so I insist on making you breakfast. What's that look for? Don't you think I can cook?"

Randi tensed. Jule calling her "buster" was just a fluke, right? She couldn't possibly know about her father. There was a time when everybody knew. You couldn't turn on the local news without hearing about it, or see a newspaper without reading about it—but that was twenty years ago. The name Buster Hartwell meant nothing to people now.

"No. I mean, yes. Of course you can cook."

Jule stopped mid-reach for a cupboard. "Are you okay? You look a little pale."

"Yeah, fine. I think I just need some air."

Randi grabbed her jacket and was out the front door before Jule could say anything else. She fumbled through the pocket then tossed it onto a chair. With shaking hands, she lit a cigarette and took a deep drag. Her impulses were screaming for her to just get in the car and floor it out of there, but she didn't think that was fair to Jule. She hopped up on the porch railing and sucked in another puff. Her lungs rebelled, launching a coughing fit that threatened to turn to tears. She sensed Jule's approach as the cough subsided.

"You're defeating the purpose of getting some air, don't you think?"

Randi forced up the corners of her mouth. "Busted."

Jule handed her a tall tumbler full of ice water.

Randi gulped half of it down. "Thank you."

"I shouldn't tease you. I still want one sometimes when I'm stressed. It's only been a month."

"Those patches really worked, huh?"

Jule nodded.

Randi avoided looking at her. She wasn't about to let Jule see tears in her eyes. What the hell? She never cried. Ever. And she had no idea why she wanted to.

"They're yours if you want them."

Randi extinguished the cigarette on the side of her shoe. "I'll think about it."

"Ready for breakfast?"

*No. I need to get the hell out of here. This is getting way too...too what? Inviting? Close for comfort?*

"Randi, would this have been easier for you if I had just let you fuck me last night and sent you on your way?"

The question slapped her hard, jerking her head back so unexpectedly that she slipped backward and thought for sure she was going to fall off the railing. Suddenly, Sirius reared up, snatched her shirttail in his teeth, and pulled. Damn, the dog was strong. And friggin' smart, too. She shifted her weight to regain her balance, but Jule's words were still stinging.

She petted the dog and asked quietly, "Is that all you think I wanted?"

"You have quite a reputation, you know."

"What, 'love 'em and leave 'em', is that it? Is that what you heard?"

Jule stepped between Randi's knees. She extended her arms on either side of her and braced her hands on the railing. Their bodies were nearly touching. Randi's breath accelerated.

"You leave 'em. But you most certainly don't love 'em," Jule said softly.

"Are you insulted because I didn't seduce you like I did the others?"

"No. I'm insulted because you won't come in and join me for breakfast." Jule grinned as she released her and headed for the door. "Now come back inside before I kick your ass." She let the screen door slam shut behind her.

Randi couldn't move. Now was her chance to escape. All she had to do was get in her car and go. The only snag was that she was still wearing Jule's clothes, and her own were inside hanging in the downstairs bathroom. She would have to come back. She should have insisted on a shower as soon as they came back. Too late now.

Maybe she could break in while Jule was at work. *Yeah, right. You dumb shit. Go in and have breakfast, change your clothes, and be done with it. What are you so afraid of?*

Maybe that she had never felt so transparent in all her life.

"You really are a pain in the ass, you know that?" Randi called, as she made her way inside.

When she entered the kitchen, Jule was at the stove preparing bacon and eggs. There were two places set at the dining table. On the counter were two small bowls of mixed fruit and two glasses of orange juice. Randi took the four slices of toast out of the toaster and buttered them. She divided them onto the plates next to the stove where Jule was cooking and took the liberty of bringing the juice and fruit into the dining room. She then helped herself to cups from a cupboard and poured them each coffee. The only words spoken were Randi asking Jule how she liked her coffee.

In a few minutes, they were both seated and eating. After anticipating a meal of unknowns, she was impressed with how delicious everything was.

"It's turkey bacon. Less fat and grease, so it's better for you, and tastes about the same as pork bacon. I go to a weekly farmer's market to buy fresh eggs from free range chickens that haven't been fed growth hormones or any other crap."

"Everything's really good. I take it the fruit is fresh, too?"

"As fresh as you can get this time of year. Everything I buy now is organic. No artificial anything."

It didn't take long for Randi to clean her plate. Jule seemed to be taking her time, chewing slowly, savoring every bite as if it might be her last.

"That was quite a trick Sirius did out there, catching me so I wouldn't fall. Did you teach him that?"

Jule looked down at her plate. She moved some food around with her fork, but didn't spear anything. "Casey did."

"Oh. I'm sorry. I didn't mean to make you sad."

"No, it's okay. They're good memories. She loved to mess around with him and invent all kinds of silly games like that. It started out as tug-o-war, but then she'd climb on the porch railing or the fence, waving his tug toy and saying 'Sirius, save me!' and he'd grab the rope or her sleeve and pull her up.

"She gave each of his toys a name and he learned every one of them. Then she'd hide one of them and tell him to go find it. He always did."

"She sounds like a lot of fun."

"Yes. Casey was all about fun." There was a hint of bitterness in Jule's tone.

Randi waited for Jule to resume eye contact, but she suddenly seemed very interested in her bowl of fruit. "Is this all because of Casey's death?"

"What do you mean?" Jule looked up at her.

"The health food. The jogging routine. Yoga, the gym, being smoke-free."

Jule downed the rest of her juice. "How do you know I haven't always been this health conscious?"

Randi stood up with her as they collected the dishes and brought them to the kitchen. "Because a month ago, you were smoking, drinking Dr Pepper, and I found fast food wrappers and a bag of dope in your truck. Now, your fridge is full of stuff I can't even identify, and you act like it's a crime to have a bottle of soda or a six-pack of beer in the house. What gives?"

Jule began rinsing off the dishes and loading them into a dishwasher that looked to be on its last legs. "Nothing gives. I'm just trying to take care of myself. What's wrong with that?"

"Nothing."

"What would you have eaten for breakfast if I hadn't fed you just now?"

Randi shrugged. "I don't know. Probably just coffee with Frosted Flakes or chocolate Donettes."

"It wouldn't hurt you to take better care of yourself either."

"Maybe. But that's what I like to eat."

"You sound just like Casey."

"Ah-ha. That's what I'm getting at. You think we'll wind up with heart problems."

Jule stabbed silverware into the basket so hard it rattled the nearby dishes. "What happened to Casey could have been prevented if she had taken care of herself."

"So now you're going through life obsessing over every little thing you eat and forcing yourself to keep up with all these exercise routines?"

"It beats the alternative."

"You mean dying."

"I mean dying *young*. I'm only thirty-one years old. I have too much I still want to do and see in my life. Don't you?" She rearranged some dishes in the top rack to make room for more. "Randi?"

Randi stared at her, trying to find the words to answer. "How do you know life after death isn't better than this one?"

Jule sighed. "I don't, but I'm not in any hurry to find out."

They stood on either side of the open dishwasher door, facing each other in silence for a minute.

Jule closed the dishwasher door and pressed the start button. The movement jolted Randi's attention back to the present.

"Randi, who did you lose?" Jule asked softly.

Randi opened her mouth to answer then snapped it shut. She swallowed hard. "I should get home and shower." She made a move toward the foyer, but Jule caught her by the arm.

"When you're ready to tell me, I'm a good listener."

She nodded ever so slightly and Jule let her go. Randi reached for the door.

"Monday at four thirty. That's when I go jogging next. Are you free?"

Randi thought for a minute. She was on desk duty until four.

"I'll be here."

She was halfway home when she remembered that her jeans and T-shirt were still in Jule's bathroom and she was still wearing Jule's jogging clothes.

*Now I have to go back.* The thought wasn't nearly as scary as it should have been.

## Chapter Seventeen

Jule steeled her nerves as she walked toward Kathy's workstation. She hadn't put enough thought into this part of the job when she accepted the quality inspector position. *I hate Mondays.*

Kathy extinguished her torch and set it in its cradle when she saw Jule approach. "Well, if it isn't Madame Clipboard. Here to bust me again, Jule?"

"Sorry, but yes. There's another leak on one of your units. Linda's sending it back now."

"You tell anyone about that shitty solder yet?"

"There's nothing wrong with the solder, Kathy—"

"Bullshit, there isn't—"

"Shh! Mr. Roberts is right over there. I can't have you swearing at me."

Kathy tipped her head back and rolled her eyes. "Oh, so sorry, your highness. Forgot about you hobnobbing with the bosses now." She chuckled. "Wouldn't want us peons makin' you look bad."

*She thinks this is funny. Why can't she take me seriously for once?* "Come on, Kath. You know I don't think of anyone as a peon. I'm looking out for you, that's all."

"Well, if that's true, then do something about that damn solder. I've been having problems ever since they changed suppliers and we've been getting this other brand."

"I'll tell them, but that doesn't explain why only your units are failing. That's the third one this week. None of the other braziers have complained. Just try to be more careful, okay? I'll see what I can do about the solder, but in the meantime, we've got to use what we have."

An hour later, it was Toni's turn.

"You forgot to fasten down your ground wires, Toni."

Toni had her hands deep inside the unit she was wiring, threading them through a hole in a metal panel. She had two wire ties clenched between her teeth and didn't bother removing them to reply.

"Hey, good thing we got inspectors, ain't it?"

"It's not up to me to fix it. You know that."

Brenda, who was wiring her own machine at a nearby station said, "I'll take care of it for you, Toni."

"No, Brenda, I don't want to slow down the line." Jule sighed. "I'll fix it this time, but that's it. I'm through covering for you guys."

She borrowed Brenda's socket wrench, grabbed tooth washers and nuts from her parts drawer, and walked back to the inspection station. She knew things were going from bad to worse when she saw the production manager, Mr. Roberts, approaching. Sometimes she was surprised that his pale bald head didn't scrape the ceiling of the factory. She and her friends joked that if he stood perfectly straight and didn't move, you might mistake him for a support pole. He leaned over to see what Jule was doing.

"Why are *you* doing that? I have seven R-50s ready for inspection on the Rampart line."

"This'll only take a second. There. Done."

"Whose unit is this anyway?"

"Uh…it's…look, it's all set now."

Mr. Roberts folded his arms and pursed his lips. "Go take care of Rampart and then I want to see you in my office."

She refrained from stealing a glance in Toni's direction. Instead, she focused on convincing herself that she didn't want a cigarette. That she didn't want to tear into Toni and Kathy for the umpteenth time. That she didn't want to put her tail between her legs and walk out the door.

She seethed over all the times during the last decade she had covered for them. Catching their mistakes at her wiring station and quietly fixing them herself in order to keep the peace. Taking over

Kathy's braising station at the start of countless shifts to get the line going in the morning—despite her fear of the torch—because Kathy was too hung over to get to work on time. Tightening hardware and installing parts that Toni absentmindedly missed because she was too busy running her mouth all day. She wondered if Brenda felt the same frustration, since she also chipped in regularly to keep the line running smoothly.

She knew what was coming before Mr. Roberts motioned for her to sit down in front of his desk—a monotone, standard lecture, spoken over steepled hands about objectivity, and the importance of expediency, and staying on schedule.

"...and I know you're partial to your old line because it's your comfort zone. I can't have you coddling your friends or not expending equal time and energy on every line. You have a responsibility to the entire firm now, Julianna."

Jule cringed at the use of her full name. Mr. Roberts didn't believe in using nicknames. Toni was Antonia. Kathy was Kathleen. They all hated it. "I'll work on that, Mr. Roberts. I just need a little time to adjust."

Mr. Roberts's smile was forced. "Don't take too much time, Julianna. Business is picking up. We have deadlines to meet and customers to keep happy. I'm counting on you to make sure those customers are not kept waiting."

Lunchtime wasn't much better, when she tried in vain to explain her situation to her friends. They resented her for abandoning them and moving up. They made a point to remind her that she wasn't their boss—Quality Assurance was a neutral department.

Only Brenda stood up for her. "I'd rather have Jule telling me I screwed up than some asshole."

"That's because you never screw up, Brenda," said Kathy.

"No shit," Toni said with a mouthful of food. "I swear, you're a freakin' robot."

"I pay attention to what I'm doing, that's all. I'm not shooting the shit all day long."

"Are you callin' me a motor mouth?" Toni replied.

"Toni, you're a fucking V8!" Kathy roared, slapping her forehead, mocking the juice commercial.

Toni punched Kathy in the shoulder. "You suck." Everyone laughed—including Toni—even though Jule didn't feel like laughing. And so it went until lunch was over. They eased up a little at the end of the day, after Jule informed them she had convinced the purchasing manager to go back to ordering the former brand of solder. The warm fuzzies wore off at quitting time—when Jule turned down the offer to go out with them for a drink because she had plans to go jogging. She didn't tell them she was going to have company.

Today, she was glad that her new position was more demanding than her previous one. Otherwise, she wasn't sure she could have focused on anything but Randi all day. Anytime she had even the tiniest break in the action, she thought about her. Randi was a puzzle. Sometimes she was sweet and playful. Every time Randi was about to open up to her, however, she either shut down, or there was something—Pain? Anger?—simmering just below the surface.

As she drove home from work, she reflected on their time together over the weekend. She thought for sure Randi was going to kiss her when they had fallen on the side of the road. What stopped her? She could still picture the smoldering look in Randi's eyes that quickly changed to fear.

Jule knew she was throwing off Randi's game. After all she'd heard, it seemed safe to assume that every other woman jumped at a one-night stand with Randi. That hadn't happened with Jule. They hung out. They talked. They fell asleep in separate rooms—after *not* having sex.

And Randi was still there in the morning. Randi had been looking for an out all day—and Jule didn't give her one. *She likes me, and it's scaring her. Why?*

She suddenly felt bad for pushing so hard when they were jogging. She'd better ease up today, in case Randi couldn't take the strain. Maybe it was foolish to think that. She was a cop, for Pete's sake. Randi had been a little winded from smoking, but otherwise she appeared to be in good shape. Very good shape. Jule felt heat low in her belly as she pictured the sharply toned legs and muscular arms. Randi obviously maintained some sort of fitness regimen.

She'd go easy on her physically, but she sure as hell wanted to find out what was going on in that head of hers.

❖

Randi arrived at Jule's at precisely four thirty. She spun her cap in her hands and tried unsuccessfully to suppress a smile when Jule opened the door.

"I believe you requested a police escort, ma'am?"

"For some reason, I thought my escort would be a plainclothes cop, *ma'am*."

"She will be in about five minutes." Randi swiveled slightly to show a small backpack on her shoulder. "I didn't want to be late, so I thought I'd change here instead of at the station."

Jule quickly scanned her up and down in a nearly indiscernible appraisal. "Oh, right. Sure. By the way, I washed the clothes you left here the other day." Jule stepped aside and let her in.

"Thanks." Randi gave her a full smile this time. It felt good when Jule looked at her like that—as if she liked her in uniform but was fighting an urge to rip it off her. *I wouldn't mind if you did.* She cleared her throat. "I've got yours, too. All clean." She headed toward the first-floor bathroom. "I'll just be a minute."

"Why don't you come upstairs and use the guest room? It'll be easier than changing in that small bathroom." Before Randi could answer, Jule started up the stairs.

Randi took advantage of the view as she followed her. She could think of better ways to spend the afternoon with Jule. She'd shaken the thought out of her head by the time they reached the landing. *Don't go there.*

There were three bedrooms and a master bathroom on the second floor. The guest room was freshly painted a warm dark beige and would have reeked of fumes had the two windows not been wide open. Forest green patterned curtains billowed out from the breeze. On the bed was a matching comforter. The furnishings were scarce. There was an old dark-stained dresser and a full-sized bed. Between them was a tiny wrought-iron stand with a lamp. An area rug with various shades of green, tan, and rust covered a good portion of the maple hardwood floor.

Jule said she'd wait for her downstairs and left her alone. Randi looked across the hall into the other room and saw a wall full of books. As she changed, she noticed the walls in this room were bare. She caught herself picturing where she would hang some of her own photos. Maybe she'd frame a few to give her for her birthday or something. *Whoa, where the hell did that come from?*

She finished dressing and hurried downstairs, resisting the temptation to check out the master bedroom. She recalled Jule's comment two nights ago about the upstairs being unsafe. It didn't appear to be unsafe at all. *Maybe she just said that to discourage me from trying to get her into bed.*

"Ready?" Jule asked.

"Yeah."

"I worked like a crazy woman yesterday so that room would be ready for you. I finished the second coat on the walls and did the trim."

"I could've used the bathroom."

"I know, but it helped motivate me to get it done. I want to finish the upstairs before summer hits and it gets too hot up there. I'm hoping I can afford to install central air next year."

After Jule led them through a stretch routine, they headed out, taking the same route as before. Randi continued her vigilant surveillance, more out of habit than necessity. At least this time she had prepared for the exertion. She'd made a point of staying hydrated throughout the day and gagged down a high-energy protein bar.

She'd even smoked fewer cigarettes today. Probably because she'd been confined to the squad room for eight hours. Whatever the reason, she was having less trouble keeping up with Jule tonight.

She stole a glance at her and her body temperature spiked. It just felt good to be with her. But she didn't know *how* to be with her. Was this leading to something? She'd only risked putting her heart out there once before. Despite the massive crush on Shawn she'd had then, she'd managed to accept that they'd never be more than friends. Even so, Randi was in no hurry to go through that heartbreak again.

It was different with Jule. She couldn't define how or why it was different. All she knew was that when she looked at Jule, she knew that friendship wouldn't be enough. What if she pursued more and fucked things up?

*This is too much. My freakin' head's going to explode. I'm better off sticking to what I know: sex and no entanglements.*

❖

They ran in silence. Jule managed to focus on her breathing and steady pace, but it wasn't easy. Randi looked so cute in her baggy navy shorts and gray Portsmouth PD tee it was hard to keep her eyes on the road ahead. Randi seemed to be handling the pace much better this time. She really hadn't been prepared to run two days ago.

Jule stole a sideways glance and saw distraction on Randi's face. If Randi really was worried about the rapist, then this wasn't fun for her. It was work.

Perhaps this wasn't fair. Randi dealt with criminals at work every day. Having to worry about them on her own time cheated her out of doing something she enjoyed. This was stress relief for Jule. It appeared to be just the opposite for Randi.

They reached the halfway mark and crossed the street to reverse direction. Jule slowed down.

"You know what, I'm a bit sore from all that painting yesterday. You mind walking back?"

"You're not taking pity on me again, are you?"

"You don't need it today. But I do."

"You okay?"

Jule sighed heavily. "Yeah. Rough day at work. I need to slow things down and unwind."

"What do you do for work?" Randi wiped sweat off her brow and brushed hair off her face, causing her damp bangs to stick up straight. Jule imagined this was how Randi looked as a kid—dusty and sweaty and uncombed from playing outside, and not giving a damn what she looked like. Typical tomboy. *God, she's adorable.*

"I work at Northeast Scientific. I just moved up to quality inspector. Before that, I was an assembler."

They fell into a comfortable steady stride, though she noticed that Randi still seemed preoccupied.

"Sounds like a lot of pressure."

"Well, yeah. There was pressure on me before—just a different kind of pressure. This is more stressful—not so much because of the job, but because my friends are still on the assembly line."

"Ah. That must be tough to get used to."

"For them and for me."

"Well, if they give you a hard time, you just give me their plate numbers. I'll take care of them for you."

Jule stopped and stared at her. "Take care of them *how?*" Randi started laughing and said she was kidding, but Jule was horrified at the thought of Randi offering to sleep with her friends to get them to back off. Jealousy swelled up so fast that her face burned. She resumed walking. "I can handle my friends. You just stay focused on catching that rapist."

"That's going to be hard to do right now."

"Why is that?" Randi didn't answer, and Jule again saw the signs of a shut down. "Come on, Randi, what's going on?"

"I'm on desk duty."

"Is that normal? Or—shit, you didn't get hurt or something, did you?"

Randi chewed her bottom lip, drawing Jule's attention to her mouth. She wondered if those lips were as soft as they looked.

"No. It's for…disciplinary reasons. Someone filed a complaint about me."

Jule grabbed Randi's arm and pulled them to a halt. "I hope you don't think it was me."

"You? Why would I think—?" Randi broke into a huge smile. "Oh yeah, I was a little out of line the night we met, wasn't I? Come to think of it, I let you off the hook entirely, didn't I? Maybe I shouldn't have done that."

"If you're suggesting I still owe you sex for not arresting me—"

Randi's grin grew even wider.

"What?"

"Damn, you're hot when you get mad."

"What…I…you…"

"Race you home!" Randi exclaimed, breaking into a run.

"Hey!" Jule ran after her. "You're supposed to be protecting me!"

"Then you better get moving!"

Within seconds, Jule caught up, only to have Randi quip, "You're not the only one who can be a pain in the ass."

"It takes one to know one."

They were still laughing as they reached the house and clambered up the porch steps. Once they caught their breaths, Randi asked, "How about I buy you dinner tonight to make up for it?"

"I should be buying *you* dinner. You're the one taking time out of your day to play bodyguard for me."

"But you made us breakfast the other day."

Jule unlocked the door and they went inside. Sirius greeted them happily. "That was the least I could do after I practically forced you to go with me, and then proceeded to run you ragged." She loaded two water bottles with ice and filled them from a filtered pitcher.

Randi followed her to the back porch, scratching the dog's head and asking if he wanted to play ball.

"I came back today, didn't I? I could've said no." Randi threw the tennis ball downward, causing it to bounce high into the air, and then guzzled down some water. "Yeah!" she shouted, when Sirius caught it in midair on the second bounce. He chomped on it a few times before picking it up and trotting back to Randi. "Good boy!" He dropped it at her feet and waited anxiously, his ears straight up and his eyes darting back and forth between the ball and his new pal.

Jule watched the transformation in Randi's face when she played with Sirius. Why did it seem as though happiness was a rare emotion for her? Randi continued to throw the ball, mixing up the manner and the direction in which she tossed it. Sirius was having a blast, and Jule's desire to see that joy on Randi's face more often sent an ache through her entire body. It multiplied tenfold when Randi knelt to receive the ball from him and gave him a big bear hug.

"So, Randi, if I agree to go to dinner with you, where will you be taking me?"

Randi scrubbed Sirius's head and stood. "Any place you want, as long as it's nothing too fancy. I don't feel like dressing up."

"How about the Gas Light?"

She nearly sighed in relief when Randi replied, "You read my mind." Randi checked her watch. "I need to run home to shower and change. What time can I pick you up?"

Jule's heart rate went into overdrive. "How soon can you get back here?"

"Give me about an hour."

She puffed out her bottom lip. "I'm really hungry." *Hungry for you, Randi.* "I hope I can wait that long." *Careful, Jule, you're losing control again. Breathe.*

"So do I." Randi rewarded her with a seductive smile and hustled out the door.

*What is it about this woman that crumbles my willpower?* Then again, maybe Jule was reading too much into this. Was this even a date? It *could* be a date. Or could it simply be Randi's way of thanking her for breakfast and her hospitality?

Besides, after the things she'd heard about her, Randi didn't seem like the commitment type. She was probably looking for another one-night stand. It just took longer this time because Jule wasn't as easy to seduce as the other women.

Whether tonight led to sex or not, she was going to keep her life on track. She wasn't going to lose her identity again. Not for Randi. Not for anybody.

## CHAPTER EIGHTEEN

Randi hurried home with an unfamiliar excitement buzzing through her veins. She had to think hard to recall when she had last felt this way. It was Christmas Eve. She was nine. It was the last year she still believed in Santa Claus. She kept sneaking into Stevie's room because she couldn't sleep. Each time, he reminded her that Santa wouldn't show up if she didn't go back to bed. After the fifth time, he bribed her with a promise to let her play with his toy rifle if she would let him sleep. It worked. She didn't bother him again, but then she was even more excited about his promise.

This was crazy. It felt like a date. Did Jule think it was a date? What was with the pout? Was she flirting or just being funny? She shook her head. *This is not me. I don't take women out on dates. I sleep with them.* Maybe that was the problem. She needed to sleep with Jule so she could move on. If things kept going in this direction, Jule might want more from her, and she couldn't let that happen. She needed to keep her distance, just as she had with Megan. *No entanglements, remember?*

She made up her mind by the time she got home. If the signs were there, she would seduce Jule tonight when she brought her home. Then she would be able to leave before she awoke under the pretense that she had to be at work early. It wasn't a lie. As far as the jogging arrangement went, Randi knew her route. It would be easy enough to cruise the streets a few times while Jule ran and keep a lookout for the van. Jule would be at the softball field on Wednesdays and Fridays.

She let out a long sigh. This wasn't going to be easy. Other than a little flirting here and there, she'd never indicated that she was pursuing anything romantic, but she didn't want to hurt Jule either.

A strange pressure suddenly filled her chest. She swallowed hard and dropped into the kitchen chair. Her eyes stung. With great effort, she steadied her breathing and fought back a horrible sense of loss.

She needed to put on the brakes before she cared too much. Caring too much meant having more to lose. *Losing someone only leads to pain. Screw that. Just sleep with her and get her out of your system, just like you've done with everyone else.* She headed to the bedroom to pick out something to wear.

She arrived at Jule's house at seven. She sat in the car for a minute, trying desperately to work her mind into a calmer state. She wanted a cigarette, but she didn't want to turn her off by reeking of smoke. She reached for the bouquet on the passenger seat, but she couldn't pick them up—her hands were shaking. She clenched the steering wheel and focused all her energy into relaxing her body. Her breathing was out of control. *What's going on with me? Get a grip, will you?*

She grabbed the flowers and got out. She knocked and Jule opened the door with a beaming smile. Her hair was down, shining golden brown, sprawled over a nylon navy blue baseball jacket with red and white trim. Beneath it, she wore a white button-down Oxford shirt, blue jeans, and white sneakers. She looked casual, fun, and sexy as hell.

"Hi," said Jule.

"Hey," she replied, standing awkwardly with her hands behind her back.

"I thought criminals got handcuffed, not cops."

"Huh? Oh!" Randi swung the flowers around and presented them to her. "For you."

"Oh wow, Randi. That's so sweet of you."

Randi shrugged, with no idea what to say.

Jule closed her eyes and smelled the flowers. "Mmm, they're beautiful. Thank you. I'll go put them in water and then we can go." She retreated to the kitchen.

Randi scratched Sirius behind the ears and talked to him while she waited.

"The flowers are all set. You ready?"

Randi looked up and caught Jule's appraising look. She returned it and smiled. "Yeah. You look great, by the way."

Jule blushed and Randi knew she was on the right track. She would definitely make her move tonight.

"So do you. Burgundy's a good color on you," Jule replied, referring to Randi's polo shirt. She wasn't really dressed up, just jeans and her leather jacket, but she was glad Jule seemed to like what she saw.

It was a short ride to the restaurant. Good thing, since they were both starving. They decided on sharing a brick-oven veggie pizza before they even arrived. The host seated them in the upper deck that overlooked the patio below, where the restaurant held live performances on summer nights. It was still too cool in May for that just yet.

When the server asked for drink orders, Jule thwarted the first part of Randi's plan by stating that she didn't want anything alcoholic on a work night. It was usually easier to seduce women who had too much to drink, but not impossible. *On to plan B.* Randi ordered a draft beer. So far, so good—Jule promptly offered to drive them home and demanded the car keys.

"It's only one beer."

"You're already benched, Randi. I don't think it's going to help your cause if you're caught drinking and driving. Hand 'em over."

"Oh, all right, fine." She pried them out of her pocket and gave them to Jule. "Hope you can drive a stick."

Jule laughed. "Please. I'm a lesbian."

The drinks arrived a few minutes later, along with a spinach and artichoke dip with cheesy bread. They dug in and ate heartily.

"Are you going to tell me what you did to get in trouble at work?" asked Jule.

"No."

"Why not?"

"Because I don't want to spoil my night out with a beautiful woman by talking about work."

Jule blushed again, obviously not expecting the flirtatious response.

"I'm not being sued for sexual harassment, if that's what you're thinking."

Jule cocked her head and eyed her curiously. "Okay, then. Since we both had a bad day at work, how about we take that subject off the table tonight?"

"I'll drink to that," said Randi, raising her mug. They toasted and drank.

"So if we're not going to talk shop, how about you tell me about your family?"

*Shit.* "You first."

Jule gave her a quizzical stare, but didn't press. "Okay. I have a sister and three brothers. I'm the youngest, so when they're not picking on me, they're being overprotective, or otherwise a royal pain in the ass." She smiled, as if lost in a fond memory. "But we're pretty tight. I've got nieces and nephews that I love to pieces and more cousins in the area than I can count."

"Big family."

"Yeah. I'm lucky. My parents are good people. They don't have a lot as far as material things go, but they don't seem to mind. As long as the bills are paid, there's food on the table, and you've got clothes on your back, life is good in their eyes."

"Sounds good to me. What do they do for work?"

"My dad's a hardworking factory man, like me. Totally devoted to his family. My mom works part-time at the Hallmark shop at the mall now, but she stayed at home when we were kids. She pretty much had to with five of us. She was amazing at keeping everything organized."

Jule looked so happy and proud that it was nearly impossible for Randi to feel jealous.

"She had this chart on the refrigerator," Jule continued. "Everything was prioritized and scheduled accordingly. Homework. Chores. After-school activities. Appointments. Everything." Jule smiled crookedly and shook her head. "You know…I don't think I realized how much that stuff was engrained in me until now. It's no wonder I'm good at what I do."

"Those organizational skills and attention to detail are paying off, huh?"

"Yeah. I guess they are." She took a drink. "Your turn. Tell me something about yourself. Anything."

Randi secretly breathed a sigh of relief that Jule left the choice of topic open, and when she didn't say anything right away, Jule asked how she spent her free time.

Randi started to tell her about restoring Stevie's car and stopped herself. If she planned to tail Jule when she went running, she might have to do it in the Camaro, not the Miata. She recovered quickly by saying, "I take pictures."

"Really?" She took a sip of her iced tea. "What kind of pictures?"

"Nature shots, mostly."

"Like what?"

Randi shrugged. She rarely touched her camera since Stevie's death. Talking about the photos she had taken during that family camping trip so many years ago would be a big mistake. "Nothing much. Birds. Animals. Flowers. Scenic shots, you know, such as mountains or sunrises at the beach and so on."

"Nice. Are you any good?"

"I like to think so."

"I'd love to see them sometime."

She needed to get the conversation back on Jule. Fortunately, the server showed up with the pizza and spared Randi from having to respond. They had each worked through their first slices when Randi asked, "So, besides softball and exercising like a madwoman, what do you do for fun?"

Jule wrinkled her brow slightly and hesitated. She swallowed her bite and washed it down with a long drink.

"Well, until recently, I spent most of my adult life wasting time. Hanging out with friends at the bar. Going to clubs on the weekends. Staying up late getting stoned or fooling around with Casey." Jule served herself another slice, looking reflective. "You were right, you know."

"About what?"

"When you asked if my lifestyle changes were because of what happened to Casey. You were right."

Her insides roiled in response to the sadness in Jule's tone. "It's understandable. Don't you think you've gone a little overboard though? You still deserve to have a little fun now and then."

Jule's lips turned upward. "I'm out with you, aren't I?" She gave Randi a seductive look and leaned back in her seat.

Warmth filled her chest and flowed through her entire body. There was little doubt she and Jule were on the same page on where the evening was heading. She needed to get them out of here fast, before they talked too much and got to know too much about each other. That could spell disaster.

She didn't want to hurt her. She had already let this go too far. She motioned to their server, ordered them each a refill on their drinks, and quickly excused herself to the ladies' room.

She splashed cold water on her face and looked in the mirror. She had never spent this much time with a woman before she seduced her. She couldn't risk getting attached to them, or vice versa. Nikki Razer was the only one she'd developed a friendship with after they had slept together, but she and Nikki knew what they shared wouldn't go any further, so it worked.

It was getting harder to keep up her guard with Jule. It was obvious that Jule was trying hard to get to know her. If she kept avoiding Jule's questions, she was bound to catch on that she was only interested in sex.

*The problem is, I'm interested in more than sex with her.* She splashed more cold water on her face. *Now what?*

Randi wasn't as talkative after she returned from the restroom. She seemed to have something on her mind, but Jule had quickly learned that it wasn't good to push or she'd shut down even more. Randi diverted the conversation to the safe subjects of sports and food.

Randi also downed two more beers. Jule hated the familiar feeling that reminded her of the nights Casey had been too drunk to drive. She liked Randi more than she cared to admit. She cared even less to admit that she was afraid of regressing into the lifestyle she was working so hard to escape. It didn't keep their time together from being fun, but it definitely made Jule pause.

Later, Jule parked Randi's car next to her own and shut off the ignition. The sport coupe had been fun to drive, but the ride itself had been confusing. She handed the keys to Randi and made the mistake of looking her in the eye. Randi hadn't been subtle about what she wanted tonight, and Jule had flirted with her enough to hint that she wanted it too. Maybe it was better if they got it out of their system. Then they could go their separate ways and Jule could go back to focusing on her new life. And Randi could go back to focusing on... whatever it was that she focused on. Randi's reluctance to share more about herself frustrated her as much as it intrigued her.

And dammit, the intrigue was winning. She reached out and stroked Randi's cheek.

"Should I drive you home, or do you want to come in?"

Randi took her hand and kissed her palm. "Do you want me to come in?"

Jule's heart pounded. "Yes."

Randi backed away and got out. She swiftly came around to the other side and opened the door for Jule. She took Jule's hand and pulled her into her arms. "Are you sure?"

Jule fell into her embrace, overwhelmed by the heat emitting from Randi's body. She thought Randi was going to kiss her, but she stood motionless, her dark eyes swimming with desire.

"Yes."

They walked hand in hand into the house. Jule closed the door and Sirius barged in between them. Jule expected Randi to be annoyed at the interruption, but instead she scrubbed his head with both hands and asked if he needed to go out.

"Be right back." Randi smiled and wiggled her eyebrows. "Don't go anywhere."

"I live here, remember?"

Jule stood at the window and treated herself to the view of Randi in the yard with Sirius. She was in black leather boots, a brown leather jacket softened from many years of wear, and a deep maroon polo shirt tucked neatly into her jeans. Her dark hair fell softly on her collar, and the warm expression on her face as she interacted with

Sirius once again took her breath away. *Slow down, Jule. You haven't been intimate with anyone since Casey died. The last thing you need is to jump into bed with someone and have Casey on your mind.*
She looked at Randi again. Her insides fluttered with arousal. There was no way she'd be thinking of Casey if she took Randi to bed. Comparing the two was absurd. This woman was nothing like Casey. Casey was a sweet girl, but most of the time what you saw was what you got—a fun-loving simple soul who partied hard and didn't think much about consequences.

There was nothing simple about Randi. Jule was dying to learn what her secrets were. She wanted to show Randi that it was safe to share them with her.

Sirius bolted to his water bowl when they came in. Randi smiled and came toward her.

Jule reached up and interlaced her fingers behind Randi's neck. "You know, I'm starting to think you like my dog more than you like me."

Randi grinned and rested her hands on Jule's hips. "What if I said it's a tie?"

"Then I'd better do something to break that tie. Any ideas?"

"This, for starters." Randi ran her hands up her torso and slid Jule's jacket off her shoulders. She then discarded her own coat and stepped into Jule's arms. "Now this." Randi kissed her with a tenderness that melted her insides. It wasn't the sex-hungry aggression she expected. *Oh God, her lips are as soft as they look.*

She leaned back against the wall and Randi deepened the kiss, teasing with her tongue. Jule moaned and opened her mouth to allow her entry. She tugged at Randi's waist, inviting her closer.

Randi braced her hands against the wall as she moved against her, the friction sending Jule higher as their tongues wrestled. Randi lowered her arms and untucked Jule's shirt. Her breath caught when Randi's hand brushed across her bare skin.

The sensations taking over her body dismissed all thoughts from her brain. Randi was unbuttoning her shirt. When she finished, she planted maddeningly light kisses down her throat.

Jule moaned at the feel of Randi's lips and hot breath on her neck. "You…are…making me…crazy."

Randi took a step back. She opened the shirt and looked at her as if she would devour her on the spot. "So beautiful. My God, Jule, you're so beautiful."

Jule's breath was ragged. She felt cold and wanted Randi's warm body back against hers. A voice in her head warned her to slow things down. "Want to go upstairs?"

"Yes."

They stumbled up the stairs and into the bedroom. She pulled Randi's shirt up and over her head and their lips met again. They unhooked each other's bras and their breasts came together. Randi's skin felt so unbelievably soft against her own. She kissed Randi's throat and cupped one breast, enjoying the full weight of it in her hand before taking the nipple between her lips. She flicked it with her tongue a few times and thrilled with how quickly it hardened.

"Oh, Jule. Oh, yeah."

Jule kissed her hard and then took in the other nipple, giving it the same treatment. She felt Randi's hands on the button of her jeans. Within seconds, they were naked, and together they turned down the covers of the bed. Randi lowered Jule onto her back and lay on top of her, kissing her hungrily as they rocked against each other's centers.

Jule pushed her up gently and broke the kiss. She placed her hands on Randi's cheeks. "Randi. Open your eyes."

Randi's eyes opened slightly, her lids heavy with raw sensual hunger. But there was something else, and when Jule held her gaze a little longer, Randi lowered her head, letting her hair fall over her face, shielding her eyes.

"Look at me, Randi." She lifted Randi's chin and their eyes met. "I want to know you." She felt Randi's entire body shiver and then her eyes shone with tears.

"Don't. Jule, please don't."

"Shh." She silenced her with a tender kiss. "When you're ready, baby. Tonight, just show me."

A long silence passed and then Randi pressed her lips to her shoulder and shifted to her side. She felt Randi's hand on her stomach. The kisses continued up her neck, and every nerve ending in her body tingled. She tipped her head back. Randi kissed her throat and slid a hand over her breast.

Jule found her lips and kissed her, savoring the softness of them, and the warmth of her tongue's caress against her own. Randi moved over her and brought her thigh against her center. Jule moaned in pleasure as she held Randi's breasts and ran her thumbs over taut nipples. Randi's body was long and muscular, but with softness and curves in all the right places. Jule drank in the pure beauty of how she looked and moved. She wondered if she'd ever get enough of her.

Randi's breathing accelerated and their lips parted. She arched back and lowered a nipple into Jule's mouth, letting out a long, guttural moan that sounded so sensual Jule almost came right then. She sucked and teased and stroked until Randi withdrew and offered the other breast.

Randi's hand slid downward. Jule raised her hips, inviting her in. She was already soaked and throbbing, and at the first touch of Randi's fingers, she cried out.

"Take me, Randi."

Randi peppered kisses across her body and began stroking her in gentle circles. Her mouth found Jule's nipple. She loved the feel of Randi's hair falling softly over her chest. She ran her fingertips all over Randi's body and moved in rhythm with each stroke. She was so close. Randi entered her, teasing and exploring, and attending to her every response. Just when she thought she'd lose her mind, Randi took her over the edge.

She screamed as her body shuddered. Randi stayed inside her and collapsed breathlessly next to her in her arms. After several minutes, she withdrew and Jule instantly missed the connection. She rolled over and placed a long, languid kiss on Randi's lips until she felt her squirm beneath her. She responded by deepening the kiss and pressing into her groin.

Randi's moan grew more urgent and she rocked against her. "Touch me. Please."

Jule smiled smugly. "Say it again."

"Please." Randi's eyes fluttered in need and her breath quickened.

"Please, Jule. Baby, please touch me."

"Are you begging?"

"Yes."

"Baby, you're beautiful." She kissed her firmly and slipped her hands between Randi's legs. "And you're so wet for me."

"Please…"

"I want to taste you."

"Please…"

She kissed her one more time and then settled between her legs. She parted the soft lips with her thumbs and took her into her mouth. Randi gasped and moaned with such need that Jule almost came again. She licked her softly and steadily. Randi scraped her fingers through her hair and urged her closer.

"Please…"

Jule slid her tongue inside and began stroking her clit with her thumb. She knew Randi was close and brought her just to the brink and then backed off slightly.

"Oh…Jule, please…please."

She resumed stroking with her tongue, slowly increasing speed and pressure and Randi came, her body jerking as the orgasm shook her. Jule kept her lips on her, and with a few more flicks of the tongue, she came again, hard. Jule fell on top of her and Randi wrapped her arms around her tightly as she rode out the spasms.

"You're beautiful, Randi," she whispered. "So beautiful." Jule pulled the covers over them and Randi fell asleep in her arms.

❖

Randi woke up and looked at the woman beside her. Not a stranger. Jule. For the first time in her life, she didn't want to leave.

Which was exactly why she needed to.

She'd had a lot of sex with a lot of women, but never before had she made love with a woman. Not until last night, when Jule had gripped her soul in one sentence: *I want to know you.* Five one-syllable words that had shaken her to the core.

She eased herself from Jule's embrace and took one long last look at her. *I'm so sorry, Jule. I can't be what you need.* She quietly slipped out of bed and gathered her clothes. She stopped short, nearly tripping over the large dark form on the floor at the foot of the bed. Sirius lifted his head and she cringed when the tags on his collar clinked together. He looked at her a moment and then sleepily put his head back down.

She crept downstairs and dressed in the first floor bathroom. She stepped out into the night, lit a cigarette, and drove home. *What have I done?*

Sex was supposed to be her release. Satisfy each other's physical needs and that was all. Nothing less. Nothing more. No one pressed for more and she was fine with that. It had always been enough.

Until now.

## Chapter Nineteen

Jule awoke before her alarm was set to go off—something she rarely did. The first thing she noticed was how satisfied her body was, but a horrendous emptiness replaced that feeling when she realized she was alone. Last night Randi had mentioned that she needed to be up early for work today. She listened for sounds of activity in the bathroom. Nothing.

She got up and slipped on a T-shirt. Sirius came to her side and followed her downstairs. Maybe she'd left a note on the kitchen table with a thank you or a phone number. Something—anything—to indicate an interest in seeing each other again. She flicked on the lights and wasn't surprised to find no such thing.

An unsettling rage surged through her. She wasn't sure what pissed her off more—her own foolishness, or Randi's selfishness. Randi could've at least let her know she was leaving. She'd thought she was different. That she was special. But no. Randi had gotten what she wanted and left—just like everyone said she would. But then, it wasn't like she'd promised anything either.

She instinctively reached for a pack of cigarettes on the phone stand and then remembered that she'd given them up. She let out an exasperated sigh and took Sirius outside. When he finished his business, she picked up the tennis ball and whipped it against the wooden fence so hard she nearly pulled a muscle. She threw it several more times. She knew she was probably disturbing the neighbors. She didn't give a damn.

She trudged into the house and got ready for work.

Four hours later, Brenda was pleading with Jule at the lunch table. "Are you crazy? Stay away from her, Jule. She's bad news."

After Toni and Kathy had gone outside to smoke, Jule had told Brenda the whole story. How she and Randi met, of Randi's proposition that night, of the budding friendship, and of the way their date ended last night.

"How do I know she didn't leave because she had to work early this morning? There's something there. I can feel it."

"And what if that's exactly what she wanted you to believe so she could get you into bed? Look how well it worked! That's her game, Jule. Everybody knows it. You should've heard what they were saying about her at the field last week, and not just about her using women for sex. Did you know her father's in prison for murder?"

The question punched her in the gut. "Are you sure?"

"Toni overheard some people talking about it on the bleachers. It could be a bunch of bullshit rumors, but I don't think so."

*Oh my God.* No wonder Randi avoided talking about her family. Her stomach churned. As her mind worked around what that meant if it were true, some of the pieces fell into place. The moments of sadness. The pain she saw in her eyes. The guarded demeanor when Jule urged her to talk about herself.

"Maybe if people showed her some compassion instead of judging her…" Jule let the sentence hang. She had done just that last night, but Randi had still run. It hadn't made a difference.

"It's not that I don't agree with you. I'm afraid you're gonna get hurt if you think last night will lead to something more with her. I'm telling you, let this one go."

That was going to be easier said than done. Part of her agreed with Brenda, but this news about her father only piqued her interest in Randi more. Not to mention that it seemed unlikely that Randi would have spent all this time putting on an act to get her into bed. She doubted she had put that much time or effort into seducing all those other women. Megan. The softball player. *Hell, she's probably slept with Nikki, too.* They were all thin and gorgeous. *Why would she be so interested in someone like me?*

Brenda sighed and looked at her sympathetically. "You're forgetting about one other thing."

"What's that?"

Brenda tipped back her head and let out a deep breath. She gave Jule's hand a squeeze. "Let's just say for the sake of argument that you two do become an item. She's a cop, Jule. Every day she goes to work, she could wind up in a situation where her life is in danger. After what you went through with Casey, could you deal with knowing she might not come back?"

It's not that it hadn't crossed her mind already, but she'd been so caught up in Randi's charm that she'd ignored it. She didn't answer and they walked quietly back to their workstations.

She began her next inspection, her thoughts drifting to the intimacy she and Randi had shared last night. The pain of waking up alone was too much. Maybe Brenda was right. Randi was a cop. What was she thinking?

She didn't need the anxiety of waiting for a police officer to show up at her door to inform her that her lover had been killed in the line of duty. And what kind of cop was Randi anyway? A cop who offered sex to get out of speeding tickets probably took other questionable risks as well. And if she never reported the marijuana she found in her truck, what did she do with it?

With Casey, she'd abandoned her orderly life and lapsed into a phase of recklessness. At first, it had been a liberating break from always being "the good girl." In the end, it had left her feeling empty and unsatisfied. She didn't want to go through that again—living life out of control and going nowhere.

*You fool. Why are you even thinking about her? Chances are that Brenda's right, and I'm not about to hang around and wait to be hurt and disappointed.* She knew damn well Randi wouldn't show up to go jogging with her today.

She zipped home to let Sirius out and then decided to do something totally out of the ordinary. She went to the mall to buy some new clothes to fit her newer, trimmer body. Knowing she had a grasp on *that* aspect of her life lifted her spirits. She could measure *that* type of progress. Sizes and numbers made sense. They reassured her she was doing the right thing for her body.

Now if she could only get matters of the heart to add up that clearly, she'd have it made.

❖

Randi called in sick and didn't feel an ounce of guilt over it. It was just as well. Showing up at the tail end of a good high would have guaranteed her a whole boatload of trouble. She had gotten home around three in the morning and resorted to smoking a joint to get to sleep, but it hadn't numbed the confusion.

What an idiot to think that all she had to do was sleep with Jule once to get her out of her system. Jule couldn't possibly be more *in* her system. *I want to know you.* The words haunted her as much as the memory of how their bodies felt pressed together. As much as how good it felt to be inside her, and the beautiful sounds she made when she came. As much as the sensation of Jule's hands caressing her breasts, of her kisses on her lips, of her mouth and tongue on her sex taking her into oblivion.

She downed the rest of her coffee and called the garage for an appointment for a state inspection. She was getting the Camaro on the road today, dammit. Mechanically, it was ready. She could replace the worn belts later, but she definitely needed new tires today, too. She stopped at the town hall to register it and picked up plates at the DMV.

It still needed the paint job and new upholstery, but maybe it was better that she hadn't had them done yet. She didn't want it to stand out. Not yet.

It was a gorgeous day, the type of day that New Englanders savored in the spring: seventies and sunny with a slight breeze to ward off the black flies. The trees were finally in full bloom, bursting with bright green foliage. She needed cigarettes, so she decided to walk two blocks to the drug store while her car was in the shop. On the way, it dawned on her that this was part of the route taken by Carly on the night she was raped. Her senses heightened, taking in anything she could observe of the surrounding area. She saw nothing out of the ordinary.

She stepped into the store only to learn that it no longer sold tobacco products. Smoking cessation aids had replaced the cigarette racks behind the checkout counter. Grumbling, she walked to the drink coolers in the back and selected, of all things, Dr Pepper. She placed it on the counter with a pack of gum and was appalled when she heard her own voice ask for a box of Step One nicotine patches.

Yeah. Getting Jule Chapin out of her system was gonna be a bitch.

Later, she was back on the road. Randi couldn't believe how smoothly the Camaro rode on four brand new tires. She splurged on chrome wheels to go with them, which made for a ridiculous look when combined with the faded paint and shitty condition of the body. *So what?* It was a work in progress, after all.

She cruised around Hampton Beach for a while, drove south to Salisbury Beach, and then around through Seabrook before returning to Hampton. She decided to take the long way home, electing to jump on Route 101 toward Manchester. At least with the sixty-five miles per hour speed limit on this road she could get away with seventy-five or eighty to keep up with the usual flow of traffic.

She rolled down the windows, the wind sweeping up memories of the first time Stevie took her for a ride in this car. She was twelve and she thought she had the coolest brother ever. He joked about what a chick magnet it would be. She'd told him he was a dork. She didn't like the idea of sharing him with anyone, much less some flakey, giggly girl who spent hours on her hair and makeup, and would rather spend the day at the mall than at a baseball game. Surely, Stevie was smart enough to see that a day with his supercool kid sister would be much more fun.

She got back to Portsmouth in time to find a good place to set up surveillance on Jule's afternoon jog. She parallel parked down the street among other cars. She couldn't see the house, but she could see the end of Jule's driveway. Once she saw Jule, she'd give her a bit of a head start before she pulled out. She hoped she could keep her distance without backing up any traffic that might come up behind her.

And so she waited. And waited. And waited. After half an hour, she started the car. Her heartbeat accelerated. *Maybe I'm too late and she's already out running.* If that were the case, she was out there alone. Would Jule be a temptation for the rapist? It wasn't likely, but still…*Shit.* She slowed down as she approached Jule's house. Her truck wasn't even in the driveway. She sighed in relief. Maybe Jule had taken her advice and gone to the gym to run on a treadmill.

She turned around in Jule's driveway and headed downtown to Avyanna. Jule's truck wasn't there either. *Damn.* She headed back out and tried the natural foods store. Nope. The home improvement store? No luck. What the hell? Was Jule so distraught over her leaving this morning that she went to the bar with her friends after work?

Great. Randi hated to think that Jule might have thrown in the towel on her healthy new lifestyle already. *I'm not worth it, Jule. Trust me.*

After an hour of searching, she laughed in frustration and recalled Jule's remark about stalking her on the night she caught her at the end of her driveway. What the hell was she doing? She needed to forget about her.

She pulled into her favorite sub shop and ordered a foot long steak and cheese before heading home to wallow in her pathetic excuse for a life.

And to put on her nicotine patch. *Christ.* First Nikki had planted a seed in her brain telling her she should give up the one-night stands and try a relationship. Now Jule had inspired her to quit smoking. *Who the hell am I?*

It was all too confusing and further proof that she wasn't cut out for relationships. Her chest constricted again. *I want to know you.*

Jule didn't know what she was asking. Once she told her about Stevie, about her father—and oh God, what if her mother's mental illness was hereditary? She'd wind up in therapy for sure, just like when she was a kid. It had been torture. One hour, twice a week, for three goddamn months. *Why didn't they understand that reliving it over and over again was driving me friggin' nuts?* Even at thirteen years old, she had been smart enough to acknowledge how ironic it was that she'd felt saner *before* she'd started therapy. The counselor had told Randi repeatedly that Stevie's death wasn't her fault. Bullshit. He wasn't there. Randi knew the truth—that if it weren't for her, Stevie would still be alive. And her father wouldn't be in prison.

How could she possibly talk to Jule about all this? Sweet, beautiful, feisty Jule, who had opened up and talked about her family, her job, and Casey. Jule had let down her guard and talked about how she'd grown dissatisfied with her life and was taking positive steps to turn it around. *I've barely told her anything about me.* A relationship would mean telling Jule everything.

Once she did that, there was no way Jule would want anything to do with her. Sadness ripped through her as she realized she was right. She had to forget about Jule.

It wasn't going to be easy. She grabbed a beer out of the fridge. She inserted a *Cagney and Lacey* disk into the DVD player and plopped onto the couch with the remote. She brought the bottle to her lips. *Bottoms up.* This was the kind of therapy she needed tonight— the kind that helped you forget.

Everything.

## CHAPTER TWENTY

Even from second base, Jule recognized Randi in the police car that stopped in the drive behind her team's dugout. A week had passed since their night together. She tried to stay angry with her, but it was a losing battle. As much as it hurt that Randi had lived up to her reputation as a player, Jule couldn't shake the feeling that they had shared something special. And it wasn't as if Randi had misled her in any way. She'd never pretended to be anyone other than who she was, and she'd never made any suggestion about wanting more than sex. Although Jule's ego took a hit, she couldn't be pissed off with Randi for being who she was. Reflexively, she flashed Randi a smile, but it was too dark to see if Randi was even looking at her. She wondered if she'd stick around.

She checked the runner on second, dug in, and readied herself for the next batter. As hard as it was to concentrate on the game, she wasn't about to make a fool of herself with another bonehead play.

The batter lined a hard base hit into right center field. Jule trotted out, took the cutoff, spun, planted her feet, and fired a bull's-eye home. The runner slid into the tag, ending the inning and preventing the potential tying run.

Thinking fast, Jule grabbed her right elbow and fell to the ground, writhing. Her teammates quickly surrounded her. Among the myriad of voices, the only one she wanted to hear came through.

"Give her some room." Randi parted the crowd and kneeled next to her. "Don't move. You okay? Where are you hurt?"

She looked up at the most beautiful law enforcement officer she'd ever seen. The genuine concern she read in Randi's eyes spoke volumes.

Randi called to Megan over her shoulder and quickly returned her attention to Jule. "Megan's an EMT. She can check you out."

"That won't be necessary."

"If you're hurt—"

Jule grinned.

"What?"

Jule motioned for Randi to lean in close and whispered, "I knew that would get your attention."

Randi leaned back and glared at her.

"Well? Are you going to help me up, or not?" She held out two perfectly healthy arms.

Instead of pulling her to her feet, as she expected, Randi nimbly lifted her into her arms and stood. Jule draped her arms around her neck.

"I see your arms are working just fine now."

She put her lips next to her ear and said, "You've got the magic touch, Officer."

"You're infuriating, Ms. Chapin."

"And you love it."

Randi's jaw tightened, and Jule could see her trying not to smile. She walked past the dugout and shouted to no one in particular, "Someone grab Jule's bag and follow me."

Jule looked up and saw Brenda running toward them. Jule winked at her and Brenda gave her a questioning look. Jule mouthed, "It's okay," and Brenda ducked into the dugout with a smile.

Randi carried her directly to the cruiser. When Brenda showed up with her gear, she followed Randi's orders to open the passenger side door, and Randi gently lowered Jule onto the seat.

"Thank you, Brenda."

Brenda looked at her oddly, as if surprised Randi remembered her name, even though they'd only met once at the club a few weeks ago.

Randi took the bag from her and placed it on the floor of the backseat. She closed both doors and addressed Brenda very seriously. "Don't worry. I'll take good care of her."

"You'd better. She's my best friend."

Randi saluted Brenda and got in. "Your friend doesn't trust me."

"Do you blame her?"

Randi winced. "No. No, I don't blame her at all."

"You're infuriating, Officer Hartwell."

A smile twitched at the corner of Randi's mouth. "And you love it." She started the car and stepped on the gas.

"Where are you taking me?"

"Someplace more private than this."

"Oh really? And what about my truck?"

"We'll come back for it. I'm still on duty. We can't go far." Randi turned slightly and gave her a smile.

Jule smiled back. "You can take me as far as you want."

Randi kept her eyes on the road, but Jule saw what looked like a struggle to maintain her cop face, and her grip on the wheel tightened. She drove quickly and deftly on back streets and then turned into a hidden wooded area Jule had never noticed before. She turned the car around so that it faced the road, but oncoming traffic wouldn't see it. Jule realized it was probably a place used regularly as a speed trap.

Randi cut the engine, turned, and cupped the back of Jule's neck to pull her into a kiss. At first, the kiss was urgent, filled with desperation and electricity, and then it grew into something so passionate and sensual that Jule never wanted it to end.

This time she didn't hesitate to pull Randi's police hat off her head and run her fingers through her hair. Randi had one arm around her shoulders and the other on her thigh. Jule became acutely aware of how easily she could feel Randi's touch through the thin polyester material of her softball pants. As if she read her mind, Randi slid her hand higher.

Jule pulled away and grabbed Randi's wrist. "Whoa. Wait a minute."

Randi retreated to her side of the car and Jule sensed the imminent emotional shutdown. She was learning to recognize the signs. The avoidance of eye contact. The tense shoulders. The clenched jaw. The silence.

"Sorry."

"Sorry for this? Or sorry for sleeping with me and then disappearing for a week?"

Randi stared out the driver side window.

"Don't get me wrong. If this is your idea of first aid, I'll fake an injury every game. But I need to know I'm not just a sex toy to you."

Randi snapped around to look at her. The fire in her eyes alarmed her, but Jule couldn't determine if it was anger or fear.

"I don't think of you that way."

"I didn't think so." Jule spoke softly. "Randi, I don't know what kind of secrets you're guarding, but you're not the only one battling demons here. You think this is easy for me? You're the first woman I've slept with since Casey died. I was so scared I'd see her face instead of yours. That I'd feel guilty, as though I was cheating on her, and that I was being unfair to you. Well, guess what? That didn't happen." She stroked Randi's cheek and managed a smile. "From the moment you first kissed me, I thought of you and only you. I've let her go. I'm ready to move on with my life."

Randi bit her bottom lip.

Jule suspected there was a debate going on in her head. She took Randi's hand and gave it a gentle squeeze. "I think there's something here worth exploring, don't you?"

Randi visibly tensed, then exhaled. She closed her eyes and gave an almost imperceptible nod.

"Hey." Jule lightened her tone. "I'm not proposing marriage or anything. What I'm saying is that I like you, Randi. I like you and life is short and I want us to give this thing a shot. I don't want to ignore my feelings and then wonder what might have been. I know you feel something for me, too."

"I'm scared. I've never done this before. What if I can't give you what you want?"

Jule smiled wider and shook her head. "In some ways, you already have. You just don't know it."

"I don't understand."

Jule kissed her lightly. "Actions speak louder than words. All I'm going to ask is that you don't run away from me again."

Randi released a deep breath. "What if I can't promise I won't?"

Jule kissed her again, this time teasing her with her tongue until she elicited a groan. "Then I'll have to find another bodyguard to go jogging with me. I'm already sick of running inside on the treadmill."

Randi finally smiled and some of the tension left her shoulders. "You really are a pain in the ass."

"Protect and serve, Officer."

"I'll see you tomorrow at four thirty."

Randi watched Jule toss the softball bag into her truck and climb in. She wanted desperately to follow her home, but she had to get back on patrol.

What a day. It started when she got to work and learned that she was off desk duty because Peterson had dropped the charges against her, thanks to a plea bargain agreement between the department and his lawyer. The wife corroborated Randi's story that he had resisted arrest. She had filed for divorce and was now staying at a safe house for battered women.

Of course, Lieutenant Baldwin delivered the news with another stern warning that this had better be the last time her temper caused the department trouble. She knew he was right. She could deal with a suspension, but there was no way in hell she was going to jail.

She hadn't intended to stop at the softball field long enough for Jule to notice her, but when Jule went down, she'd shot out of the car so fast she nearly bowled over everyone in her way. She couldn't get to her fast enough. When Jule admitted that she'd faked the injury, Randi realized just how much she cared. When she had picked her up and carried her to the car, she'd felt such a need to protect her that nothing else mattered, even though she knew Jule wasn't actually hurt. She hadn't even asked Jule if she wanted to finish out the game. Randi couldn't have waited that long to kiss her.

She dropped her keys on the kitchen table when she got home and slumped onto her couch. She didn't understand what was happening to her. No matter how hard she tried, she couldn't stay away from Jule, and saying no to her was proving impossible.

For the first time in twenty years, life wasn't…gray. For the first time in twenty years, she felt alive.

It scared her to death.

## CHAPTER TWENTY-ONE

They ran in silence. There was definitely something on Randi's mind, but Jule was unsure whether she should ask her what it was or not. She was beginning to wonder how long she would have to play this balancing act. Yet, she didn't want to risk scaring her off with all the questions she wanted to ask her.

It wasn't so much that Randi seemed sad and distant, but rather there was anger simmering just below the surface. Randi had no problem matching Jule's pace this time. Jule sensed a need to get some stress out of her system.

With a quarter mile to go, Jule slowed down to walk the remaining distance. As they let their breathing settle back to normal, Jule decided to test the waters.

"Randi?"

"Yeah?"

"What's wrong?"

"What do you mean?"

"You've barely said two words all afternoon, and you look like you want to kill someone."

"I'm fine."

Jule stepped in front of her, forcing Randi to stop and face her. She touched her cheek and Randi closed her eyes and let out a shuddered breath.

"You don't fool me for a second. Haven't you figured that out by now?" Randi's look softened, but Jule could tell she was struggling with a decision. "That's what scares you, isn't it? That I can read you so well."

"You have no idea what I'm thinking."

Jule took Randi's hand. "You're right," she said softly. "So tell me."

"I don't know if I can."

"Why not?"

"I'm not who you think I am," Randi grumbled as she brushed past her and resumed walking.

Jule didn't move. She gave Randi a few minutes alone before jogging to catch up. She smiled and nudged her shoulder. "So tell me, who do I think you are?"

"Please, Jule, I'm not in the mood for games. I had a bad day on the job, okay? I just want to get you safely home, then I can get home, and you won't have to put up with me being an asshole."

*Ouch.* Okay, so she'd pushed too far. Jule knew she should probably let it go. But now she was getting pissed. Pissed at Randi. Pissed at herself that she couldn't figure out a way to get her to open up, and pissed off that she cared enough to keep pushing, even though it could end in disaster.

"I didn't ask you to do this, you know. You're the one who keeps insisting on running with me."

Randi continued to look straight ahead when she answered. "I need to protect you."

"There's a whole town that needs protecting, not just me. Is there something you're not telling me? Did you spot the rapist in my neighborhood?"

"No."

Jule left her alone the rest of the way back, but there was no way she was letting Randi leave without one last attempt to improve her mood. When Randi came inside to grab her keys, Jule darted past her toward the bathroom.

"I really have to pee. Would you mind taking Sirius out before you take off?" She didn't wait for an answer. When she finished, she went outside expecting to see them playing their usual game of fetch. Instead, she found Randi sitting on the back step hugging Sirius with her face buried in his fur.

Jule sat next to her. Randi raised her head and turned in her direction. Her eyes were drenched and red. Jule gently wiped the moisture from her cheeks and waited.

"We raided a house today."

Jule swept a lock of hair from Randi's face. "And?"

"We found six dogs, seventeen cats, twenty-three rabbits, and four birds. Starved. Sick. Abused."

"Oh, Randi."

"One of the dogs…a shepherd pup, reminded me of Sirius. The asshole had kicked him so many times he broke his ribs. He was too weak to get away or fight back because he was starving to death."

Jule's blood boiled. She put an arm around her and tugged her close.

"I went ballistic. I kicked the suspect in the balls and when he went down, I kicked him in the stomach. I just kept kicking him, and I was screaming at him, 'How do you like it, motherfucker? How do you like it?' It took two cops and the Animal Control officer to get me off him."

Randi stood and lumbered out into the yard. She picked up a tennis ball and whipped it against the fence. Jule almost laughed, thinking of how she did the same thing when she was angry.

"I would have wanted to do the same thing."

"Yeah, but just 'cause you wanted to, you wouldn't have. I did. Don't you see? I'm no better than he is!"

Jule jumped up and went to her. "Are you shittin' me? How can you even think that?"

"How can I *not* think that?"

"For crying out loud, Randi, you kicked him because you care about those animals, not because you're an abusive person!"

"It doesn't matter what the reason is! When I get that angry, I can't control myself, and it scares the shit out of me. What if they hadn't been there to stop me?"

"But they were."

"But there are times there's no one to stop me." Randi looked like she was about to say more, but instead she looked away.

Sirius picked up the ball and circled them twice before giving up and dropping it.

"Hey," Jule said softly. "Are you saying this isn't the first time you've done something like this?"

Randi's jaw tightened and she slowly shook her head.

"Is that why you were on desk duty before?"

Randi nodded.

"Oh man. So what happens now?"

"I'm suspended indefinitely."

Sirius let out a whine and nudged Jule's hand. She petted his head and said, "Someone's ready for his supper. How about you?"

Randi nodded before letting out a long, slow breath. "Yeah. Okay."

After eating quietly, they curled up on the couch together and watched a movie. Then they climbed into bed, and Randi promptly fell asleep in her arms. There wasn't any need for a discussion about it or a long talk about expectations. It was unguarded and easy, and the understanding that they weren't going to talk about anything deeper than what to watch or drink was a given.

When Jule's alarm awoke her the next morning, Randi was still there, nestled in between her and Sirius. Her arm was draped over the dog, both of them sound asleep. It felt so natural to see them there, together, in her bed. Her insides warmed with affection and... something else she couldn't quite name. A need to make her feel safe, perhaps. Or...no, she couldn't quite admit it might be something beyond simply caring for her. She wasn't sure she was ready for *that*.

Maybe she wasn't ready because it was too soon and because Randi was still a puzzle. Was the anger she carried around because of her father? Was he really a murderer? She couldn't imagine how difficult it would be to live with that knowledge. Was that why Randi became a cop? Was she trying to atone for his crime?

She had witnessed Randi's tremendous capacity for compassion. It was evident in how badly she'd been affected by finding the rape victim and the abused animals. *And in the way she'd rushed onto the field when she thought I was hurt.*

What concerned her was the way Randi dealt with those emotions. Yet *she'd* been the one who'd pushed Randi for a chance to be together. She couldn't give up on her when Randi had begun to let down her shield. She wanted to help her, but she couldn't be her savior and neglect herself in the process. She needed to be careful. Maybe if she gave Randi time to open up, she could give her a safer outlet for her feelings, so that she wouldn't act out in anger.

She smiled. Randi had said she liked to take pictures. *I have an idea.*

❖

Randi woke up alone. She rolled onto her back and stretched out her entire body. She wore only underwear and one of Jule's T-shirts. She couldn't recall feeling this rested in ages. She turned onto her side and hugged Jule's pillow into her body, breathing in her scent. The bright sun streaming through the gap between the curtains told her it was late. The clock on Jule's nightstand told her it was well past ten. *Holy shit.* She had slept more than twelve hours.

The jingle of dog tags made her smile, and she sat up to find Sirius lying on the floor beside the bed. On *her* side of the bed. He looked at her anxiously with his ears perked.

"Morning, buddy." She scratched his head and behind his ears before making her way to the bathroom. When she returned, she made the bed and marveled at the realization that she'd spent the night in a woman's bed without having sex with her. Without ducking out in the wee hours. Without feeling guilty.

She'd slept. She'd felt safe. She'd felt…cared for.

Her heart sped up. Sirius followed her to the guest room down the hall, and she slipped on her jeans. She started to pull off Jule's shirt, changed her mind, and scooped up the rest of her own clothing. She found a note on the kitchen table in handwriting so neat it belonged on an architect's blueprints.

*Good morning beautiful,*
*As I'm sure you've figured out, I've gone to work. You were sleeping so soundly I didn't want to wake you. Have some breakfast and stay as long as you want. I'm on vacation starting tomorrow. I'd love to spend some time with you—if you're interested—since you're suspended anyway. I'm going hiking tomorrow. I thought you might want to come along and bring your camera. I've done this trail before and I think you could get some awesome shots. (Plus I need to fill some empty wall space—ha ha!)*

*Anyway, call me tonight and let me know. No game tonight, so I'll be home.*

*Jule*

At the bottom, Jule had written her cell phone number and a request to take Sirius out before she left. Randi tucked the note into her hip pocket and heated a cup of coffee in the microwave.

"Come on, let's go out." She tapped her thigh and Sirius followed her out the back door. She leaned on the rail, watching him and sipping her drink. She closed her eyes. Warm sunshine washed over her face while thoughts of Jule warmed her inside. She knew in her heart there was no turning back now. Something—everything—had shifted. She'd never let herself cry like that in front of anyone. That had to mean something, though she wasn't sure what.

She eased into one of the porch chairs, feeling lazy and unambitious, and let Sirius linger in the yard. She should get home and work on the car. The interior needed detailing, and she still had belts to replace. Having it painted might have to wait now, since she had no idea when she'd see another paycheck.

The department could only let her slide so far. Tim had been taking the heat for her for years. She couldn't expect him to save her ass all the time. It wasn't fair to him or the other officers. God, she was such a loser. *What does Jule see in me?* Jule didn't seem like a desperate person. Maybe she was just a sucker for lost causes. Had Casey been a lost cause, too?

Maybe it was about time to get Jule to open up more, too.

Yeah, something had definitely shifted. She never cared this much about getting to know anyone before. It felt good for a change, as if finding out what made Jule tick was awakening something buried deep inside her.

## CHAPTER TWENTY-TWO

How long *is* this trail anyway? It looks like you've packed enough stuff for a week." Randi heaved a backpack onto Jule's shoulders. "Holy shit. This thing weighs a ton." They were taking the gear out of the back of her SUV. Sirius darted back and forth in the backseat, barely containing his excitement.

"I like to be prepared."

"Prepared for what, Armageddon?"

Jule opened the back door, attached Sirius's extendable lead, and he bounded out and headed for the nearest tree to relieve himself.

"Yes. I prepared us for the end of the world. I hope you brought your bazooka to fend off the fools who didn't plan ahead."

"Sorry, but the only bazooka I brought was the bubble gum out of your softball bag."

She chuckled and handed Randi her camera bag. "It'll have to do. Don't forget, you're taking pictures so I can finish decorating my house."

Randi grinned and settled into her gear.

She had never seen Randi so relaxed. Randi's job took an emotional toll on her, but she still suspected that the root of Randi's stress had something to do with her family. If the rumors about her father were true, it couldn't be easy to be a cop who was the daughter of a murderer.

She had chewed over going online to look for more information, but couldn't bring herself to invade Randi's privacy. When Randi was ready to talk about it, she would. The more time they spent together, the more Jule was sure they might be headed in that direction. *Cross that bridge when you come to it.* If Randi was in no hurry to spill her guts, then that was probably a good thing. *You have enough work to do on your own shit.*

Something had definitely changed since Randi stayed over Thursday night. Jule thought for sure she would have left during the night as she had before. What a wonderful feeling to wake up with Randi beside her. It must have been a cute sight, the three of them spooning each other: Jule's arm around Randi, Randi's arm around Sirius.

Neither of them brought up the animal rescue during the long ride this morning. Their moods were surprisingly light, and they enjoyed easy conversation and effortless banter. Randi always seemed like a different person when she wasn't working or talking about her job. Jule wondered why Randi was a cop if she hated it so much.

She took one last look through the truck to make sure they hadn't forgotten anything and they headed off into the woods. This was a popular hike because it was a small mountain and suitable for just about anyone who wanted to enjoy a nature walk without roughing it too much. She liked that she could take the short trail and circle back down in less than two hours, or continue higher if she wanted more of a challenge. She hoped Randi would be up for the long trail. Not only did she think it would be good for her—mentally and physically—but because she wanted to spend as much time with her today as she could.

"You quit smoking," Jule said after about an hour. Randi was sucking on her third lollipop since they'd started, her choice of a healthier alternative.

Randi gave her a wry smile. "Bought some patches. Maybe that's why I've been on edge."

They exchanged brief smiles before returning their attention to the path. It was going to be hard to keep her hands off her today. Well, that applied every day, but Randi was especially adorable right now. Her faded jeans had a hole in one knee, which she found charming, and like Jule, she was wearing suede rough terrain sneakers. She'd thrown a gray zip hoodie over a black T-shirt and she'd taken advantage of her unexpected day off yesterday to get a haircut. Her hair was above the ears and collar now, and her bangs were shortened a bit to show off more of her gorgeous face, but were long enough to keep that mysterious sexy look.

Randi patted her back pocket. "I made sure I brought plenty of patches so you won't have to put up with me being an ass if they wear off."

She doubted Randi would *be* an ass, but she certainly didn't mind *looking* at Randi's ass. Especially with how good it looked in those jeans. *Yikes. Down, girl.* "I'll have to make sure you have a good time today so that won't happen."

Randi surprised her by taking her hand. "What did you have in mind?"

"If I told you, we wouldn't even make it halfway through the kiddie trail."

Randi raised an eyebrow and smiled mischievously. "Oh really? I have ways of getting it out of you. I could be a detective instead of a street cop if I wanted to."

"So why don't you?"

Randi shrugged. "No use contemplating that now. The rate I'm going, I'll be lucky to keep my job."

"What'll you do if you lose your job?"

"Haven't thought about it."

*Odd.* Jule would stress to the max if she thought she might be out of a job. She'd had the security of a steady paycheck for so long, it was hard to imagine having to find work elsewhere on short notice. But Randi seemed relieved. Of course, maybe that was the difference—Jule liked her job. Randi hated hers.

"If you could do anything you wanted, what would you do?"

Randi looked at her long and hard. She either didn't have an answer, or was debating if she was going to share it if she did have one. Suddenly, her eyes widened and her gaze moved over Jule's shoulder. "Shh. Don't move."

Jule was frightened for a second, but when she saw Randi smile, she was curious. Randi slowly kneeled and slid off her camera bag and opened it. She removed a 35mm camera from a leather case and expertly replaced the normal lens with a zoom as if she could do it in her sleep. Jule slowly turned and saw Randi's target—three deer through the woods about twenty yards away. Randi snapped away.

After a few minutes, the deer meandered out of sight. Randi's face glowed with a smile so beautiful that it was all Jule could do not to jump her right there.

"That's what you should do. Take pictures for a living."

Randi's smile faded.

"What? Why not? It makes you happy. You should do something that makes you happy, not rip your heart to shreds like the job you have now."

"I can't."

Jule shook her head. "Why not?"

"I just can't. I'm a cop. It's what I do."

Randi packed up the camera bag but left the camera around her neck. She resumed walking the trail.

Jule caught up, trying to figure out what that meant. "But it's not who you are."

"It's not that simple."

"So you keep saying. There are other jobs, you know. Are you a cop because you want to be a cop, or because someone else wants you to be a cop?"

"It doesn't matter."

"How can you say it doesn't matter? It's your life, Randi. You have a right to live it the way you want to."

Randi stopped. There was fire in her eyes. "No. I don't."

Jule stared at her. "Okay. If you say so." She walked by her. "By the way, you might want to change that patch now."

Randi glared at her, dropped her gear, and shrugged off her sweatshirt. She pulled up her sleeve and peeled off the old patch.

Jule fought back a smile. "You are so sexy when you get mad."

"Is that why you enjoy pissing me off?"

"Nah. You're always sexy. That's just a bonus."

That triggered a smile. Randi tied the sweatshirt around her waist and slapped on the new patch. "There. That ought to keep me out of trouble for a few hours." She hoisted her bags back into position.

Jule refrained from commenting. As tempting as it was to keep flirting with her, she was starting to see that flirting was one of Randi's defense mechanisms. And she was damn good at it. No wonder she had the reputation she did.

They walked for another hour, stopping twice for Randi to take shots of a chipmunk scampering across in front of them and up a tree, and again for several shots of a pair of cardinals.

They reached a small clearing and stopped to rest. The sun was high in the sky, indicating it was around noon. The temperature had risen at least ten degrees since they'd begun and Jule guessed it was close to eighty. Her stomach growled.

"You ready for lunch?"

"I'm freakin' starved." Randi removed her packs. She rubbed her neck and shrugged her shoulders, trying to stretch them out. She unclipped the canteen from her hip pocket and took a long drink.

Jule followed suit. She withdrew two collapsible bowls from one of the bags and gave Sirius food and water. After smoothing the ground with her foot, she spread out a blanket and set out a picnic lunch of sandwiches, chips, baby carrots, and cucumber slices. They ate heartily and then chowed down on the homemade chocolate chip cookies Jule had made last night. When she noticed Randi rubbing her neck again, she scooted around behind her.

"Let me do that."

Randi dropped her hands into her lap.

Jule worked her thumb and fingers in circular motions on Randi's neck. Man, she was tight. "Hold on a sec."

She went to her backpack and took out a small tube of lotion. She lathered up her hands and began working kinks out of Randi's muscles. Little by little, she felt them relax.

"Oh, Jule. This feels like heaven."

Jule gravitated to the shoulders, cursing the fabric between her hands and Randi's skin. It wasn't as if she could undress her here— they had already crossed paths with other hikers a few times today. When Randi dropped her head and vocalized her pleasure, Jule was tempted to say the hell with it and strip off Randi's shirt anyway.

"If you keep this up, I'll be ready for a nap."

Jule wrapped her arms around her and whispered into her ear. "If I keep this up, neither of us will be napping."

Randi turned within the embrace and caught her lips. Like horny teenagers, they were all arms and legs, fighting for position and determined to keep the kiss going. Randi slipped Jule's denim shirt off her shoulders and slid a hand beneath her T-shirt. In one smooth motion, Randi eased Jule onto her back and lowered herself on top of her.

One thing was for sure: they couldn't make love here, but Jule sure as hell wanted to when they got back to her house tonight.

❖

Randi wanted Jule so bad it hurt. This was turning out to be one of the best days of her life. Except for when Jule brought up the career change thing. *What an ass I am.* She'd only gotten angry because she knew Jule was right. Of course, she couldn't tell Jule the truth—that she was only a cop because she owed it to Stevie.

*Focus.* She didn't want anything to screw up this day. She slowly drew away and looked Jule in the eye. There was so much…emotion, in those eyes. No one had ever looked at her that way before. It was going to be her undoing. She just knew it. She leaned in and kissed her again, this time with such hunger she was afraid she'd strip her and take her right there, putting on one hell of a show for any passersby to see.

Jule deserved better than that. She pulled away again, though it took a tremendous amount of energy to do so, and stroked her cheek. "If I don't stop now, I won't be able to stop."

Jule's breathing was heavy, and she gave Randi a pleading look that begged her to continue, yet acknowledged agreement that they needed more privacy. "You'd better get off me then, because I'm about to explode."

Randi sat back and extended her hand. They packed and continued up the trail. The terrain was rougher on this stretch, as well as steeper. As they forged on, the trees were scarcer and they could see more of the sky peeking through ahead. The air was cooler, which wasn't a bad thing since they had both worked up quite a sweat. Sirius panted heavily. They stopped one more time to give him a drink and to replenish their own fluids. There wasn't a lot of conversation, and what they did say was light, surface stuff. It felt so carefree and simple, something Randi couldn't remember ever feeling before.

A little past three o'clock, there was a noticeable decrease of foliage. The trail twisted into an s-shape littered with sparse shrubs. They rounded a corner and stood atop a wide-open plateau. There was nothing but the clear blue sky above and the magnificent view of the surrounding forest and mountains.

They grinned at each other like kids and put their arms around each other's shoulders, taking it all in.

"Wow," said Jule.

"Yeah. Wow."

Jule's eyes were sparkling. The bright afternoon sun accentuated the golden streaks in her honey-brown hair. *My God, she's an angel.*

"Isn't it the most beautiful sight you've ever seen?"

Randi thought of that night in Montana when she lay on her back in the grass, with billions of stars as far as she could see. Before her life was torn to pieces in a matter of seconds. Before she knew such unbearable pain. Before she imagined anything could shatter her ambitions of a photography career. Before she gave up on falling in love.

"Not even close." She rested a hand on Jule's cheek and put the other on the small of her back. She drew her close. "You are."

Jule pulled her in for a kiss. A cool breeze swept over them, blowing Jule's hair, tickling her face. Randi imagined it falling over her naked body as they made love. Goose bumps erupted all over. She was weakening fast.

Jule seemed to read her mind. "We better head back down so we can get to the bottom before dark."

"Yeah. Okay."

They couldn't get there fast enough. Going downhill was a little easier, but they were setting a pace that was far quicker than the leisurely stroll they'd taken on the way up.

They didn't talk much. They focused on the ground ahead, carefully avoiding tree roots and dodging stray branches. Randi even passed up a few photo opportunities. Jule probably noticed but didn't say anything. It wasn't like they couldn't come hiking again.

And there it was. A plan for a future. A hope that they could do this again sometime. Things to look forward to—something she rarely granted herself permission to do.

Randi's imagination was running rampant with visions of dinner dates, going to the movies, attending all her softball games, walks on the beach together, playing with Sirius, and hanging out at each other's houses. Jule didn't even know where she lived. She never had company. No one had even been over since Shawn moved out when she and Jaymi got back together. Nikki's brief stops for a quickie didn't count.

She should have shut off these thoughts, but whenever Randi stole a glance at her companion, they crept up on her. She wasn't paying attention to her surroundings.

Her foot caught the root so hard, her toes almost wedged themselves beneath it. Her lower leg twisted awkwardly. Before her mind grasped what was happening, she hit the ground, landing on her shoulder. A searing pain ripped through her ankle.

"Randi! Shit." Jule dropped her bundle and finagled Randi out of hers. "Where are you hurt? Your knee? Shoulder?"

"Ankle. Damn, it feels like it's on fire."

"Put your arm around me. Let's sit you up." Jule started to scootch her toward a tree.

"No! Not there!"

"Huh?"

Randi pointed to an area near the tree. "Poison ivy."

"Shit." Jule looked around. "Over there. I hate to drag you that far. Can you stand?"

"I'll have to lean on you, but yeah."

Jule planted herself firmly and they stood up together.

Randi tried to put weight on her left foot and immediately regretted it. "Argh!"

"Don't try to walk." Jule securely grabbed her around the waist, placed her other hand on her stomach, and waited until she steadied herself. She looked into Randi's eyes. "Trust me."

Randi bit her lip and nodded. Her ankle throbbed and the pain was worsening.

"Take it nice and slow. We're gonna hop over there. Whenever you're ready, okay?"

Randi took in a deep breath and blew it out. Despite the agony she was in, she resisted telling Jule just how badly she'd like to take *her* nice and slow.

When she didn't answer right away, Jule said again, "Trust me."

"Yeah. I do." She managed a smile and Jule smiled back with an earnest look of reassurance.

"Ready?"

"Ready."

As if he knew what was going on, Sirius came to her other side. Randi latched on to his leather collar and he gave her the added balance needed as she hopped along.

"Good boy, Sirius," said Jule. "He never ceases to amaze me."

"Takes after his mama."

Jule was much stronger than Randi expected. She settled her against a giant oak, and Randi wasn't the least bit surprised when she unzipped an outer pocket of her pack and removed a first aid kit. She balled up her jacket and Randi's sweatshirt and gently guided one under her injured ankle and the other beneath her knee. After carefully removing Randi's shoe, she activated an instant ice pack and applied it to the ankle.

"I've got some ibuprofen in here, too. That and the ice should help minimize the swelling." She handed it to her with her canteen. Randi swallowed it down, praying it would take effect quickly.

"Thanks, but I'll probably be okay in a few minutes. Just give this a little time to kick in."

"You might have a nasty sprain there, Randi, or worse. We can rest here a bit."

"We can't sit here long. We won't make it back before dark. Especially if I'm gimpy."

"Then we'll spend the night."

"What, just sleep on the ground in the middle of the woods? Are you crazy?"

Jule grinned. "You afraid the big bad wolf'll get you?"

"Wolves. Bears. Bugs. Snakes. Where you going?"

Jule laid out her backpack and unzipped it all the way. She peeled back the flap and pulled out something made of fluorescent-yellow nylon and started unrolling it.

"Unbelievable. You have a pop-up tent?"

"Yup. It's only thirty-six square feet, but it can sleep two. I also have blankets, matches, flashlights, biodegradable toilet paper—"

Randi laughed. "No wonder these things are so friggin' heavy."

"And you teased me about over-packing."

Randi swung an arm across her stomach and bowed slightly. "I promise that will never happen again."

"Shame, though. I only have one self-inflating sleeping pad. We'll have to share."

"Yeah. What a shame."

## CHAPTER TWENTY-THREE

It didn't take Jule long to set up camp. Fortunately, there was a small but level clearing nearby. After she erected the tent and stowed everything inside, she helped get Randi settled on the air mattress. It wasn't easy convincing her to lie down. She kept insisting she was fine and that she felt bad that Jule was doing all the work.

But when Randi attempted to stand, she was in obvious pain and gave in. "Stop fussing over me, Jule. I'm a big girl."

Jule bent over and kissed her forehead. "Stop being so stubborn. Maybe I like fussing over you."

"I'm not used to being fussed over. I feel guilty sitting on my ass while you're stuck doing everything."

"Am I going to have to shut you up with a kiss?"

Randi laced her fingers together and put her hands beneath her head. Randi's T-shirt rode up, revealing a teasing glimpse of her toned abs. She wiggled her eyebrows. "Isn't that what got us into this mess in the first place?"

Jule's center pulsed. *Shit, how do you do this to me?* "I don't recall hearing you complain."

"How could I with your tongue in my mouth?"

She moved within an inch of Randi's lips. "Let me take care of you or I'll be keeping my tongue to myself for, oh, I don't know, a week? A month?"

"I'm in pain and you're threatening to punish me?"

"Punish you? Torture myself is more like it. Do you have any idea how irresistible your lips are?" She straightened up and backed off. "Now behave, because I'm way too tempted to kiss you right now."

Randi grinned like a fool. "Pain in the ass."

"Touché." She went to work gathering kindling to start a fire so she could heat up some food.

Jule was grateful to put a little distance between them so she could gather her thoughts and get her hormones under control. It was encouraging to see Randi loosen up a little.

She sucked in clean air and the familiar scents of pine and the other various plant life. She loved this place. Everything was so green and alive. She'd done this trail with Brenda many times. And once with Casey—a total disaster. If she were in this situation with Casey right now, it would have been because Casey had stumbled from being drunk off her ass. *Who are you kidding? You would've been drunk, too.*

She had spent so much time over the past year in shock and grief that she was just now realizing that she had fallen out of love with her before she'd died. Now she questioned whether she was ever in love with her in the first place. It was a sobering, uncomfortable thought.

She got back to the tent and thought about Randi. She hadn't felt for Casey what she was beginning to feel for Randi, and as scary as that was, it was also incredibly exhilarating.

She set down her armload of sticks and poked her head through the tent's opening. Randi was stretched out on her back, with Sirius beside her looking as content as could be.

"Hey, I'm back."

"Good. You need any help?"

"Nope. I'll have a fire going in a few minutes and then we can eat."

"Eat what? What did you do, hunt rabbits while you were gone?"

"Yeah, right. Like I could hunt anything. I'm an animal lover like you, remember?"

They smiled at each other. Randi propped herself up on her elbows and asked, "Can I please come sit out there with you? I'm bored stiff in here. You could've at least given me some reading material before you went foraging for firewood."

"Sorry, I didn't bring any. Reading wasn't exactly in my plans for the day. Oh wait, I've got my iPod." She reached into one of the many pockets of her cargo pants. She fussed with it and handed it over.

Randi looked pleased with her taste in music, but then she set it aside and reached out her hand.

Jule took it, assuming she wanted help sitting up. Instead, Randi pulled her down on top of her. Randi's body was solid, but soft and warm in all the right places. She could feel Randi's nipples straining through her T-shirt. Their eyes met. Jule said, "You're looking for trouble."

"Always."

Jule kissed her forehead and ran fingers through her hair. Randi pressed her lips to her neck and then traced an earlobe with her tongue. The hot breath sent heat coursing through her veins. Jule gave in and their lips came together.

Again, the sweet tenderness of Randi's kiss took her by surprise, despite the fire and hunger, she sensed she was holding back. As if she were saving it for later—or afraid to let go.

She slipped a hand beneath Randi's shirt, relishing the smooth skin and the tempting swell beneath her bra. *Not yet.* There was still enough daylight left that a passing audience was a possibility. She grazed her palm one more time over Randi's stomach and then traced a finger up her right arm. When she reached just above the bicep, she discovered the sleeve was stuck to Randi's arm as if glued down. She ended the kiss and sat up.

"What's wrong?" Randi asked.

"You've got blood on your sleeve. Shit, I was so worried about your leg I didn't check the shoulder you landed on when you fell."

Randi twisted her head to look. She was about to lift up the sleeve, but then looked at Jule strangely and stopped. "I'm sure it's nothing. Just a scrape."

Jule fetched the first aid kit. "Let me take a look."

"Jule, don't worry about it. I'll wash it off later."

"It could get infected."

Randi gave her another stubborn look.

"Let me take care of you. Please?"

Randi shook her head slightly and sighed. "You make it difficult to say no, you know that?" She closed her eyes, looking resigned.

"Good to know."

She gently pried up the fabric and separated it from the flesh. The abrasion was about two inches wide and deep enough to make her nervous. She rolled up the sleeve. On the rounded part of her shoulder was a tattoo of a silver police badge detailed in dark blue and the name Stevie.

*Huh.* She hadn't noticed it the night they'd slept together. It had been too dark. Randi had clearly been hesitant to let her see it just now. Why?

She looked at Randi and saw an almost indiscernible shake of the head. Her jaw was clenched shut, and Jule wasn't quite sure what she saw in her eyes. Warning? Pain? Once again, Jule set aside her curiosity and focused on the task at hand. She soaked a cloth with water from the canteen and dabbed the cuts clean.

"This might sting a little," she said as she shook the can of antiseptic spray. Randi winced as it hit the wound but seemed to relax when Jule respected her unspoken message. She quietly tended to the scrapes and applied a gauze bandage before handing Randi a long-sleeved T-shirt from the clothing partition of her pack.

"Where'd you learn all this first aid stuff?"

"I'm on the safety committee at work."

Randi smiled. "Of course you are."

Sirius let out a loud whine. He was scratching at the tent opening. She gave Randi a peck on the cheek and said, "He has to go. Why don't you get changed while I take him out and start supper?" She tossed Randi the shirt.

As she walked with Sirius through the woods, she thought of the many questions she wanted to ask but wasn't sure she could yet. *Who's Stevie? A friend on the police force? An ex-girlfriend?* She doubted Randi would tattoo a girlfriend's name on her body—not with her playgirl reputation. Unless…maybe she became a playgirl after a woman named Stevie broke her heart? The thought made her wince, but somehow, she thought it must be something more than that. How was she ever going to get answers, when she couldn't even ask the questions?

She sighed and tried to focus on their surroundings. For now, she'd have to be content with taking care of her and spending time with her. The other stuff could wait.

❖

Randi watched Jule and Sirius disappear into the woods. She scooted across the floor and crawled out the tent's door hatch. She zipped it shut and picked up the thick branch Jule had found for her to use as a cane and stood. She grabbed a packet of the toilet paper, limped away from the site, and managed to brace her body against a tree as she squatted to relieve herself. Nothing could ruin the mood more than needing help to pee.

Back at camp, she decided to surprise Jule by starting the fire. She saw two foldable pans next to the fire pit Jule had made. She peeled open two food pouches and emptied them into the pans. She set the pan on the wire cooking frame she'd set up above the flame so it would be heated through by the time Jule returned. Although her shoulder and ankle ached horrendously, she didn't want to just lie around with her thoughts.

She knew Jule was dying to ask about the tattoo. She'd forgotten about it until she rolled up her sleeve. She had panicked, but as usual, she was helpless to resist the way Jule so gently took care of her.

In that moment came a fleeting temptation to tell her about Stevie. No one in her circle knew about Stevie, not even the two people she could loosely call her closest friends, Nikki and Shawn. Why start now? Speaking of Nikki and Shawn, she noticed Jule had both Passion Play albums on her iPod. She rested against a boulder and scrolled through the menu on the device.

Her collection was quite extensive. Jule was definitely a rocker girl. Big into '60s classic rock and women rockers: Led Zeppelin, Janis Joplin, Pink, Rolling Stones, The Who, Jefferson Airplane, Melissa Etheridge, and Sheryl Crow, just to name a few.

It was a bad move, but she couldn't help herself. She wedged in the earbuds and selected Passion Play. She skipped over the first track, one of Nikki's songs. As soon as she heard Shawn's voice, she closed her eyes and relaxed. Yeah, definitely a bad move. Shawn's sexy voice always kicked her hormones up a notch.

If there was anyone who could get her over Shawn, it was the remarkable woman emerging from the woods and walking toward her right now. Even in khaki cargo pants, a denim shirt, and a baseball cap, she was the sexiest thing she'd ever laid eyes on. Shawn's song ended and the voice of Shawn's lover, Jaymi, took over.

She tuned out Jaymi's voice and heard only Jule's in her head: *I want to know you.* Was she ready to give her that? Jule had to be wondering about the tattoo, and probably all the other stuff Randi wouldn't talk about, but she hadn't pried. If Randi was going to open up about herself, it started with Stevie. Everything started with Stevie.

She pressed stop, removed the earbuds, and sat forward. Sirius, refreshed and happy, scampered to her side for a hug.

"Glad to see you're getting around on your own. How's the ankle?"

"Still sore, but better. I think the painkillers helped. That should be hot enough by now," Randi said, pointing to the pans of chili and sweet corn.

"Great. Thanks. I don't know about you, but I'm starved."

Jule wrapped the handle with a potholder and divided the contents into two aluminum bowls.

"I still can't believe you brought all this stuff."

"Good thing I did, huh?"

"Yeah." Randi blew on a spoonful and took a bite. *Not bad for vegetarian.*

Jule told Sirius to lie down, since he was trying desperately to put his nose in her bowl. "I already fed you, now be good." He reluctantly obeyed. "What were you listening to?"

"Passion Play."

"Good choice. I love that new song they just put out, don't you? With the mandolin in it? That Jaymi Del Harmon can play anything with strings, can't she?"

Randi blurted, "That's Shawn."

"Oh." Jule gave her a strange look and washed down a bite with a swallow of water. "So, what's the scoop on you and Nikki, anyway? How'd you guys meet?"

*Shit.* The honest answer? She could easily tell her they'd met when Nikki tended bar at the club before the band hit it big. But damn it, she didn't want to lie to Jule. It was no secret that she hit on women she pulled over—that's how she met Jule for Christ's sake. She hadn't done it since. *Don't be a coward. Do it.*

"I pulled her over for speeding."

Jule eyed her suspiciously. "And I take it she didn't turn you down like I did."

"No, she didn't."

"Wow. Are you saying you were able to charm a rock star into bed easier than a nobody like me?"

Randi might have been irked if it hadn't been for Jule's playful tone. "Hey, first of all, you're not a nobody. And in my defense, she wasn't a rock star yet. And you've seen her—she's hotter than that campfire."

"Uh-huh. And I bet she's even hotter in bed."

"Leave me alone."

"I suppose you've had your way with everyone in the band by now."

She knew Jule was teasing her, but a wave of heat rose through her face. Her reputation was coming around to bite her in the ass. "You didn't by chance bring anything stronger to drink than water, did you?"

Jule's smile dissipated. "Sorry, but no. Is there something more between you and Nikki? Shit, Randi, you're not cheating on her with me, are you?"

"No, we're...no. Not her."

Jule scooted over to her side. *Shit, Jule, don't do this.*

"Someone else in the group?"

"If you must know, I had a crush on Shawn, but that was it. I'm not involved with any of them, all right?"

Jule stroked her cheek, kissed her lightly, and said, "I don't want you thinking of Nikki, or Shawn, or any other woman right now."

The way Jule kissed her, that wasn't going to be hard. The sun was setting. The world was slipping away. An unfamiliar sense of peace was settling within her. Randi deepened the kiss and pulled Jule in close. Her body felt so good, despite the wrinkled, dirty clothes, damp with sweat from their long day. She wanted Jule out of them. Naked, with nothing between them. She wanted to explore her inside out and sate her every sense with Jule and nothing else.

She made a move to get up so they could take this to the tent, when Jule spoke two words that made her freeze.

"Who's Stevie?"

A lump lodged in Randi's throat so fast she had no time to raise her shields. She couldn't see. She couldn't breathe. Her heartbeat thundered so loudly in her ears she thought her head would explode.

Her eyes stung. She released Jule and stumbled away on her hands and knees. She couldn't look at her.

Jule's voice echoed through the madness as if they were in a tunnel. "Randi, sweetheart. Please, I know what it's like to lose someone you love. I have to live with Casey's death every day, but I won't let that stop me from loving someone else. Whoever Stevie is, she obviously means something to you—"

Randi shook her head violently. Her mind cleared, and she forced herself to her feet. She looked at Jule. She had that same look of love and concern she'd seen in Stevie's eyes right before he died.

Jule stood and waited.

"Randi?"

"No, please…" Randi choked on her words.

"Baby, don't be afraid. Let me in."

"Why? Because you want to know me?" Her voice was hoarse and sounded alien to her own ears. Her ankle was screaming, but she had no choice—she was too worked up to sit, and she couldn't walk away.

"Yes. I want to know you." Jule spoke so softly that Randi's next words sounded like a lion's roar.

"You want to know who Stevie was? I'll tell you! Stevie was my brother. He was murdered right in front of me when I was thirteen." The fucking dam had broken. She was powerless to stop it. "My father went to the courthouse and put five bullets into the bastard that killed him. He's doing time for it right now. You want me to keep going? How about my mother was so fucked up over it all they had to put her in a fucking mental hospital! Is that what you want to know?"

Jule's face was soaked with tears and Randi realized that hers was, too. She was shaking so badly she thought her legs would collapse beneath her. Jule took a step toward her and Randi flinched.

"Yes." Jule's voice was barely above a whisper.

Randi stared at her.

Jule moved within arm's length and very cautiously placed a hand on her cheek. "Yes, baby. That's what I want to know."

Randi's vision blurred. Her tears continued their downpour.

Jule closed the gap and took her into her arms. "It's all right, baby. It's all right. I've got you."

Randi sobbed even harder when she felt Jule's tears against her shoulder. It was a strange and wonderful feeling. *Jule's crying for me. With me...as if she knows my pain. Something I didn't think anyone else could feel.*

She vaguely remembered making their way into the tent. Jule tucked a blanket around them as she curled into Jule's embrace. "We can talk more tomorrow. For now, just let me hold you."

The relief of saying the words out loud nearly made her dizzy. She wanted desperately to sleep, but a slideshow of memories with Stevie bombarded her. She shivered when it reached the final frame. Stevie struggling with the intruder. The deafening gunshot. Stevie folding in half with a jerk as the bullet ripped through him.

"It's okay, sweetie. I've got you." Jule squeezed her tighter.

With great effort, she willed her breathing to slow down. She relaxed into the safety of Jule's arms. "We used to play cops and robbers." She wasn't sure Jule had heard her. She barely heard herself.

"Tell me about it."

"Stevie hated playing the bad guys, but I didn't mind. Big surprise there, huh?"

Jule smiled against her cheek. "I plead the fifth."

"Smart move. We were cops most of the time, you know, partners. I liked it best when we acted out episodes of *Cagney and Lacey.* I used to tease him about being Lacey, 'cause he'd have to play a woman, but he said it was only fair, since I played the male roles in other games. That's how I knew he would've been okay with me being gay."

Jule caressed a damp lock of hair off Randi's forehead. "He sounds like a cool guy."

"The best." She swallowed back tears. "He's the one who started calling me Randi. Said Miranda was too girly for me."

"I think it suits you better, too. So he was cool *and* smart."

"Yeah." She was surprised that she actually wanted to tell Jule more, but she didn't know where to start. Her eyelids were suddenly very heavy. She succumbed to their weight and closed her eyes. "Thank you, Jule."

"For what?"

"Just...for everything."

Jule kissed her cheek and whispered. "You're welcome. Thank you for sharing this with me."

"There's a lot more I haven't told you."

"I know. We have time. Right now, you need to sleep."

"G'night."

"Good night."

## CHAPTER TWENTY-FOUR

Jule barely slept. In all the times she'd contemplated Randi's secrets, she had never imagined such horrors. Randi hadn't even filled in the details, but as she broke down and choked it out, Jule's heart ached for her. *It certainly explains why she didn't want to talk about her family.*

The sun began to filter through the yellow canvas. Randi had tossed and turned much of the night, waking them twice when doing so exacerbated the pain in her ankle. Jule wondered if she ever had nightmares about her brother's death.

Right now, Randi was breathing steadily with intermittent light snores, indicating she was sleeping more soundly now than she had all night, most likely from sheer exhaustion than anything else. Jule hated to disturb her, but she had to pee. Sirius stirred and she had no choice but to get up. She carefully extracted herself and they slipped outside.

She started a fire when they returned. She boiled the water she'd collected from a nearby stream and made a cup of instant coffee. She'd never admit it to Randi, but she'd also thought she'd gone a bit overboard with all she had packed for a one-day hike. She was grateful now that she had.

She sat against a tree with her coffee. Sirius finished his breakfast and lay down beside her. It would have been heavenly to have spent last night at the peak and watched the sunrise together this morning. *Maybe next time.*

If Randi gave her a next time, that is. Had she pushed her too far? When she saw the tattoo, it hadn't occurred to her that Stevie could be a guy, much less a relative. What was the significance of his name in the badge? Was Stevie a cop?

She finally had some answers, and now she had more questions than ever. She'd have to wait to contemplate them, though, because she could hear movement inside the tent. The door flap unzipped and Randi poked her head outside. She gave Jule a bashful smile and wordlessly disappeared, limping into the brush to relieve herself.

She handed Randi some coffee when she returned.

"Thanks."

"You're welcome. How're you feeling?"

"Better."

"Think you can make it down today, or should we plan to spend another night?"

"You have enough supplies for another twenty-four hours?" Randi let a small smile escape. "That's probably a stupid question."

Jule smiled back. "You're getting to know me too well."

Randi looked down at her cup and took a sip. "Ditto."

She wanted so badly to touch her, not in a sexual way, but to comfort her. She held back for now, careful about what to do or say next. "I'm so sorry about your brother."

Their eyes met. The connection between them had intensified, and she was sure Randi felt it too. She rested a hand on Randi's thigh.

"I can see he meant a lot to you."

Randi took a deep breath. "He was everything."

"How old was he when…when it happened?"

"Seventeen."

*Ouch.* Jule pictured the tattoo and another piece fell into place. "He wanted to be a policeman, didn't he?"

"It's all he talked about."

"Is that why you became a cop? As a way to honor him?"

Randi laughed humorlessly. "Believe me, I've done him no honor as a cop. God knows I've tried. But yeah, that's why I joined the force."

"I don't understand."

"It's my fault he died." The fire was back in her eyes. "I took away his dream. I'm a cop because I owe it to him, but I'm not the cop he wanted to be."

"Randi, you're not making sense. How can it be your fault he was murdered? What happened?"

Randi scrubbed her face in her hands.

Jule gave her leg a gentle squeeze. "Tell me."

"You don't know how hard this is."

Their conversation was interrupted by the sounds of an approaching group of early morning hikers. They greeted them as they passed.

Once out of earshot, Randi slowly stood and said, "I need you to understand something—and don't take this the wrong way—but I've never told this stuff to anyone. I just need a little more time to get my head around that. I'm also in desperate need of a shower and clean clothes."

Jule swallowed the rest of her coffee and stood. She picked up the tree branch cane and handed it Randi. "Okay. Whatever you need. Let's get packed up and head out."

"Yeah, okay."

Jule brushed her cheek with a kiss. "I want you to know you can tell me anything. Whenever you're ready, baby."

They touched foreheads and Randi closed her eyes. She pulled Jule into a hug and whispered, "Thank you."

Soon, they were on their way.

Randi moved much better today. The swelling wasn't gone, but had lessened. She took another dose of ibuprofen and assured Jule that she was okay as long as they took it slow. Jule led the way, keeping an eye out for any trip hazards, and was relieved when Randi didn't hesitate to lean on her or Sirius when the footing was tricky.

Once at the bottom, she tossed the gear into the back of the truck and helped Randi into the passenger seat. It was a good thing they hadn't needed to spend another night. The sky clouded and there were showers all the way home. Randi slept for much of it, leaving Jule to her thoughts about life and death.

It wasn't until she pulled into her driveway that she remembered that Randi's car was a standard shift. That'd be tough on a sprained ankle. She was about to bring it up when Randi beat her to the punch.

"I think you'll have to give me a lift home. If you don't mind."

Only two days ago she had given Jule her cell phone number. Now Randi was going to let her see where she lived. Despite all the progress Randi had made in trusting her recently, she was still a bit shocked.

They drove about ten minutes to a white Cape with black trim. It had a garage and a small yard surrounded by trees and shrubs that provided plenty of privacy. She helped Randi out of the truck, and Randi directed them in through the garage entrance. Jule was amazed at what she saw: a muscle car enthusiast's dream of a classic Camaro. She wasn't sure how old it was, but she guessed it was a late '60s or early '70s model. There was a wall-length workbench, a tool chest, and two large storage cabinets. A pegboard filled with tools hung on the wall above the bench. The tools were neatly organized by type and size, making the quality inspector in her drool. The entire garage was spotless.

Randi grinned and gestured to the car. "You like it?"

"Like it? Are you crazy? It's beautiful!"

"Just needs a paint job and a few final touches and it'll be done."

"What, you mean…you're restoring it yourself?"

"Yep."

Randi chewed her lip and stared at the car for a minute before she opened the driver's side door.

"Get in."

Jule looked at the newly reupholstered seats. "Me? No, I can't. I mean, I'm all dirty."

"Oh, come on. Don't be a fussbudget. Get in."

Jule sank into the leather and groaned with pleasure. "Oh my God. This is the coolest car I've ever been in."

Randi raked her fingers through Jule's hair and kissed her. "And you are the second coolest person who's ever been in it."

"Thanks. Wait. What do you mean the *second* coolest person?"

Randi smiled sadly. "It's Stevie's car."

*Holy fucking shit. Randi's letting me sit in Stevie's car.* "Randi, I'm touched. Really."

Randi shrugged. "You're still pretty cool, you know. You're definitely the sexiest person to ever sit in it."

"No, I'm pretty sure you have that honor."

"Come inside. I'll show you the house."

They went through a door to a finished basement. Now Jule could see how Randi kept in such good shape. She had an entire home gym set up, including a universal, free weights, and a treadmill. There was an old couch and small table along one wall and a TV on the other side. There were several plastic storage totes stacked in one corner and a door to what Jule assumed was the boiler room. In another corner was a bathroom.

Jule helped Randi up the stairs to the main floor. Randi dropped her keys on a table in the eat-in kitchen. It was simple and small, but laid out functionally well. Next was a living room. Randi didn't decorate much and her tastes were modest. There was all the standard necessary furniture and a 32-inch flat screen TV. Jule noticed photography magazines on the coffee table, a cabinet full of DVDs, and beautiful framed photos on the wall.

"Did you take all these?"

"Yeah. You like 'em?"

"Randi, they're spectacular! They look like something you'd see in a gallery."

"My family went on a cross-country camping trip when I was twelve. I took most of these in Montana."

Jule took in the collection of wildlife, mountains, flowers, sunrises, and night skies. "Look at all those stars."

"I know. They don't call it the Big Sky state for nothing. I'd never seen so many stars in my life. It was like you could see all of them at the same time."

"They're beautiful." Absent from the pictures were any people. It wrenched her heart to think it must have been too painful for Randi to display family photos. She quickly did the math. Stevie had died a year after these were taken.

Randi led her down a hall and showed her a bathroom and a master bedroom on the left. Opposite her room was an office. Randi said she'd never done anything with the upper floor, so there was no point showing it to her.

They returned to the kitchen and, knowing how badly they both wanted to shower and change, she reluctantly said she should get going. Randi pulled her into a tight hug.

"Thanks for the ride."

"You're not exactly in any shape to drive."

"And thanks for, you know, everything else."

"Anytime. Are you going to be okay? You need help with anything before I go?"

"I'll manage. I won't attempt a shower, but a long, hot bath is calling my name."

"Call me if you need me, okay?"

"I'll need to get my car back."

*I hope you want to see me for more than that.* "True. Any ideas?"

Randi smiled. "You wanna bring it over later? I'll make you dinner."

"And how will *I* get home?" *Two can play this game.*

"I should be okay to drive you home tomorrow."

"Tomorrow? Are you inviting me to stay the night?"

Randi gave her a long, slow kiss. "Only if you want to."

"Mmm. I definitely want to. What about Sirius?"

"He can stay over, too."

"Good. What are you cooking us?"

Randi opened the refrigerator and pulled a face. "Damn." She snatched her wallet off the kitchen table and pulled out two twenties. "Here. Pick up some Chinese food on your way over."

Jule refused the cash. "I'll get it. You paid for dinner at the Gas Light, remember? It's my turn to treat."

"Fair enough. What time?"

"Six?"

"Five hours should be enough time to get the slime off me."

"I sure hope so." Jule kissed her and left, feeling both happier and sadder than she had in years. She wondered if Randi planned to share more with her when she got back. *Am I ready to handle more?* What if Randi couldn't bring herself to tell her the rest? Where did that leave them? If there was any chance of a future with her—*wait just a minute, there, girl. Future?*

Randi had trusted her to open up about her pain—something she said she'd never done before. *Would she have done such a thing if she didn't feel something for me, too? Is she thinking about a future with me?*

Future or not, she'd let Randi into her heart, and she wasn't at all confident that she had the will—or the ability—to keep her out of it now.

❖

Randi closed the door behind Jule and was acutely aware of how empty the house felt without her in it. Her heart, however, was full. Just like her head, which was now swirling with thoughts of Jule and Stevie and Dad and Mom and the Camaro and Sirius and...*slow down.* She needed a smoke as badly as she needed a bath. No wonder—she hadn't changed her patch since last night, before she'd imploded.

She started the bathwater and went to her room for clean clothes. Jule was coming over and Randi wanted to look good for her. She was staying the night, and that opened up a whole new path of thoughts. *In my house. No one stays the night in my house.* Not even Nikki. Well, other than that one time she hid out here for about a week because she was pissed off at Jaymi. *Shawn lived here for a month.* That was different. She'd never slept with Shawn. She sure as hell wanted to at the time.

And tonight Jule was coming over to eat, hang out, and maybe watch a movie. *What did I get myself into?*

She smiled when she looked in the bathroom mirror and saw herself in Jule's shirt. She shook her head and chuckled. She was smiling at her own reflection—*now that's a switch.* She stripped and shut off the faucet. Getting into the tub was going to be a challenge. If she stepped in with her bad foot first, she'd have to stand the weight on it while she lifted the other one. Yet she couldn't do the opposite either. Maybe she should have had Jule stay to help her after all.

Then again, she needed this time alone. She needed to figure out how to proceed from here, now that Jule knew about Stevie and the other bits about her family she'd spilled.

She sat on the edge of the tub and, using the toilet and wall for support, swung her legs over. Bracing her hands on the sides, she lowered her aching body into the steaming water. She closed her eyes and took a deep breath. She slid forward and sank beneath the surface, staying under until she knew if she remained there much longer, she would drown. A month ago she might have contemplated staying under. She would have been thinking of Stevie. She would have been thinking about how much she hated her life. How much she hated the ugliness in the world. How much she hated the pain that just wouldn't go away.

And now, she only hated every minute she wasn't with Jule. Hell, even being without Jule's dog sucked.

Her oxygen was running out. She pushed herself up and sucked in as big a breath as her lungs would take, and let it out slowly. She slicked back the hair from her face, relaxed her head on the inflated bath pillow, and closed her eyes again. Calm washed over her as thoughts of Jule took over again. How many nights had they spent together now? Four or five? They'd only made love once. How was it possible that she wanted Jule more than she'd wanted any other woman, and yet she'd fallen asleep on her every other night? What kind of message was she sending?

That she wanted more than just sex with Jule, that's what. That she cared for her. She felt safe with her. She actually *slept* when she was with her. Even after a joint or sleeping pill, she didn't sleep as long or as soundly as she did with Jule.

The water was cooling off and she hadn't even washed yet. She turned on the hot faucet and quickly shampooed her hair and washed before she began to prune. As she dried off and dressed, she thought about how much she wanted to make love with Jule again.

And then, afterward, how badly she wanted to sleep.

## CHAPTER TWENTY-FIVE

Jule hurried home and showered. She didn't know why she was rushing. She didn't have to leave for hours, but she was so anxious to get back to Randi, she couldn't help herself. She walked naked from the bathroom to the bedroom and opened the closet door. She was glad she'd bought new clothes, because now she had several outfits from which to choose. She tried on three combinations before deciding on a navy and gold plaid cotton button-up shirt and a new pair of carpenter jeans.

She changed her mind several times about whether to put her hair into a ponytail, a braid, or leave it down. In the end, she left it down. The next thing to do was to pack an overnight bag and whatever Sirius would need. She unpacked the hiking gear, threw in a load of laundry, started the dishwasher, and spent an hour tidying her already neat house. She still had an hour before she had to leave.

She thought of calling Brenda. She almost called her sister, Denise, who had been her steadfast confidant most of her life. For some reason, she didn't want to talk to them about Randi yet. She knew they would just bug her for more details, and that would feel as if she were betraying Randi's trust. She knew it hadn't been easy for Randi to divulge what she did. As excited as she was about their budding relationship, she still wasn't sure where it was going. She wanted it to be on firm ground before she started telling people there was someone new in her life.

Inviting her over tonight had to be a good sign. Randi would have driven herself home, or even taken a taxi, if Jule had scared her off in any way. She was obviously interested in more than sex. She'd had several opportunities since that one night to take off and never call again, but she hadn't. But then, she hadn't seemed to want sex either… *Shit, Jule, quit overanalyzing every damn thing. Randi likes you.*

She arrived at Randi's house a half-hour early. As always, Jule caught her breath when Randi opened the door and flashed a smile. She looked so gorgeous in jeans and a heather blue pullover that she nearly dropped the food and tackled her.

"Hi. Let me take those for you."

Jule knew she had a stupid smile on her face. Sirius barged in beside her and started sniffing everything in sight. Randi set the bags of food on the counter and then pulled Jule in for a hug and a quick kiss.

Jule said, "Did you miss me?"

Randi kissed her again, teasing her tongue with her own, and holding her closer. She finally pulled away. "No. I didn't miss you at all." She grinned and her eyes twinkled.

Jule's heart danced. "You hungry?"

Randi's pupils darkened. "Starving."

Jule didn't think she was talking about food—and that was more than okay with her—even though she knew they still had some serious stuff to talk about, it was getting harder and harder to keep her libido in check.

"You look beautiful, Jule." She ran a hand through Jule's hair and twirled a lock between her fingers.

Jule felt her face flush. "You clean up well yourself. Come on. Let's eat before it gets cold." She reluctantly extracted herself from Randi's arms.

They filled their plates and sat at the kitchen table. Sirius aborted his explorations to plant himself on the floor between them.

"Whatever you do, don't feed him from the table. I've worked hard on teaching him to wait until we're finished. But we're not at home, so he's going to see what he can get away with."

Randi pouted. She looked at the pitiful furry face. "Sorry, buddy. Mama said you have to wait, and I'm really hoping for a good night kiss tonight—from her, not you! That means we better do what she says."

Sirius twitched his ears as she spoke to him, as if considering his options. He let out a whine and slid down onto the floor, keeping his head up and eyes on their forks.

"You're amazing with him, you know that?"

Randi shrugged. "I'm sure he just listens to me because you've got him so well trained."

"No, he definitely responds to you better than he does to anyone else I know."

"Magic touch, I guess."

Jule smiled. "Seems to be working on me, as well."

Randi returned the smile and tore off a generous bite of beef teriyaki.

Jule turned her attention back to her meal. She loved the nights they'd spent together so far. She loved that they were sharing more. She loved that Randi was starting to open up more. She cherished the increasing closeness.

And there were times like now, when she just wanted to tear off Randi's clothes and have her way with her.

They finished eating and fixed a plate for Sirius. He slurped it down in ten seconds and then did the same with his water bowl. After cleaning up and taking him out, they settled on the couch to find a movie to watch.

Randi picked up the remote, but instead of turning on the TV, she set it on the arm of the couch and turned to Jule.

"Aren't you going to ask me about my screwed-up family?"

Jule swiveled to face her and folded one leg up on the couch. "Your family isn't screwed up. You all suffered a terrible tragedy. Do I want you to tell me about it? Of course I do. But I think your need to get it out is more important than my need to know." She added softly, "I already care about you either way."

Randi's look pierced through her. She looked confused and touched and many other things Jule couldn't read. She returned a look she hoped was inviting and safe. Randi held her gaze and touched her cheek.

"You...God, Jule you do things to me. I don't even recognize myself anymore. This sounds crazy, but that's a good thing, not a bad thing. I know I'm not making any sense—"

"It makes perfect sense. Maybe I'm the one you're meant to share it with. Just like maybe you're the one who's meant to give meaning to my life, too. I've wasted so much of my life without it having any meaning. Trudging along in a job, going through the motions every day, and never doing anything with my life that matters. Then, just like you, someone I care about is struck down—right in front of me. Casey and Stevie were taken away sooner than either of them deserved. We're left behind to pick up the pieces. We're the ones who suffer and wonder what could have been if only they had lived. It makes you think they were the lucky ones, doesn't it?"

Jule didn't expect the tears any more than she expected to say all she just said. Sometimes Casey's death did that to her—blindsided her just when she thought she'd made peace with it. She'd wanted to give Randi a chance to open up, and here she was turning the conversation on herself.

She reached up to wipe away the tears, but Randi beat her to it. Before she knew what was happening, Randi was rocking her in her arms and stroking her hair. When she finished crying, Randi pulled away and kissed her cheek.

"I'll make a deal with you," Randi whispered. "I'll tell you my story if you'll tell me yours."

"Deal."

"I want to know you, too, Jule."

Now she knew the impact of those words for herself. She shifted in Randi's arms and their lips came together. The tenderness was there again, but this time it changed quickly to hunger. She maneuvered Randi onto her back and hovered over her, searching for Randi's tongue with her own. When she found it, she released a groan from the back of her throat. She slowly lowered her body and pressed her center between Randi's legs, eliciting a groan from her, too.

Randi grabbed her ass and encouraged the contact, thrusting her own hips upward, matching her every move, driving Jule closer and closer to her breaking point. She didn't want to go over the edge so fast—especially when they were both still fully clothed—so she backed off and broke the kiss.

"God, Randi. How do you get me so hot so fast?"

"I told you. You do things to me no one's ever done before. I want to devour you. I want to—"

*This is too much.* Jule placed her palm on Randi's chest and gently nudged her back. "I'm sorry."

"What?"

"I think we should slow down. We said we'd talk. I can't just give in to my hormones like I did before, when I thought it would only be that one time. I need to know you, Randi. I want you to know me."

She saw a brief flicker of hurt, then apology in Randi's eyes. "You're right. I'm sorry." Randi slowly stood and limped toward the kitchen. "You want something to drink?"

"Sure. Water's fine."

Randi disappeared and Jule flinched when she heard Randi open what sounded like a beer. She didn't want to panic and jump to the conclusion that Randi used alcohol to relieve stress the way Casey did. *Give her a break, Jule. This is hard for her.* Still, she needed to proceed with caution.

Randi returned, handed Jule a glass, and sat at the other end of the couch with her beer. She sighed heavily. "Are you sure you want to hear all this?"

Jule touched Randi's knee. "You can tell me anything." She took a generous drink of her ice water and braced herself.

Randi let out a long breath. "My brother…shit. Nothing's going to make sense if I don't start at the beginning." She took a swig of her beer and shifted uneasily into the corner of the couch. "That means I have to start with my father."

"Okay. Tell me about your father."

"He's a cop—*was* a cop. I come from a family of cops. Stevie wanted to be a cop. It was all he ever talked about."

"But not you."

Randi shook her head. "I wanted to take pictures." She gave Jule a sad smile. "But you already figured that out, didn't you? Stevie was all set to go to the academy after graduation. But he couldn't enroll until after he turned eighteen in July." She ran a hand through her hair. "Anyway, earlier that year, Dad testified against a man he'd arrested who was accused of abusing his wife and kids. The court took away his visitation rights. A week after Stevie graduated, the guy broke into our house." She picked up her beer. "It was a Sunday afternoon. My parents weren't home. I was in the kitchen." Randi picked at the label on her bottle. She peeled it off and crumpled it tightly in her hand. "Stevie was downstairs and I heard him yelling at someone. So I went down to see what was going on." She downed the last swallow of her beer and set the bottle on the table. She leaned forward onto her thighs. Her hands were shaking.

Jule softly covered them with her hand. After a minute, Randi turned her hand palm up and let Jule interlace their fingers.

"It happened so fast." Her voice cracked as she spoke. "When I showed up in the doorway, I saw a strange man in the room. Stevie shouted at me to run back upstairs and call 911, but I didn't. I froze. The guy pointed a gun right at me and said, 'Your old man thinks he can take my kids away from me? Well guess what? I'm gonna take his kids away from him.' And then Stevie grabbed his arm and tried to get the gun away from him. He pushed Stevie away and aimed at me again, but Stevie tackled him."

Randi was shaking. Jule gently ran her thumb back and forth on Randi's hand, not wanting to distract her, but needing to let her know she was there.

"They struggled on the floor, and then the gun went off."

Jule put her arm around her when she began to sob.

"Don't you see? That bullet was meant for me. It should have been me that died, not Stevie."

"Randi, what makes you think he wouldn't have killed Stevie after he'd killed you? He was going to kill both of you—"

"But he didn't. After he saw what he'd done, he got scared. He dropped the gun and ran from the house."

"And you've spent all these years feeling guilty because your brother lost his life saving yours?"

"He didn't deserve to die," Randi said through clenched teeth.

"No, he didn't. Neither did you."

Randi scrubbed her face with her palms.

"What happened next?"

"Everything got weird, like I was watching myself in a dream. I remember calling 911. I remember someone pulling me off Stevie's body when they showed up. I remember that my mom was hysterical. My dad, he was just numb. The next few days are a blur. The day after the funeral, two police officers came to the house and told us my father showed up outside the courthouse as they were bringing the guy in and opened fire on him."

"Oh, Randi."

Randi pushed through another onset of tears. "So Stevie's gone. My father's in jail. And my mom's a basket case who couldn't take care of me. Or herself. We couldn't stay in that house anymore, so we moved in with my aunt."

Randi stared across the room. She absentmindedly stroked Sirius's head and gently drew circles with her thumb in Jule's palm.

"Randi, look at me."

Randi slowly turned her way.

"None of that was your fault."

"How can you say that?"

"Because if the situation were reversed, you would have done the same for Stevie, and you know it."

"I'm not sure I would have—"

"I do. You refused to leave the room. Even with a gun pointed at you, you wouldn't leave him. Come on, I've seen how protective you are with people you care about. You're like that with me and Sirius. Look at the way you reacted over those animals you rescued last week. You'd give your life in a second to protect any one of us. I don't know if I'd have the guts to risk my life for someone else. I'm too scared of dying."

"Some things are worth dying for."

Jule let out a long breath. "That may be true, but there are also things worth living for."

Randi looked at her. "That doesn't mean I deserve those things."

"Bullshit. Tragedies happen every day. If there was anything different you could have done to save Stevie, you would've done it. I beat myself up for months after Casey died. I kept telling myself that I should have seen the signs. She complained about heartburn a lot. I brushed it off and blamed it on all the fried food she ate. She seemed to tire out and get out of breath easily. I just figured she was out of shape because she didn't exercise."

"Jule, you're not a doctor. If you noticed it, I'm sure other people did, too. It's not your fault she didn't take care of herself."

"That's exactly my point, Randi. Stevie loved you enough to protect you. That was his decision. That's nothing to feel guilty about."

"But—"

"You need to let yourself off the hook. He died because of that maniac, not because of you. You need to stop blaming yourself for the actions of others. This was not your fault. None of what happened was your fault. Your father made his own decision, without thinking of the consequences to his family. That's on him. Not you. And I would give anything for you to believe that so you can stop hurting like this."

Randi folded herself into Jule's arms and cried like a baby. She couldn't even begin to comprehend the pain Randi had been living with for all these years, and Randi's belief that she was responsible for her brother's death only added to that turmoil.

As she let Randi cry, she thought about how differently Stevie's and Casey's deaths had affected them. The image of Casey dying was imprinted in her memory. She would never forget the agony and confusion on Casey's face as she suddenly pressed a palm to her chest. Or the shock as she collapsed to the floor. Or the helplessness Jule felt as she pulled her lifeless body into her arms. Or the terror she felt when she placed an ear to Casey's chest and heard nothing.

She and Randi had both suffered terrible losses. But Jule had allowed herself to grieve for Casey. Since then, the focus had been on fear of her own death, not on the life that Casey never had the chance to live. She didn't have the guilt to deal with over the cause of death, but rather the self-deprecation for her own lifestyle. Maybe she needed to let herself off the hook a little bit too.

Randi grew quiet. Jule gently released her and wiped the wetness from her cheeks before placing a kiss on each of them. "Are you okay?"

Randi shrugged. "What do you think?"

"I think it's a good thing that you finally got that off your chest. I'm glad you told me."

"Hmm." Randi excused herself to the bathroom. She then went to the kitchen and came back to the couch with two more beers. She handed one to Jule.

Jule hadn't had a beer in over a month. She hesitated for only a moment. *What the hell. You deserve to give yourself a break right now, too.* Her resolve intact, it went down easily. "Randi?"

"Yeah?"

"Where's your mother now?"

"She moved back in with her sister."

"And is she...okay?"

Randi again picked at the label on her beer bottle. When she managed a small tear, she peeled it off and began folding it into squares until she could fold it no more. Then she flicked it onto the coffee table. Jule wondered if this was another new habit she'd developed since she quit smoking.

"My mother drank herself into oblivion every day for two years. I came home from school some days and she was so wasted that she thought I was Stevie's ghost coming back to haunt her. Or she thought she was dead and talking to him in Heaven. Sometimes she couldn't even look at me because I know I looked like him, and she couldn't handle the fact that I wasn't him." Randi set the unfinished drink on the table and pushed it away. "Aunt Sandy finally made her get off her butt and get some help."

Jule ached inside. How in the world did a thirteen-year-old handle all that? She looked at the grown woman next to her right now. Her skin was damp with tears and sweat. Her hair was mussed. Her dark eyes were distant, yet full of fire and vulnerability. Jule knew Randi was dealing with an explosion of emotions that were crashing through all at once.

"And were they able to help her?"

Randi nodded slowly. "It took a long time, but yeah. She's better now. She even works part-time at a bakery and does okay. It's good for her, you know? Gets her out of the house."

"Do you ever see her or talk to her?"

"She calls once in a while just to be a pain in my ass."

Jule smiled. "So I'm not the only one, huh?"

She combed her fingers through Jule's hair. "She'd like you. You don't let me get away with shit."

"I'd love to meet her sometime."

"I'm not sure if that's a good idea."

"And why is that?"

"You might give her some pointers."

Jule laughed. "You mean you listen to me but not your own mother?"

"Well, you do have…" Randi cleared her throat and traced Jule's jawline with a fingertip. "…other weapons at your disposal that are much more persuasive than her guilt trips."

Jule leaned in to kiss her. "Oh really? Such as?"

Randi looked at her lips and ran her hand up Jule's thigh. "Do you really have to ask?" She stood and led Jule to the bedroom. Randi sandwiched Jule's face between her hands and kissed her. A slow, achingly tender kiss that was full of promises of what was coming. She fingered the buttons on Jule's shirt, eased it open, and then lightly brushed her hands around her torso and unfastened her bra.

They continued to kiss. Randi pushed the shirt off Jule's shoulders, and when Jule lowered her arms to let the shirt and bra drop, Randi yanked off her own shirt. She pulled Randi closer, pressing their breasts together into a delicious bonding of flesh as Randi explored her mouth with her tongue.

Randi's hands moved to Jule's jeans, and in a matter of seconds, both had pulled off their pants and come back together, still standing by the side of the bed. Randi broke the kiss, and before she knew what was happening, Randi lifted her into her arms. They kissed again, and then Randi slowly lowered her onto the bed and settled on top of her. The strength and weight of her was intoxicating.

Randi looked into her eyes. "Are you okay with this?"

"Yes." Jule pulled her down into another long slow kiss. "More than okay." She placed one hand on Randi's breast. Randi gently took her hand and interlaced their fingers.

"I don't want you to touch me. Not yet. I want all my focus on you." Randi placed a light kiss on the side of her neck, sending shivers down her entire body. Randi hovered over her as she continued to kiss her neck all over. She went across her throat, up and down, placed a peck on her chin, her forehead, and then gave each cheek a turn before moving to the other side of her neck.

"You taste so sweet," Randi whispered into her ear. She caressed her earlobe with her tongue and expelled a warm breath, sending a jolt through every nerve ending.

"Oh God, Randi, you're going to make me come just by doing that."

"Don't you dare."

Her kisses traveled downward, and she sucked on her shoulder as she wet it with her tongue. She followed the pattern across her chest to the other.

Jule put her arms around her.

Randi sat up, breaking the contact. She interlaced their fingers and then lowered their joined hands onto the bed on either side of Jule's head. "I said no touching. Not yet."

"I can't help it."

Randi grinned mischievously. "Do I have to handcuff you to the bed?"

Jule's imagination went crazy. "I'll try to behave."

"Don't try too hard." Randi released Jule's hands and went back to kissing her body. She flattened her tongue across a nipple and then took it softly between her teeth. She then spread her lips around the areola and sucked on the hardened nub.

Goose bumps swarmed all over Jule's skin. Randi's touch was feather soft as her hands caressed her all over. Her kisses traveled downward and the anticipation of having Randi's mouth on her only made her crazier.

"Oh God, Randi, if you don't take me soon—"

Randi slid a finger inside her.

Jule nearly screamed and Randi said, "Tell me what you want."

"Baby, please let me hold you. I need to hold you."

"Yes." Randi's voice was breathy and ragged. "Hold on to me. Hold on to me and don't let go."

Jule wrapped her arms around her and savored the smooth skin tinged with sweat. "I've got you, baby."

Randi kissed her abdomen and continued to tease her with her fingers. Just when she didn't think she could stand another instant, Randi opened her with both thumbs and replaced them with her lips and tongue. She could have climaxed immediately, but Randi expertly took her time and everything seemed to shift into slow motion.

She raked her fingers through Randi's hair, guiding her and moving in rhythm with every stroke and flick until she was so high she grew dizzy.

Suddenly, Randi pulled away. Jule cried out and opened her eyes. Randi looked right at her and said, "You're beautiful," and quickly resumed, sending Jule into an ecstasy she'd never experienced in her life. Moments later, Randi moved to Jule's side and fell asleep within her embrace.

She held Randi close. She fit as if she belonged there. And it felt wonderful.

## CHAPTER TWENTY-SIX

Randi awoke wrapped in Jule's arms. Without opening her eyes, she smiled contently and replayed last night in her mind. Despite all the women she'd been with, she couldn't recall ever experiencing anything remotely close to the connection she had with Jule. She rolled over and stretched her arm around Jule's waist. She was surprised to feel clothing.

Jule stirred and opened her eyes. The sunlight streaming through the window highlighted the golden streaks in her hair and her amber-specked eyes sparkled as she smiled. "Good morning, baby."

"Morning, beautiful." Randi kissed her lightly and brushed back a lock of Jule's hair. "You're dressed."

Jule looked down and murmured, "Yeah, I got up to pee and was a little cold."

"I'll have to do a better job keeping you warm." She kissed her again. Jule's mouth tasted fresh and minty—she'd also brushed her teeth when she got up during the night. She ran a hand down Jule's side and slipped her fingertips beneath the waistband of Jule's sleep shorts.

Jule grabbed her wrist.

"It's a little late to be playing hard to get, don't you think?" Randi said in a teasing tone. She slid her hand upward and underneath Jule's shirt.

Jule tightened her grip and stopped any further movement.

"What's wrong?" asked Randi. *Shit. Reality's sinking in and she's having second thoughts about me.*

"Nothing. I just…I need to get up." Randi recoiled and Jule's expression turned apologetic. "I'm sorry. I'm just not ready for you to see me naked. You know, in the light of day kind of thing."

Randi almost laughed, but the look on Jule's face told her she was serious. "Honey, unless I dreamed it, we've been naked together twice now. I must be losing my touch if—"

"That's different. It was dark."

Randi hadn't seen this coming at all. "Jule, are you ashamed of your body? What is it? Scars? A tattoo you regret?"

"I still have seven pounds to lose, and I need to tighten my stomach muscles some more."

Randi couldn't believe what she was hearing. "Don't you know I think you're beautiful? Wasn't it obvious last night?"

Jule bowed her head, as if she couldn't face her.

Randi lifted Jule's chin and waited for their eyes to meet. "Jule, you are the most amazing, most beautiful woman I've ever known." She tapped Jule's chest above her heart. "And I'm not just talking about how you look. I'm talking about what's in here." She kissed her tenderly.

Jule kissed her back tentatively, as if she still didn't fully believe her words. It only made Randi more determined to show her just how much she meant it, but for now, she wanted to respect Jule's feelings and not make light of her insecurities.

"Is that why you're so obsessed with working out?"

"I'm not obsessed. I'm disciplined. Speaking of which, today's my workout day."

For the first time since their hike on Saturday, Randi realized that being with *her* wasn't the only activity on Jule's vacation agenda. *How selfish of me to assume that.* It was Monday morning. If she wasn't suspended, she'd be at work right now, and Jule would be going about her day without her. She didn't want to crowd Jule, but with everything they'd shared over the last few days, she relished the thought of spending as much time with her as possible. Her thoughts were interrupted by a whine and a wet nose touching her elbow.

Jule reached over her and petted Sirius's head. "Hey, bud. Need to go out?" She got out of bed and went into the bathroom. She emerged a few minutes later dressed in baggy nylon shorts, a T-shirt, and sneakers. "I need to take him out and then I'm heading to the gym. How about I take you to breakfast when I get back?"

Randi's heart sank. Where was this distance coming from? An emptiness pulled at her that she couldn't bear. She didn't want Jule to leave feeling as if she had to have the body of a goddess to be attractive to her. Randi propped up on her elbow and the sheet dropped off her bare shoulder. She quickly pulled it back up.

"I have a better idea. Stay here. I have everything you need to work out in my basement. I'd join you, but between my shoulder and my ankle, I'm not much good for it today."

"Oh, Randi." Jule's face softened. "I'm sorry. I still owe you a back rub, don't I?"

"Yes, you do." Randi gave her a mock stern look. "But I'm willing to take a rain check if that offer for breakfast is still on the table."

Jule smiled. Finally. "Deal."

"I'll take care of Sirius and take my shower while you work out, okay?"

Jule gave her a peck on the cheek. "Okay."

Jule completed her stretch routine, guzzled some water, and adjusted the seat on the leg press. With each push, she scolded herself. What the hell was that all about? Randi was completely vulnerable last night and finally opened up about everything. *And you act like a total idiot this morning because of a few extra pounds?*

She moved on to leg extensions and thrust each rep as if she was kicking someone. Namely, herself. She knew her weight wasn't the only issue here. It was the fact that Randi's reputation suggested that she'd slept with a lot of women—including Nikki and Megan, who were more attractive and in better shape than she was—and she couldn't stand the thought that she might not measure up enough to hold on to her when the lights were on.

She felt like a jerk for thinking that way. Did she think Randi was that shallow? She continued her workout, replaying the events of the past three days in her mind. It definitely felt like something special was going on between them. By the time she stepped onto the treadmill for a five-minute cool down, she felt confident that she wasn't going to let her stupid insecurities get the best of her.

She went upstairs and found Randi sitting at the kitchen table sipping coffee. Sirius was sprawled out on the floor nearby gnawing a giant bone. She smiled. Randi must have gone to the pet store recently. She leaned over, hugged Randi from behind, and kissed her cheek. "I'm sorry for being such a grump earlier."

Randi rested her head back on Jule's chest. "I'm sorry I called you obsessive."

"It's okay. You're right. I can be obsessive, and I have gone a bit over the top since Casey died."

"I actually admire your dedication. I wish I was more self-disciplined."

Jule moved to Randi's side so she could face her. She touched Randi's cheek and then kissed her softly. "Let's not waste any more time apologizing to each other for not being perfect. What do you say?"

Randi's lips curled up. "I say you stink and you need to get your beautiful body in the shower so we can go, because I'm starving."

Jule gave her a lingering kiss and then sauntered down the hall. She knew Randi was watching her the entire time.

And she was starting to feel pretty damn good about it. For a change.

❖

Randi grinned from ear to ear as she watched Jule walk away. Whatever this thing was between them, it felt good. She didn't know what to do with all this newfound energy surging through her. Well, that wasn't entirely true. She could think of many ways to expend that energy, but they couldn't spend all their time in bed. She fantasized about what she'd love to be doing to Jule in the shower right now. She jumped when the doorbell rang and checked the clock. She'd been drooling over Jule for twenty minutes. It was her mother.

"Hi, Mom. What're you doing here?"

"I'm sorry. I know you prefer that I call first, but I wanted to talk to you in person."

Randi hesitated. She wasn't sure if she was ready to subject Jule to any more of her family drama just yet. She pondered a few excuses to send her away, but then felt Jule's hand on her shoulder.

Her mother said, "Oh! I'm sorry. I didn't know you had company. I can come back later."

"It's okay, Mom. Come on in." Her mother stepped in and Randi gestured to Jule. "Mom, this is Jule Chapin. Jule, my mother, Aida Hartwell."

Jule shook her hand. "Hi. I'm so happy to meet you, Mrs. Hartwell."

"Please, call me Aida."

"Okay."

"Here," said her mother, handing a cake saver container to Randi. "I brought you a coffee cake. I made it this morning. It's still warm."

There was an awkward silence. Jule must have seen something in Randi's face, because she said, "Well, I don't want to intrude on your mother-daughter time. I should get going. I hope to see you again soon, Aida."

Randi said, "I'll call you later, okay?"

"Okay. Oh, I forgot to tell you I have a game tonight at six thirty. A makeup for a rainout." Jule gave Randi a peck on the cheek and left with Sirius.

"I didn't expect you to have company, sweetie. I'm sorry if I interrupted your plans."

"She's not company, Mom. She's—"

"Is she a girlfriend?" Her mother's face lit up. She looked so much younger when she smiled. Other than the salt-and-pepper hair and shorter stature, Randi saw much of her own features in her mother. She was still trim and in great shape for her age, too.

"No. I mean, maybe. She's great, but we haven't really talked about what we are."

She followed Randi to the kitchen. "She seems very sweet."

Randi couldn't help smile. "Yes, she is."

Her mother sliced them each a piece of the cake and sat at the kitchen table with the cup of coffee Randi had just fixed her. "How long have you been seeing her?"

Randi sat down with her own cup of brew. She took a generous bite to stall. "Mmm, this is delicious. We've been spending time together for a couple of months. We got to be friends and it just happened."

This was weird. Randi never talked about this sort of thing with her mother. It actually felt good.

Her mother patted her arm. "That's a good sign, you know. Friendship makes a solid foundation for a relationship. That's how it was with your father and me."

Randi felt her mood change with the mention of her father. She braced herself for the impending guilt trip. She sipped her coffee and waited for it.

"His parole hearing is next month." *Here it comes.* "Our lawyer is very confident that the judge will grant it."

"Forget it."

"Honey, it would mean a lot to both of us for you to be there."

"I said, no way. The minute he pulled that trigger, he abandoned us. Don't you get that? I'm glad the bastard's dead, but it didn't bring Stevie back. All he did was destroy our family because he couldn't control his damn temper."

Her mother was silent, but there was fire in her eyes. "You're one to talk about tempers, Miranda. I know you were suspended. And I didn't even have to ask Tim why."

*Damn it, Baldwin!* She wasn't surprised her mother had heard about it from the lieutenant.

Randi mustered every ounce of energy to refrain from throwing her empty coffee cup across the room. That would only prove her mother's point. With her back to her mother, she braced herself at the counter, took a moment to catch her breath, and set it in the sink.

"He had no right to call you."

"He's worried about you. Frankly, so am I. What were you thinking beating up that man? You'll wind up in jail yourself if you don't start dealing with your own anger issues."

Randi turned around and began to pace. "If you saw half the shit I do, you'd lose it, too, Mom."

"When are you going to stop being so selfish?"

Randi shook her head, confused. "Excuse me?"

"You've done nothing but wallow in your guilt and anger since Stevie died."

Randi gritted her teeth. Her breathing sped up and she could feel her temperature rising. "Selfish? *Selfish?* How the hell am I being selfish? You weren't there!"

"You're right!" Her mother jumped up so fast she nearly toppled her chair. "That's exactly my point! I wasn't there. You think you're the only one who feels guilty? It was my idea to drag your father out to the furniture store that day. You think I don't live with that every day? How do you think your father feels, knowing that it was his testimony that caused that man to snap? That he wasn't home to protect his kids? That he lost control, and his anger and need for revenge tore his own family apart? Hasn't he suffered enough with those regrets? Haven't we all? You're not the only one who lost Stevie, Miranda. We all lost him. It's time for you to recognize that."

Randi was stunned. She couldn't move as she watched her mother grab her purse and walk away. She shouted at her mother's back, "Who's losing her temper now?"

"Enjoy the cake." She slammed the door behind her.

Randi staggered into her chair. Her mother had never spoken to her like that before.

She needed to get the hell out of the house. She grabbed her keys and leather jacket. She bounded out of the house into the garage. She jumped into the Camaro and burned rubber at the end of the driveway.

As soon as she was on Route 1A, she sped up, negotiating the sharp turns and squeezing the wheel so tightly her fingers cramped. After several miles, the lines on the road began to blur as much as the trees on her right and the ocean on her left. She came up behind another vehicle and slammed on the brakes to avoid ramming it. It was the freakin' middle of the day in June and she couldn't pass because there was too much traffic coming in the other direction. The entire stretch was a no-passing zone, but Randi didn't give a shit. She watched for an opening and took it. Her eyes flew open wide when an approaching car came up right in front of her.

"Shit!"

She downshifted and veered back into the right lane, cutting off the car she just passed and nearly forcing the oncoming car onto the shoulder. She turned awkwardly into the first side street she saw and pulled off the road to an abrupt stop. Her breathing was out of control as she gripped the top of the wheel and dropped her forehead onto her hands. She heard the sound of tires crunching on the gravel behind her. She looked in her rearview. Officer Fisk, the policeman who had helped her with the second rape victim, was approaching. His blues were on. Randi rolled down her window and expelled a deep breath.

"Hartwell? Are you all right?"

Randi let out a humorless laugh. "Just ducky."

"We got two calls with complaints about you in the last three minutes. Passing cars on this road, Hartwell? Are you out of your fucking mind?"

"Yes. I think I am."

"You trying to get yourself killed?"

"Just give me the fucking ticket and leave me the hell alone."

"If I write you a ticket, it's for reckless driving and a long list of other violations. That'll buy you a court date and who knows what else. Aren't you in enough hot water already?"

"So you're gonna let me slide? Don't do me any favors, Fisk. I get enough flack from the squad as it is."

Fisk leaned in through the window. "I have no beef with you, Randi. We all have our demons to deal with because of this job. I'm not going to add to yours. Go home and find some other way to cool off that doesn't involve getting behind the wheel, okay? Go get drunk or get laid like the rest of us do." He straightened up and turned to go.

"Hey! Wait!"

"What?"

"The rapist. You catch him yet?"

Fisk's jaw visibly tightened. Anger flared in his eyes.

"Shit, Fisk. Don't tell me he struck again."

"Where you been, Hartwell? It's been all over the news."

"What? Don't fuck with me, just tell me—"

"He killed this one. Raped her then strangled her."

Randi's heart clenched and her lungs constricted. "No no no no."

"Sorry, Randi. I know how you feel about this case. We're doing everything we can—"

"Bullshit you are! Why the hell can't we catch this bastard?"

Fisk raised his voice. "Hey, it's not helping that we're short an officer. In case you haven't noticed."

"Fuck you." Randi started the car. "Fuck all of you." She punched the accelerator, strangely satisfied with the gravel that flew out from beneath the tires as she took off.

## CHAPTER TWENTY-SEVEN

Jule reluctantly trotted out to second base to take her position. In between warm-up tosses with the other infielders, she scanned the sidelines for Randi. She was worried about her. Randi hadn't called as she said she would, and when Jule stopped by Randi's house on her way to the game, she wasn't home. She still didn't know enough about Randi's relationship with her mother to speculate about what had happened after she'd left them this morning.

She took a throw from Megan at shortstop and fought back her insecurities.

"Batter up!" The umpire's shout reminded her to get her head in the game.

Two innings later, they were losing by four runs, and their starting pitcher was moping on the bench as Brenda warmed up to relieve her. Jule was hitless so far and had just made her second throwing error of the game.

Jule took a few steps into the outfield and let out an exasperated sigh. Megan jogged over and clapped Jule on the shoulder. "Hey, shake it off."

"Sorry."

"You okay?"

It was easy to see why Randi had hooked up with Megan on more than one occasion. Megan was beautiful with puppy dog brown eyes and a sincere sweetness that Jule assumed soothed those she helped as an EMT.

In the distance, a familiar figure caught her eye. Randi was alone on the bleachers just outside the center field fence. She had a beer in one hand and her legs stretched out in front of her crossed at the ankles.

"Jule? You all right?"

"Yeah. I am now."

Megan followed her line of sight and smiled. "I can see why. She is a sight for sore eyes, isn't she?"

Randi caught Jule's eye and raised her can in a toast. "She sure is."

The ump hollered, "Let's go!"

The next batter grounded out to end the inning. Jule's team managed a comeback over the next few innings to bring them within a run in the bottom of the seventh, the last inning. The game had become intense, with the opposing team fighting to keep the lead. While Jule's team cheered louder and louder in hopes of pulling off a walk-off win, the other team's players grunted with frustration and impatience over the possibility of blowing the game.

Jule led off with a single. Brenda came up and drove a hard bouncer to short. Jule took off at full speed and hoped they could avoid a double play. She dropped into a slide, but her cleat caught in the dirt and jolted one leg to an abrupt stop. Her momentum carried her body into a sideways roll and she plowed into the second baseman, who was covering the bag and awaiting the toss from the shortstop. The fielder tumbled over her and Jule spotted the ball sailing over her head toward the outfield.

"Safe!" shouted the field ump.

Jule and the other woman disentangled themselves and got to their feet. Jule made sure she kept contact with the bag.

"You okay?" asked Jule.

Before she could answer, the shortstop was in Jule's face. "What the hell was that?"

"I stumbled."

"Like hell you did. You did that on purpose."

"Trish, I'm all right," said the second baseman.

Trish turned to the umpire. "That's interference! She's out!"

"Incidental contact. Rule says to slide. She slid. And your throw was way out of reach whether she'd fallen or not."

"Bullshit!" Trish turned back to Jule and violently slapped her palms into Jule's shoulders. "You were trying to knock her over!"

"Hey," said the umpire to Trish. "Knock it off or you're out of the game."

Trish ignored her and shoved Jule again, hard enough to cause her to stumble backward and off the base. She wasn't about to fight this girl, but she'd defend herself if she had to. Out of the corner of her eye, she saw Randi jumping down off the chain link fence onto the outfield grass. Jule saw her leg buckle slightly when she hit the ground. Her sprained ankle was still weak. Randi ran toward them.

Jule could smell the beer on Randi's breath before she reached them. *This can't be good.*

Randi grabbed two fistfuls of Trish's shirt. "You keep your hands off her!"

Trish was as tall as Randi, but huskier. She shoved Randi back and suddenly both teams were on the scene. Trish took a swing at Randi's face. Randi blocked it with her forearm and used the other arm to put her in a headlock. The umps shouted in vain for everyone to get back to their positions, but there were shoving matches breaking out everywhere. Everyone, except for Jule and the second baseman, was either pushing someone, or shouting, or trying to pull someone off another.

Jule watched in horror as Randi threw Trish to the ground. Randi pinned her hands over her head with one hand and had her other hand wrapped tightly around her throat. "You killed her, you bastard! You fuckin' raped her and killed her!"

"Randi! Stop! Let her up!" Jule tried to pull Randi back, but it was no use. She was too strong. She fell to her knees so that Randi could see her. Trish's face was red with terror and an inability to breathe. "Randi! Look at me, Randi! She's not the rapist! She's not the rapist! Let her go!"

Randi's face contorted to a look of fear and agony. She jerked her hands off Trish as if they'd been burned and looked at Jule. She shook her head slowly side to side.

"Oh God no. Shit, I...what's happening to me?" She slid off Trish onto the ground and curled in on herself. "I'm sorry. I'm sorry."

Jule rested a hand on her shoulder.

Trish scampered off into the arms of the second baseman. *Must be her girlfriend. No wonder she was flipping out.*

No one was fighting anymore. They stood motionless and stared at Randi.

Someone muttered, "Apple doesn't fall far from the tree, does it?"

Jule turned to the spectators. "Who said that?" When no one answered, she added, "Whoever you are, you're a coward. You have no right to judge her. You don't know her."

She stared everyone down until the crowd dispersed. Relieved, she brushed the hair back from Randi's face. Her eyes were wide with fright, but her gaze seemed locked elsewhere.

"Come on, honey." Jule snaked her arm beneath Randi's shoulders and sat her up. "Let me take you home, okay?"

Megan came up to them and knelt on one knee. "Randi, are you all right?"

Randi stared at her, as though trying to figure out who she was. "Megan?"

"Yeah, it's me. Randi, you're drunk." Megan looked at Jule. "How about you? You okay?"

"Yeah, I'm fine."

"You want some help getting her up?"

"Did I kill her?"

Jule lifted Randi's chin. "No, baby. You didn't kill anyone."

"She shouldn't have shoved you."

Megan looped her arm under Randi's armpit. "Randi, come on. Let Jule take you home. Jule, don't worry about the game. We'll put in a pinch runner for you."

*Oh yeah.* She'd forgotten about the game. They got Randi to her feet.

She let out a moan. "Shit. My ankle."

"You landed pretty hard when you jumped the fence," said Megan. "Impressive stunt, but not too smart."

"Had to get to Jule fast."

They ignored the gawking players, who by now were just anxious to get on with the game.

As they neared the dugout, Jule said, "Megan, I think I can manage her from here. Do you mind grabbing my gear for me?"

"Sure."

They continued to the parking area and Jule realized they had a problem. Two vehicles. They stopped at Jule's truck. Megan set her bag on the ground and asked if they needed anything else before excusing herself and hurrying back before it was her turn to bat. Jule opened the passenger door.

"No," grumbled Randi. She pointed. "Camaro."

"Randi, you're in no shape to drive."

Randi fumbled keys out of her hip pocket. "Not leaving Stevie's car. I'm fine."

"No, you're not. Brenda rode here with Toni and Kathy. We can sit tight here until the game's over and I'll have her follow us home in the Camaro."

"No! Nobody drives Stevie's car but me!" Randi made a move to walk around her, but Jule quickly got in her path.

"Okay, okay," Jule said softly. "We'll take the Camaro, and Brenda can drive my truck, okay?" She caressed Randi's cheek. "But you need to let me drive."

Randi pursed her lips and furrowed her brow, contemplating the arrangement.

"I won't let anything happen to Stevie's car. I promise."

Randi looked at the Camaro. The sadness in her eyes tore at Jule's heart. "Stevie loved that car."

"I know. But he loved you even more, and he wouldn't want you to get hurt if you drove it after you've been drinking, would he?"

Randi's tears spilled over. "I miss him."

Jule pulled her into her arms. "I know. It's okay. Let me take care of you, baby." Jule fought back her own tears. She wasn't just hurting for Randi. This situation was all too familiar, and she didn't like the way it felt.

How many times had Casey put her in this position? Too drunk to drive. Too drunk to make good decisions. Too consumed with her own shit to think clearly about how her actions were affecting those around her.

The game ended minutes later, and when Brenda came over, Jule explained what needed to happen. Randi was silent, emotionally stuck somewhere in a terrible mixture of the past and the present. After picking up a change of clothes at Randi's house, Jule helped

Randi into bed. She closed the door behind her and fell against it. She stayed there in the hall for what seemed like an hour before heading downstairs to take Sirius out for his nightly walk.

When they came in, she took a long, hot shower and then dropped onto the couch. She thought about Casey. Did she really want to go through this again?

Casey was a party girl who didn't want to grow up. At least things were simpler with Casey, though. Randi was broken, and it wasn't up to Jule to fix her. Randi had to do that herself. Randi needed help, and not just a shoulder to cry on.

She wasn't sure she wanted to be that shoulder. Randi's rage frightened her. Although her gut told her that Randi would never harm her, she worried about the lengths she'd take to protect her.

Something must have happened today for Randi to get so drunk. They'd had a few beers together before, but she'd never seen Randi this wasted or disoriented. She seemed to think she was apprehending the rapist. *Did she say "you raped her and killed her"?*

Jule jumped up and grabbed her phone. She quickly navigated to a local news page. Bingo. Not only was he still at large, but he had escalated to murdering his latest victim. Randi must have found out. No wonder she was so distraught. Jule didn't know how her visit with her mother had gone this morning either. She knew very little of their relationship, other than her feelings of abandonment after her mother was hospitalized after Stevie's death.

She'd planned to sleep on the couch. She thought she needed to put some distance between them. But the thought of staying away from Randi when she was this vulnerable made her change her mind.

With Sirius at her heels, she lumbered up the stairs to her bedroom. Randi was sound asleep. She slipped under the covers and kissed her cheek. Randi stirred and rolled over to face Jule.

She snuggled into Jule's embrace and pulled her close. "I'm so sorry."

"Shh. Go back to sleep."

Randi tipped her head back and looked directly into Jule's eyes. "I need you. Please don't leave me."

Jule's heart seized. "I'm right here, baby."

Randi tucked her head under Jule's chin. Jule wrapped her arms around her trembling body. She stroked her hair. They stayed that way until she heard Randi's soft breaths slow as she drifted off to sleep.

Sleep evaded Jule. Casey had needed help. She had missed the signs completely. *I failed her. And now she's dead.* She would never have the chance to make it up to her. She would never know if it would have made a difference. Now, with Randi, signs of trouble seemed to be all Jule saw. Randi could be so tender and loving, yet her pain and anger were constantly simmering just below the surface, ready to erupt at any moment. Randi's compassion was a strength as much as it was a weakness. Tonight, she had turned to alcohol. Jule only saw her drink one beer at the game. She must have driven there drunk.

Randi had hallucinated and lost sense of reality. In the process, she had very nearly strangled someone. What if she hadn't been able to snap Randi out of it? What if Randi had killed her? *Will Trish press charges?* It was a possibility. She had plenty of witnesses. If convicted, Randi could go to prison.

Maybe she wasn't strong enough to handle a relationship with Randi. Maybe she wasn't ready. Maybe neither one of them was. So far, they'd shared some good times—not to mention some great sex—but it seemed that most of their relationship had revolved around Randi's pain. She hated to think of what would happen to Randi if she broke things off, even temporarily. Would she go off the deep end? *Maybe it would be the wake-up call she needs.* Then again, was she just being a coward and bailing on Randi at a time she needed her? *What would that say about me? That when things get tough, I can't be counted on?*

Randi had finally let herself be vulnerable. No wonder her emotions were all over the place. Her wounds were open and raw. Opening up to Jule was only the beginning of the healing process. It was going to take a long time to overcome twenty years of anguish.

Jule had made some serious life changes over the last few months and she'd faced them head on. So far, she had succeeded. It felt good. She didn't want to lose that feeling.

She tossed and turned, trying desperately to get comfortable, and to quiet the confusing conversations that were jostling around in her head. She debated again if she would be better off sleeping on the couch, away from the complex woman next to her who stirred up everything inside her without even trying.

She needed to talk to someone. Someone who could be objective and offer some solid advice. *Denise.* Her sister had always been there for her. She needed her now. She would call her in the morning.

With her mind made up about that one thing, finally, she slept.

❖

Randi woke up and for a moment wasn't sure of where she was. *I'm at Jule's house.* The room was completely dark except for muted moonlight filtering through sheer curtains. The sounds of steady rain pelted the windows and the roof. She ached all over and her skull was pounding. Her shoulder was throbbing. Her ankle burned and felt stiff. She had to pee.

Jule was cuddled up to her with an arm around her. Her breath was warm on her neck. She felt safe, yet uneasy. She couldn't recall how she got here. She was wearing only a T-shirt and underwear, but she couldn't remember changing her clothes. Vague images of the scuffle at the softball game teased her brain, but there were gaps in her memory.

She kissed Jule's head and slipped out of bed to the bathroom. When she returned, Jule was looking right at her. She got back in bed and pulled the covers over them.

"Sorry. I didn't mean to wake you."

"It's all right. How are you feeling?"

"Like shit. Confused. Did I drive you home?"

"You didn't drive at all."

She gasped. "Stevie's car!"

"Relax, it's here. I drove us. Everything's fine. Go back to sleep."

Her vision blurred and her head swam. She fell back onto the pillow and groaned. "Oh man. How much did I drink?"

"Too much. You need to sleep. You'll feel better in the morning."

The images were flashing back, and she didn't like what she saw. Her hands around a woman's neck. The woman's face swollen and red. A look of sheer terror in her eyes.

Randi trembled. She had been so afraid of someone threatening Jule that she'd completely lost control. If Jule hadn't brought her back to reality, who knows what might have happened.

"Hey." Jule rolled over and caressed her cheek. "Honey, tell me what's happening. You're shaking like a leaf."

"I almost killed her, didn't I?"

"Baby, you'd been drinking. You were protecting me. You didn't know what you were doing."

Randi sat up. Her head protested, but she ignored it. "You're right. I didn't. That's what scares me. What's happening to me, Jule? Even when I lost my temper before, I was always in control. I knew what I was doing."

Jule looked at her with a strained expression, as if she wanted to say something, but wasn't sure how to say it. She closed her eyes and released a long breath. "I'm scared, Randi."

"Scared of me? Jule, I would never ever hurt you. You have to know that."

"I'm not afraid of you, Randi. I'm afraid *for* you. I'm afraid for us. I'm not sure I can handle what's going on with you."

Randi's blood ran cold. She swallowed hard and forced out the question she didn't want her to answer. "Are you going to leave me?" She saw Jule stiffen. Panic surged through her veins. "I'll save you the trouble." She swung her legs over the side of the bed and scanned the room for her pants. The room spun. *Where the hell are my pants?* She felt Jule's hand on her arm. "Randi, don't."

Randi stood and fumbled in the dark, feeling her way around the room. "Where the hell are my clothes?" She flicked the wall switch. Pain seared her eyes as the bright light illuminated the room. She saw her clothes tossed over a cedar chest against the wall and walked toward it. She grabbed the bottom of Jule's shirt and began to lift it off.

Jule's arms came around her from behind and covered her hands in a firm grip. "Randi, please. Come back to bed so we can talk."

Randi stopped struggling and stared at the wall. Jule pressed her warm body against her, pulling her into a hug from behind. Randi's defenses were crumbling fast. Jule did that to her. It scared the shit out of her the way she could do that.

"I need help, don't I?"

Jule sighed heavily. "Yes." Jule stepped back slightly and Randi turned around within her embrace. "I want to help you, but I can't give you what you need."

"So you're giving up on me?"

Jule shook her head. "No, honey. I'm not giving up on you. I'm giving up on being the person I used to be."

"I don't understand."

"I can be here when you need to cry or talk. I can show you I care and give you my support. What I can't give you is the guidance you need to deal with the tragedies you've experienced. It's not fair to you because you're not getting everything you need to get through this, and it's not fair to me to take on that responsibility myself." She combed her fingers through Randi's hair. "It kills me to see you in pain and not be able to take that pain away. To see you suffer and know that I'm not enough."

Randi rested her forehead on Jule's and squeezed her a little tighter. She inhaled deeply and let out a slow breath. She knew what she needed to do. She needed Jule in a way she'd needed no other human being. Even more so, she needed to keep her safe. *Until I fix what's wrong with me, I'm no good for either of us.*

She framed Jule's face in her hands and wiped tears from her cheeks with her thumbs. She kissed her softly and slowly. Jule responded tentatively, as if she was trying to hold back, but didn't really want to. Randi didn't push, but kept the kiss gentle. Jule was in control, and Randi wanted to make sure she knew that, and that she didn't have to feel guilty for voicing tough love. Randi knew it hadn't been easy for her.

Their lips parted and Randi lifted Jule's chin. She looked into Jule's wounded eyes and knew they were at a critical place in their young relationship.

"Do you trust me, Jule?"

"Yes."

"Then trust me when I say that you are enough. I want to be enough for you. That's why I need to leave. I need to get my shit together, and I don't want you getting hurt in the process." She withdrew from Jule's arms and reached for her clothes.

Jule grabbed her arm and stopped her. "Wait. Please, don't go. I never said I wouldn't stand by you. You don't have to go through this alone, Randi."

"I can't expect you to be my shrink."

"You're right. And I don't want to be."

"If I'm this messed up, I don't know how I can be any good for you. How can I give you what *you* need if I can't even deal with what I need?"

Jule caressed her cheek so lightly it sent shivers through her entire body. "Baby, we'll deal with it together. If that means I need to give you some space, then I'll give you some space. But I'm not going to let you walk away and shut me out. This isn't all or nothing."

Randi shivered from the inside out. "I don't know what to do."

"Then I'll tell you what to do. Right now, you're going to come back to bed. We'll figure it out in the morning." Jule placed her palm to Randi's heart and then kissed her cheek. Randi shivered again at the feel of Jule's lips on her skin. Jule continued to place kisses on her face. Randi's breath caught when she moved to the edge of her jaw and then to her neck.

"Jule…"

"Hmm?" Jule's voice vibrated against Randi's throat. Jule slid her hand under her shirt and glided it around her waist, triggering goose bumps.

"Jule, please."

"Are you begging again?"

"If you don't stop, oh—" Randi's sentence was cut short when Jule's other hand brushed over her breast.

"If I have to"—Jule kissed her firmly on the lips—"give you space"—she nipped Randi's bottom lip—"then I need something"—she ran her tongue across Randi's upper lip—"to hold me over." She caught her lips fully in hers, claiming her tongue, pushing her toward the bed.

Jule walked her backward, their lips and bodies maintaining contact the whole way. The backs of Randi's knees hit the bed and she fell onto it. Jule peeled off her own shirt and stripped off her panties. She lifted off Randi's shirt and then eased her back down before sliding off her boxers. Randi lay helpless as Jule braced herself above her and brought a thigh up between her legs.

"Jule? Are you sure?"

Jule lowered herself just enough to touch their breasts together. Randi's nipples hardened at the tease.

Jule asked, "You want me to stop?"

"Never. I never *want* you to stop. I can't say no to you."

"I'm not going to let you give up on us that easily, you hear me? But we're going to do it right, okay?"

"Yes."

Randi arched up into her, taking her in and letting Jule fill her, as she pulled Jule down and kissed her.

Randi surrendered herself, savoring every sensation, every ounce of Jule's amazing compassion that flowed through her touch. She willed her body to hang on, not wanting this to end, yet needing release so badly she thought she'd lose her mind.

Jule slowed her motions slightly, teasing her, and fully aware of the torture she was inflicting.

"Come for me, baby."

"So close."

"Look at me. I want you to look at me."

Randi opened her eyes. Jule's pupils were wide and fiery with desire. "Oh, Jule. You are so beautiful."

Jule never took her eyes off her as Randi rode out the waves that just kept coming. She continued to stroke her until Randi had to push her soaked hand away. Randi collapsed into a boneless puddle.

Jule gave her only a few minutes to recover. She pulled Randi over on top of her and kissed her. She took Randi's hand and brought it between her legs. She was drenched.

"See what you do to me?"

"Jule, you're amazing."

"You're so beautiful when you come for me."

"I want…I…Jule, oh God…"

Jule seemed to sense her loss of words. "Show me."

Randi kissed her with everything she had. Jule was right. Randi wasn't going to be able to let her go.

But how the hell was she going to make everything right?

## CHAPTER TWENTY-EIGHT

The sounds of heavy rainfall woke up Jule. Randi was sound asleep in her arms, snoring lightly. The last twenty-four hours had been a difficult test and she knew it. She had no doubts about her feelings for Randi, but she needed to make sure those feelings weren't clouding her judgment. Either way, she was in too deep now. She knew Randi needed her, even when Randi was trying to push her away. She wanted to be who Randi needed her to be, even if that meant slowing things down between them. There was a chance Randi wouldn't be able to overcome her demons, and Jule had to figure out how far down the rabbit hole she was willing to go before that world, one she was far too familiar with, sucked her in again.

Casey had needed her and she hadn't been strong enough to confront Casey about her drinking. She wasn't about to do the same thing with Randi. If Randi needed professional help, then she would encourage her and support her in any way she could. She wasn't going to stand by again and let someone she loved continue on a downward spiral. She was going to be strong this time. Or, if she had to, she was going to get out. But she'd wait and see what the road looked like before she made any permanent decisions.

She kissed Randi's cheek and eased her arm out from underneath her. She quietly got some clothes out of the dresser and got in the shower. When she came out of the bathroom, the bed was made and Randi was gone. Her heart sank. *Maybe Randi decided she couldn't stick this out after all.*

She descended the stairs slowly. She landed heavily on each step, the anticipation of finding Randi's car gone almost too much to bear. It was probably for the best. She promised to give her space. She reluctantly glanced out the front door window. The Camaro was still there.

Weirdly, it wasn't until then that she realized Sirius hadn't accosted her as soon as she came out of the bathroom. She walked through the kitchen and out the back door. Randi was on a deck chair, watching Sirius—oblivious to the rain—meandering around the yard. Jule quietly sat next to her and placed a hand on her knee.

"Hey. How you feeling?" asked Jule.

Randi looked at her blankly. She shrugged. "Not great."

Sirius bounded onto the porch to Jule and rubbed his wet body against her leg. She bent over and hugged him around the neck as he showered her with kisses. "Morning, you spoiled brat. Ready for some breakfast, buddy?" Sirius responded with a small bark. "How about you, baby?"

Randi rubbed her brow and groaned. "I think I just need a strong dose of ibuprofen."

"Well, you can't take that on an empty stomach. Toast?"

"Yeah. I guess."

"I'm starved myself." Jule grinned. "Someone helped me burn off a few calories last night."

"Hmm. Glad to be of service."

They went inside and Jule fixed breakfast and gave Randi a pain reliever. Randi remained quiet as they ate. When they finished, Randi stared at her empty plate.

"I need to take care of some things today," she said.

"I understand." Jule took Randi's hand and brought it to her lips. When Randi met her eyes, Jule said, "Whatever you need, I'm right here."

"I don't know what I did to deserve you."

"You deserve to be happy. You are a beautiful person, Randi. You need to believe that in here." She tapped Randi's heart. "As far as you and me goes, we'll work it out, eventually."

Randi shrugged. "Yeah, maybe one day."

Jule continued to clear the table. "I have errands to run today, too. I need to go to the gym, and I'm going to see if my sister is free for lunch."

Randi got up and helped load the dishwasher. She walked Randi to the door and hugged her.

Randi gave her a lingering kiss and said, "I better go."

"Yeah." Jule touched her arm. "Hey. It's going to be all right."

Randi nodded and walked out the door.

Jule watched her climb into the Camaro and pull out of the driveway, wondering when she'd see her again. *Please let everything be okay.*

Randi sat in Lieutenant Baldwin's office alone, bouncing her leg nervously and chewing a knuckle. She'd been waiting for almost twenty minutes for him to get out of a meeting. She could have gone out to shoot the shit with the guys, but other than Fisk, who was out on patrol, there was no one she cared to see.

Baldwin finally came in and settled himself behind his desk. "You want some coffee?"

"No, thanks."

"I was going to call you today. Looks like they're willing to lift your suspension, but you'll have to meet some conditions first."

"I'm not here about coming back to work." She leaned forward on her thighs and let out a deep breath. "I need you to set me up with the department's psychologist."

Baldwin leaned back in his chair and raised his eyebrows. He slid open a desk drawer and took out a package of gum.

"Want a piece? Juicy Fruit. I hate that sugarless crap."

Randi shook her head and grew more restless as he unwrapped two pieces and shoved them into his mouth.

"You've got good timing. That's one of the conditions. You need to meet with our anger management counselor."

Randi nodded. She was both relieved and proud of herself for mentioning it before he did. She wondered if he would have waited this long with his other officers. "What are the other conditions?"

"You can come back to work on desk duty once you start your therapy, so you won't lose any more pay. You'll need to pass some psychiatric tests before going back on patrol. Once you're declared fit, you'll partner up with Officer Fisk or another senior officer at all times. You'll continue to meet with the counselor on a weekly basis and be reevaluated every month until the department is confident you can be on your own again."

Randi swallowed her protests. The sooner she got her act together, the sooner she could get back on the beat to help catch the rapist. She was going to do this. She needed to do this, not only for herself, but also for Jule and her mom. "Okay. Yeah, whatever I have to do."

Baldwin's eyebrows shot up. He had probably expected her to put up a fight.

"Okay then. Let's get this ball rolling." He picked up the phone and dialed. "Yeah, Baldwin here. I've got an officer that needs an appointment." He scribbled something on a notepad as he listened. "Yes. The sooner the better, I'd say. She's right here, I'll put her on." He handed Randi the receiver.

After answering a few basic questions, she made an appointment for the following day. She hung up and started to leave.

"Not so fast, Officer," said Baldwin.

Randi dropped back in the chair. "If this is about my mother, I already know you talked to her."

"Yes, I did."

"You had no right to do that."

"You can get mad at me all you want, Randi. I promised your father I'd look after you two. It took some time, but I think your mother's come through this pretty well, but I'm afraid I've let you down—"

"No, Tim. I'm the one who's let everyone down."

"I'm just as much to blame, here, kiddo. I *have* let you down. I didn't fully understand how much until recently. I thought I was helping you by cutting you some slack all these years."

"You didn't have to. I don't need any favors."

"You're right. I know that now. That's why I'm the one who pushed for your suspension."

"What?" Randi shifted forward to the edge of her seat.

"I'm glad I did. You needed a wake-up call. The fact that you came to me on your own today tells me I made the right decision." He leaned forward and added, "I'm not going to pull any punches with you. There are no guarantees here. If you show even the slightest irrational behavior, the department could declare you mentally unfit. If that happens, it could cost you your job. You got it?"

Randi pictured the animal abuser and the wife-beater she'd assaulted before she'd arrested them. Last night she'd nearly caused a head-on collision and then had driven drunk to Jule's game. She pictured the softball player pinned to the ground. She recalled the fear Jule had expressed afterward. It was one thing to not give a shit about herself, but lately, she was putting innocent lives at risk.

She had become a danger to the community she'd sworn to protect. In her desperate need to protect others, she'd become a criminal herself.

Just like her father.

## CHAPTER TWENTY-NINE

Randi had barely stepped through the doorway when Aunt Sandy pulled her into a bear hug. She felt as if an overstuffed pillow was trying to swallow her whole. Sandy took her hands and held her at arm's length. Randi squirmed at the usual scrutiny.

"Randi, honey, I swear every time I see you, you're more beautiful than the last time. You need to put some more meat on your bones, though."

"You always say that."

"That's because I know what I'm talking about. You don't have to worry about getting plump like me. You have your mother's metabolism. You're lucky I love you both to pieces or I'd have a much harder time hiding my jealousy."

Sandy dragged her to the kitchen and opened the refrigerator. She began listing options for something to eat, all of which Randi politely declined, much to Sandy's dismay.

"If you're not going to eat anything, then I'm sending some of this home with you. I swear your mother's working as a spy for Weight Watchers and she's on a mission to destroy my willpower. All she does is bake!"

"Don't you touch that stuff." Her mother walked into the kitchen. "I told you, those are donations for a charity bake sale." She turned to Randi. "See what I have to live with? She knows I have to practice recipes for class. She's always such a brat."

Sandy retorted, "Takes one to know one."

"If I'm a brat, I learned it from you, old lady."

Randi laughed. She loved when they teased each other. It reminded her of how she and Stevie had been together sometimes. She also knew that her mother was probably still upset with her, but didn't want to bring it up in front of Aunt Sandy.

Randi said, "I need to talk to you, Mom."

"Well, that's my cue!" said Aunt Sandy. "I'll be in the living room watching my soaps if you need anything."

They watched her leave and her mother asked, "Would you like some coffee?"

"Sure."

Her mother poured them each a cup and sat down. She clasped her hands together on the table. She began a familiar habit of rubbing her thumbs together. Randi got up and began pacing.

"I'm sorry for the way I acted the other day, Mom."

Her mother's face relaxed. "I am too, dear. I shouldn't have stormed off the way I did, but honestly, dear, sometimes you simply frustrate the hell out of me."

"I know. I frustrate me, too."

"Sweetheart, please sit down. I'm worried about you. What are you going to do if you lose your job?"

Randi slumped into her chair. "They lifted the suspension. I'm not going to lose my job."

"Well, I suppose that's good news. But don't you think this might be a sign that it's time to look into a new career?"

"I don't know how to do anything else, Mom. This is all I've known."

"I know it must feel that way, but you need to be realistic." She covered Randi's hand with her own and looked at her seriously. "You and I both know you never wanted to be a police officer. You may have fooled everyone else, Miranda, but you can't fool me. I know it's not where your heart is."

Randi wanted to tell her she was right, but couldn't quite find it in her to say so. Her mother continued, seemingly unfazed by her lack of response. She was used to it, after all.

"Honey, you have other talents and interests. Start with those. You're great with cars. You've always wanted to be in the K-9 unit. Maybe you could do something with animals, or see if the shelter has any paying positions. Lord knows you've devoted enough of your own time there. And there's always your photography."

Randi shivered. She remembered that she had rolls of film to develop from her hike with Jule. It had felt so wonderful to have the camera in her hands again. After some trepidation that she had forgotten how to use it, it had all come back like riding a bike. *That feels like years ago now.*

"I don't think I'm really qualified for any of those jobs." Randi got up again, refilled their cups, and returned to the table. "I've got no experience, and I've never been to college."

"If you want to go to school, I have the money for you to go."

"What? Where would you get that much money?"

Her mother stared into her cup. "When you and Stevie were kids, your father and I started college funds for each of you. We withdrew some of yours when you went to the academy, but the rest of that money's still there. It's yours if you want it."

She had Stevie's car. How could she justify taking his money, too? "You should keep it in case you need it. I'm thirty-three years old, Mom. I'm too old to go back to school."

Her mother chuckled. "If I'm not too old, then neither are you."

"You're going to college?"

"Not quite. I'm taking a baking course at the community center. It's not for credit or anything. I love my job at the bakery, but I always feel a little inadequate working alongside real chefs. I thought it might be fun to hone my skills. It gets me out. I've met some wonderful people, and it makes me happy. It would do you some good to do the same, don't you think?"

Randi shook her head. "I don't know, Mom." School was tough enough the first time around. She wasn't sure if she could handle it.

"Just promise me you'll think about it. You're not trapped unless you allow yourself to be, honey."

"Okay."

Her mother squeezed her hand. "If you want to honor Stevie's memory, I think he'd rather you did it doing something you love, sweetheart. He loved your pictures."

The defensive walls she usually erected for these conversations were losing the battle today. Randi geared up for what she needed to say next.

"Mom, there's something else."

"What, sweetheart?"

"I went to see a counselor at work yesterday. I was going to go anyway, but Tim told me that if I don't, they won't let me go back to work."

A smile tugged at her mother's lips. "I'm glad. Sweetie, don't be afraid to tell the truth this time. Let them help you."

Randi nodded and stared at her hands in her lap.

"I'm going to tell you something, though."

Randi looked up at her.

"Do it for your peace of mind. Not just to get your job back. The job isn't what's important here. Take the help while you have it available. You deserve to be happy."

"I've been hearing that a lot lately."

"Speaking of happiness..." Her mother grinned. "Tell me about Jule."

Randi was starting to believe there was a reflex built into her face that formed a smile every time she heard Jule's name.

"She's stolen your heart, hasn't she?"

Randi chuckled. "There's a warrant out for her arrest."

"My goodness. You really are smitten with her."

"Mom." Randi whined like a teenager. She could feel herself blushing as she stood and brought their mugs to the counter.

"Okay, okay." Her mother got up and came to her side. "Maybe you could bring her over for dinner sometime so we can get better acquainted. That way Aunt Sandy can meet her, too."

"I'll think about it."

"Don't think about it. Ask her today."

Randi surprised her by pulling her into a hug. "Thank you."

"No need to thank me, sweetie. You're my daughter. I love you."

"I love you, too, Mom."

Her mother pulled away and looked at her with her mouth gaping open. "You haven't told me that in years."

"There are a lot of things I haven't done that are overdue. I'll look into some jobs. You know, just in case."

"And think about school too, Randi. Even if this thing blows over and you keep your job, I think you owe yourself that much."

Randi chewed her bottom lip. "Yeah. Okay."

Her mother smiled widely. "I mean it about bringing Jule over. I'm even more anxious to spend time with her now. I think she's been a good influence on you."

Randi kissed her cheek, said good-bye to Aunt Sandy, and headed back out on the road. That was easier than she thought it would be. *And damn, that felt good.* One therapy session and a lot of talk about forgiving herself and misdirected anger had already gone a long way. After years of dismissing her pleas for her to go to counseling, it wasn't so difficult to admit her mother had been right all along.

Her mother was right about another thing, too. She was right about Jule. She was a good influence on her.

And she'd stolen her heart.

## CHAPTER THIRTY

Jule slipped under the covers. It had only been three days since she last saw Randi, and it still felt strange crawling into bed alone. She didn't like it, but she knew the separation had been necessary. It had given her time to clear her head. A long talk with her sister had confirmed that she'd made the right decision. She had no intentions of rescuing Randi or changing her. She was going to do things differently this time around, which meant she was even more determined to remain her own person. She was giving Randi the space she needed to deal with her past. If there was any chance of a future together, it would be worth it in the long run.

It was harder to tell her heart that. She missed Randi. Especially at night, when she didn't have her job or daily routines to distract her. Not that they distracted her much. Randi was always on her mind. Now it was Friday night and she had lined up enough projects over the weekend to keep her from going crazy.

A phone call wouldn't hurt, would it? Just to see how she was doing and say good night? She grabbed her cell off the nightstand and tapped Randi's name on the speed dial.

Randi answered on the first ring. "Hi."

"Hey. How're you doing? You okay?"

"I am now that I'm talking to you. How was your week?"

Jule wrapped her arm around the spare pillow and squeezed. Hearing Randi's voice only made it worse. *I can do this.* "Not bad. You?"

"Good. Exhausting, but good."

Jule heard shuffling noises, as if Randi was in bed changing position.

"Jule?"

"Yeah?"

"I miss you."

Jule released a sigh. "I miss you, too."

"You're an angel, you know."

Her face warmed. Randi wasn't even near her and she could feel herself blushing. Sirius whined. She motioned for him to jump onto the bed with her. "What are you doing tomorrow?"

"I might work on the car or catch up on housework. Why?"

"Sirius misses you, too. I thought maybe we could stop by…if that's okay. I'll bring over some takeout."

"I would love that."

"Good night, baby."

"Good night, angel."

She disconnected and cuddled up to Sirius. Next thing she knew, it was morning. She had slept peacefully and wondered if Randi had done the same. She worked like a bat out of hell on her latest house project to pass the time.

When she finally arrived at Randi's doorstep, she was almost relieved that Randi seemed as nervous as she was. She set the packages of Chinese food down on the counter and didn't hesitate when Randi held out her arms. She fell into Randi's embrace as if it were the most natural place in the world for her to be. They shared a brief kiss and then enjoyed their meal as they talked about their week. She wasn't sure what to expect and had prepared for the worst. She was relieved when Randi sounded genuinely grateful for the two therapy sessions she'd had so far and that she'd had a good talk with her mother.

After cleaning up, they played with Sirius in the backyard. They ran into the house laughing.

Randi said, "Can you stay for a bit? I'll pour us some iced tea."

"Sure." Before Randi could take another step, Jule grabbed her hand and pulled her in for a kiss. Randi seemed tentative at first, but Jule hungered for more. She'd suffered for three days already. She teased Randi's tongue with hers and deepened the kiss. Randi moaned and tightened her grip around Jule's waist.

Randi's cell phone rang.

"Shit. That's my ring tone for the station. I have to answer."

Jule reluctantly pried herself away. She couldn't help overhear Randi's end of the conversation.

"What? Shit. Where is she? I'm on my way." Randi disconnected the call and told Jule she had to go. She disappeared down the hall and emerged a moment later in running shoes and a sweatshirt.

"Randi, what is it?"

"Carly. Uh…the teenager that was raped? Remember? She's out on the Memorial Bridge, threatening to jump."

"Oh my God."

"She's asking for me. They said she'll only talk to me. God knows why."

Jule slipped on her shoes. "I'll drive you—"

"No, Jule. You shouldn't see this. I mean…if she jumps, I don't want you seeing that."

Jule put her hand on Randi's shoulder. "Hey, if she jumps, I need to be there for you. Got it?"

"You're a pain in the ass, you know. Fine, let's go." She reached for the door and hesitated when Sirius scampered over. "Bring him, too. Carly loves animals. But I'm driving. Uh-uh—don't give me that look. No one drives like a cop."

They bolted down the stairs and Randi headed to the Camaro. She swung open the door and tipped the seat forward so Sirius could get in the back. They jumped in and buckled up. Randi pressed the garage door opener, and with barely enough clearance, she gunned the engine and the car flew through the opening.

Jule held her breath as Randi wove through the streets at high speed and honked the horn at any car that got in her way. In a drive that should have taken much longer than it did, they arrived to a scene of a police car, an ambulance, and a small Coast Guard rescue boat.

Randi parked next to the cruiser, got out, and released her seat forward. "Come on out, Sirius. It's okay." They each gave him a stroke and a scratch behind the ears. When Jule gave the lead a gentle tug, he came out. The three of them walked together to one of the officers.

"Thanks for coming, Hartwell."

"Yeah." Randi brushed by the officer and headed toward the bridge with Sirius. "Jule, hang back here. But I'm bringing Sirius with me. Are you okay with that?"

"Whatever you need, sweetheart."

Randi gave a curt nod, clearly already in cop mode.

Jule folded her arms for warmth and watched them walk up the bridge. With the aid of the spotlight, Jule could see the figure of a girl sitting atop the rail at the highest point of the arch with her arms wrapped around a vertical support beam. About twenty feet away stood a police officer and a fortyish-looking woman.

Someone nudged Jule's arm. She turned and saw her teammate, Megan, dressed in her EMT uniform.

"Hey," Megan said.

"Hi."

"If anyone can talk her down, it's Randi."

"God, I hope so."

"I'd change my mind if I saw her coming my way."

Jule was suddenly sick to her stomach. *Let's just say we take care of each other.* Picturing Randi and Megan in bed together wasn't what she needed on her mind right now. Or ever.

"She'll break your heart, you know. She's not one to stick around."

She ignored the comment and walked away. If Megan thought she was being rude, she didn't care. All she cared about right now was that Randi would be able to bring that poor girl back safely. But the comment was an unwelcome reminder of who Randi had been. The question was, who was she now?

Randi was talking to the officer and the woman whom Jule now assumed was Carly's mother. After a brief exchange, Randi and Sirius slowly walked toward Carly. Carly shouted something and they stopped. Randi said something to her.

Randi made a slight motion with her arm and Sirius stepped ahead of her. Jule strained to hear above the howling wind, but she couldn't make out what they were saying. They kept talking as Randi inched her way forward.

Jule's heart jumped into her throat when Randi climbed onto the rail next to Carly. After all they'd talked about, she suddenly hoped Randi's own state of mind was where it needed to be. *Be strong, baby.*

❖

Carly barely looked at her when Randi approached her. She was staring straight ahead, rocking slowly, her jaw set. Sirius sat and waited.

"He raped another girl."

"I know."

"You promised you'd catch him."

Carly's words were quickly swallowed by the sound of the river passing below them and the wind whistling overhead.

*I belong in that river, not her.* Guilt was a feeling that had been a part of her for so long that it felt normal—as if she was supposed to feel this way all the time. She was sick of it.

"I *will* catch him."

"It's taking you long enough."

"Is that why you asked for me? So you can tell me I suck at being a cop? Get in line, honey."

Carly gave her a strange look, and Randi nearly panicked when Carly removed one hand from the beam. She didn't jump. She rubbed her eye and then brushed back a lock of unruly hair before grabbing the beam again.

"She's in my English class. Everybody treats us like we're freaks. Like it's our fault."

Randi stiffened. She knew exactly how that felt.

"We're not Jennifer and Carly anymore. We're 'the girls that got raped.' Some of them call us sluts. Even Tiffany won't hang out with us anymore, because she's afraid she won't be popular anymore if she does. Nice, huh?"

Randi noticed an embroidered picture of Snoopy hugging Charlie Brown on the front of her gray hooded sweatshirt. Randi wanted nothing more right now than for Carly to cling to her like that. She wanted to be a source of comfort, a lifeline, a person she could trust to take care of her. She wanted her to have faith that there were people in the world who loved her and she could depend on.

Randi's heart twisted inside her chest at the realization. Isn't that what her mother had wanted for her all these years? Why hadn't she seen it until now?

She wanted to go to the school and wring the necks of every one of those insensitive kids. She stared out over the water. "Let me guess.

They won't look you in the eye. You know they're saying stuff behind your back. You never quite hear what it is, but you have a good idea. They shut up as soon as they see you."

She turned and looked Carly directly in the eye.

"How do you know?"

"Because that's how I was treated in high school."

Carly's eyebrows shot up. "You were raped, too?"

Randi shook her head. "No. But something bad happened to me and it was all anyone talked about after that."

"Oh."

Randi held her gaze. Maybe that was a mistake, maybe not. Randi felt the moisture forming in her eyes. She was so adept in fighting them off, but lately…it was no use. She swiped her cheek with the back of her hand.

"What happened to you?"

"My brother was murdered. I saw it happen." When Carly said nothing, she continued. "Then my father—who was a cop, by the way—shot and killed the guy at the courthouse."

Carly pursed her lips and gave her another skeptical look. "You're making that up."

Randi sighed. "God, I wish I was. My dad went to prison. It was all over the news. The kids at school didn't know what to say to me, so they said nothing. Nobody wanted to talk to me. They just shut me out."

"People suck."

Randi smiled. "Yeah, sometimes they do. But I think it's more that they don't understand things they haven't been through themselves."

Carly shrugged.

After another long silence, Randi said, "I'm sorry I didn't come see you at the hospital."

"It's okay."

Randi thought back to the night of the rape, when she had considered driving to the hospital and then didn't have the guts. Instead, she'd sat in front of her old house thinking about Stevie and feeling sorry for herself. "No. It's not okay."

"Why didn't you?"

"Because I was a selfish coward." When Carly said nothing, she added, "I thought about killing myself once. Not long after I got my driver's license. It was about three years after my brother died."

Carly glared at her. "Liar."

"I drove too fast on a winding road and tried to flip my car. Didn't work, obviously. Jumping off a bridge, now that might've worked."

Carly narrowed her eyes. She wasn't stupid. She knew Randi was trying to psyche her out. The silence grew and Randi knew she couldn't afford to waste time. She lifted her leg over the rail and perched next to her.

"What are you doing?" Carly asked.

"I'm jumping with you."

"Yeah, right."

"How do you know? I've spent most of my life thinking I shouldn't be here anymore. But I never tried to do anything about it. Now we can do it together."

"Are you crazy?"

"Yup. Maybe I am. There's only one problem, though."

Carly furrowed her brow. "What?"

"The dog. His name's Sirius. He's very protective. If either of us jumps, he's gonna jump in there to save us."

"I don't believe you."

Randi leaned forward over the water and hollered, "Save me, Sirius!" In a flash, Sirius took hold of her sleeve with his teeth and pulled her back.

Carly yelled, "Oh my God!"

"Told ya."

"Yeah, but he doesn't know me."

"Doesn't matter. He'd save you, too."

Randi knew what was coming next. Carly loosened her grip, and as soon as she did so, Randi and Sirius both grabbed for her. As she reached for the girl, Randi slipped off the rail. Her left foot hit the narrow concrete and she felt her sprained ankle give. She caught Carly's outstretched arm and caught the rail with the other hand.

"No!" screamed Carly.

She found her balance, but now stood on the wrong side of the barrier with her back to the river. Sirius started barking. She looked up into Carly's terrified face, and in that moment, with the river rushing below her and a terrified young girl in front of her, she understood things in a way she never had before.

"Officer Hartwell! I don't want you to jump!"

"What's it matter to you?"

"Who'll take care of your dog?"

"Why do you care?"

"But…"

"Are you telling me that if I jump, you care about what happens to Sirius?"

Carly looked from Sirius to Randi and back again. Randi could tell her wheels were spinning.

"Carly, I'm going to tell you something right now. Something I've never told another living soul. I've been unhappy my whole life because I lost my brother, and I blamed myself. It's a terrible way to live. I know now that he wouldn't have wanted that for me. Do you want that for your mom? She loves you more than anything else in this world. Don't you care about what happens to her if you jump?"

Carly started to cry. "I don't really want to die." Her cries escalated into sobs.

Randi shifted toward her, moving closer so she could get a firmer grip on her. "I know."

Carly let go of the beam.

Randi's heart leapt into her throat as Carly wrapped her arms around her. "I just want to feel normal again. I want the pain to stop."

"I know. Me too. And one day, it will. But you can't let the bastards win."

Carly slipped off the bar so fast, Randi could only react on reflex. She gripped Carly in one arm and simultaneously grabbed the railing with her left hand. She arched backward. She knew she couldn't hold them for long. Carly was screaming. Pain raced up her arm and into her sore shoulder. She yanked with all her might and managed to hook her elbow around the railing. The momentum threw Carly back onto the rail.

Sirius grabbed Carly's hood and pulled, his legs braced firmly as he leaned backward. In a blur of activity, Lieutenant Baldwin and another officer were suddenly there and tugging them both over to safety. Carly's mother cried hysterically as she scooped Carly into her arms.

Randi's legs collapsed beneath her as she slid down against the cold metal post that only moments before had been Carly's lifeline.

Sirius pressed his body against hers. He ducked his head under her chin and whimpered. Someone knelt beside her and placed a hand on her shoulder. She knew the touch immediately. When she looked into Jule's eyes, her heart swelled. She recognized that look. Concern. Fear. Sympathy. Love. And something else that was entirely Jule. Admiration? Pride? She didn't have time to analyze it further. Megan walked up behind Jule.

"Sorry to break up the love fest, Randi, but I need to check you out."

Jule's look morphed into something that looked an awful lot like jealousy. *Shit. What has Megan told her?*

"I'm fine, Megan."

"You took a beating up there, between catching yourself and then catching the girl. You sure you're okay?"

Randi knew Megan well enough to know that her concern was sincere.

"Probably pulled a few muscles, but other than that, yeah, I'm okay."

Jule stood and faced Megan. "If she's hurt, I'll make sure she sees a doctor. In the meantime, I'll take care of her."

Megan opened her mouth to respond and hesitated before saying, "You'd better." She winked at Randi. "Later, Hartwell. Jule, see you at the game Wednesday." She took two steps backward and added with a smirk, "That is, unless you've got a bum arm."

Randi said, "Trust me, her arms work just fine."

"That's good. I need my double-play partner back."

Jule asked, "Can I help you up? Is it your ankle?"

"Honestly, my whole body is killing me. I think I'm going to need another hot bath."

Jule looped an arm behind her as she helped Randi to her feet. "I'll take care of you."

Carly and her mother walked over to them.

"Mom, this is Officer Har—"

Before Carly could finish introductions, her mother engulfed Randi in a bear hug. "Debra. We met at the supermarket, remember?

Thank you. Thank you so much." She kissed Randi's cheek and patted Sirius on the head. "And thank you, too. Your dog is amazing."

"Actually," Randi nodded toward Jule. "*Her* dog is amazing."

Carly looked at Jule. "He's your dog?"

"He is. But he and Randi are best buds."

"He's awesome."

Jule said, "I know. He thinks you're pretty awesome, too. I'm glad you're okay. You're welcome to come visit him anytime."

"I can?"

"You bet." She pulled a notepad and pen from her jacket pocket. "Here's my name and phone number."

Randi said, "Hey, put my number on there, too." She turned to Carly. "You can call me anytime you want. I mean it. *Anytime*. I don't care if it's three in the morning, okay?"

Carly wrapped her arms around Randi and squeezed.

"If you need me…for anything. Promise me."

"Okay. Promise." Carly released her and went back to her mother.

Debra thanked them and then said to Baldwin, "I hope you know how valuable this woman is to the community."

Baldwin gave Randi a stern look. "Try telling *her* that. She won't listen to me."

As Carly and Debra walked away, Randi heard Carly say, "Mom? Can we get a dog?"

Randi kept her eyes on Carly until the car was out of sight. Jule came up beside her and slipped an arm around her waist. One by one, the emergency vehicles left until they were alone.

Jule asked, "Are you all right?"

Randi didn't know how to answer that question. Everything felt different. Her head was buzzing as the past and present swirled together in a jumbled mess that for some screwed-up reason was making everything crystal clear. "I'm gonna be."

Jule gave her a puzzled look. "Ready to go home?"

She turned and looked into Jule's eyes. Her heart swelled with love. *When I look at you, I am home.* "Let's go."

## CHAPTER THIRTY-ONE

Randi was silent as she drove. Jule wanted to scream at her for scaring the living daylights out of her. Even more so, she wanted to hold Randi in her arms and never let her go. The thought that she could have lost her tonight—forever—terrified her. It only took seconds—endless torturous seconds—when she and Carly almost fell off the bridge, to erase any doubt about how she felt about Randi. She loved her.

Should she tell her? She had no idea how she'd react. It would probably scare her off. But Casey's death was a bitter reminder that you never knew how much time you had left on this earth. If Randi had fallen off that bridge tonight and died, Jule would have regretted never telling her how she felt.

Had Randi even considered the consequences? Jule wouldn't put it past her to dive in after Carly if she had jumped. Wasn't losing one girlfriend to an early death enough? What was she doing with this woman? Randi wasn't even on duty and she'd put her life on the line. She was a hero.

She looked at her stoic profile. Sometimes Randi's expressions were so hard to read. She looked zoned in and zoned out at the same time. The longer Jule watched her, the more she noticed how seamlessly Randi's face turned from angry to sad, tough to tender, and bitter to loving in a matter of minutes. Jule knew that if she truly wanted to be with Randi, then she had to accept all facets of who she was. But could she?

Randi backed the car into the garage and shut off the ignition. Neither of them moved. Sirius waited in the backseat, his tail thumping rhythmically against the leather.

Jule brushed back Randi's bangs and rested a hand on her shoulder. "Would you rather be alone tonight?"

"No." Randi turned and looked at her. "I need you tonight." Sirius poked his head between the bucket seats. Randi scratched his head. "I need you, too. Come on. Let's go play some ball."

They took turns tossing the ball around for a good twenty minutes and then went inside. Jule gave Sirius a fresh bowl of water and a treat.

Randi opened a beer. "I hope you don't mind, but I could really use this tonight."

Jule shrugged. "What the hell. Give me one, too. I think we've earned it."

They went into the living room and plopped down onto the couch. They sipped their beer and sat in an expectant silence.

"Randi?"

"Yeah?"

"What did you say to her?"

"Just talked to her. Turns out we have a lot in common."

"Like what? Don't tell me you've been raped, too."

"No." Randi picked at the label on her bottle. "After Stevie died, I was treated like an outcast at school. She's going through the same thing right now."

"Poor kid." Jule took a drink and set the bottle on the coffee table.

"Yeah. Hope she'll be okay."

Jule ran her fingers across Randi's cheek. "I was talking about you."

"Stop it."

"Stop what? Stop letting you know I care about you? Not gonna happen. You scared the shit out of me tonight."

"That makes two of us." Randi looked at her apologetically. "I let her down."

"Let her down? You saved her life!"

"She was pissed at me for not catching the rapist yet."

"Do you really think that's why she was up there? Think about what she's been through. Why do you think she asked for you?" She didn't give Randi time to answer. "You mean something to her, Randi. Isn't she the same girl you talked to about shoplifting? I'm telling you, you made an impression on her. That was obvious tonight. She knew you could help her."

"What if this had happened the night we were camping? I wouldn't have been there to save her."

"If they had gotten in touch with you, nothing would have stopped you from being there for her."

Randi finished off her beer and brought her bottle to the kitchen. Jule expected her to come back with another, but she came back empty-handed.

"You're right," she said, slumping onto the couch. Randi rested her head in her hands. She shook her head slightly and let out a long breath. "If I were a better cop, he would've been behind bars by now."

Jule got up off the couch and knelt before her. "That's not all on you, and you know it. It's not like you're the only cop on the force looking for him." She placed her hands over Randi's and took them away from her face. Her eyes and cheeks were drenched with tears. Jule swiped them away with her thumbs, but they kept coming. She returned to her side and wrapped her arms around her.

"Come here."

Randi hugged herself within Jule's embrace. After several minutes, she unfolded her arms and encircled them around Jule's waist. Jule held her and let her cry as long as she needed. When Randi finally withdrew, Jule pulled a handkerchief from her back pocket and handed it to her.

"Always prepared, aren't you?" Randi teased her.

"Good thing, huh?"

"Yeah." She blew her nose and stuffed it into her own pocket.

"Keep it. I have plenty."

"I seem to need them a lot lately."

"Why is that?"

Randi shrugged. "Since I met you, I can't stop it. I used to be able to stop it."

"And just how long have you gone without letting yourself cry?"

Randi shrugged.

"You deserve to let yourself mourn for him. You deserve to let yourself cry."

"I know that now."

*Something happened to me out on that bridge.* When she had told Carly that she would jump with her, there was a moment that she had actually meant it. If they had both ended their lives tonight, not only would she have ended her own suffering, but Carly would have been spared from a similar fate. Of course, no one else would have understood that logic. When she'd climbed onto that rail, she had felt something unexpected: a will to live, woven into a vision of a future she was unwilling to sacrifice. Then she'd slipped and Sirius hauled her back. And she was *grateful.* For once, the only regret she felt was for the time she would have lost with Jule if she'd fallen. She didn't want to lose a minute of it. What would it have done to Jule if she had died tonight? Especially after what happened to her last girlfriend? How cool would it be to be someone's girlfriend? What was that like? She wanted to know.

She'd used flirting and sex to divert conversations away from herself for years. It always worked, since there weren't many people who wanted to dig any deeper. She flirted with Jule too, but Jule had a way of getting her to talk. She brushed Jule's lips with her own. She felt such a release from spilling her secrets to Jule that it made her want her in a way she'd never wanted anyone else.

She wanted to be inside her right now, yet this wasn't about sex. This was about connecting with the only person that she had allowed into her soul.

As the kiss continued, Jule caressed her body, but made no other move to take things further. Randi sensed that Jule was letting her take control. She shifted on the couch with the intention of lowering herself on top of her when a pain shot through her shoulder and radiated down her arm. She had to break the kiss.

"What is it?" asked Jule, with a look of concern that again tugged at Randi's heart.

"I think I wrenched my shoulder when I caught Carly on the bridge." She sat up with a grunt and winced. "And I think my back just tightened up, too."

Jule shook her head. "You're a wreck. I knew you should've let the EMTs check you out."

"No way. I wasn't about to get into that ambulance with Megan."

"Oh really? And why is that?"

*Oh shit.* "Uh…"

"Maybe because she'd be trying to sneak a little mouth-to-mouth action on you?"

Randi felt her face grow hot. *Megan's been talking.* She decided to have a little fun. "She is a good kisser, now that you bring it up."

"If you're trying to make me jealous, it's working." Jule's ears turned red.

"Are you trying to tell me something?"

"I, uh, well—"

Randi moved within inches of Jule's face. "Well?"

"I don't want to share you. There. I confessed. You happy?"

*Yes. Holy shit, I really think I'm happy.* "Only if I don't have to share you either."

"Deal."

Randi's heart pounded. She smiled mischievously. "Does that mean we're goin' steady?"

Jule laughed. "Going steady. You are so cute." Jule moved closer. "I'd say we're almost going steady."

"Almost?"

"It's not official until we seal it with a kiss." Jule closed the gap.

When another pain traveled through her arm, Randi had to pull away.

"Stay right here," ordered Jule. She left the room, and a few minutes later, Randi heard water running. Jule returned and offered her hand. "Time for that hot bath."

She helped Randi to her feet and led her to the master bath. She had clean towels and washcloths ready. The bath was almost full and had filled the room with a soothing warm steam.

"It's awfully bright in here," Jule said. "Do you have any candles?"

"Sorry, no."

"Just thought it might be more relaxing than that vanity light." She shut off the faucet.

"Don't worry about it. I feel like I've been run over by a truck, so at this point, I don't really care."

Jule gently removed Randi's shirt. She unbuttoned Randi's jeans and slid them down. Randi put her hands on Jule's shoulders for balance and kicked off the pants. Jule removed her socks and bent down to kiss her swollen ankle. She ran her hands up Randi's torso and reached behind to unclasp her bra, their chests touching as she did so.

Randi held her gaze. "Join me."

An odd look crossed Jule's face. Was that shyness? Insecurity? Still? "Next time. Tonight, just let me take care of you. Okay?"

Randi searched her face and decided not to push it. "Okay."

Jule slipped off the bra and stepped back, openly appraising what she saw. She placed a forefinger in the hollow of Randi's throat and grazed it downward between her breasts to her panties. She hesitated only briefly before pulling them off. "You are so beautiful."

Randi caressed her cheek and placed a quick kiss on her lips. "Thank you."

"Ready?"

Randi nodded and Jule held her steady as she stepped in and sank down into the tub.

"Oh, this feels so good."

"Do you have everything you need?" Jule took a step toward the door.

"You're leaving?"

"The point is for you to relax and soothe your aches and pains. If I stay, you might pull more muscles." She winked.

"Good point, but it would be worth it."

"Save your strength, babe. You might need it later."

"I like the sound of that."

"It's called incentive. Besides, I think Sirius needs to go out."

She smiled and left the door ajar behind her.

Jule knew she'd panicked when Randi asked her to join her in the bath. If the room had been darker, she wouldn't have turned down the invitation. She'd been working out for months now. She shouldn't be ashamed of her body anymore. Even her sister had complimented how good she looked. And Denise didn't pull any punches.

Jule knew that tonight things had taken a serious turn. Did they really just agree to be exclusive? Was she ready for that? Was Randi? *Yes. I think we're heading in the right direction now. I can feel it.*

She brought Sirius inside and made sure his food and water bowls were full. Other than the dim glow of the light over the stove, the house was completely dark. It was after midnight. It had been a very long day. She was exhausted and knew Randi had to be just as tired. The house was silent. Sirius followed her down the hall to Randi's bedroom.

"I was afraid I'd scared you off." Randi's voice came from the direction of the bed.

"So was I."

Randi reached for the side lamp and turned it on. She turned down the covers and stretched out on her back with her hands beneath her head. She was in navy blue boxer shorts and a heather gray sleeveless tee. How in the world did she look so sexy in such casual attire?

"Sorry. I put you through hell tonight."

Jule sat on the side of the bed and draped an arm over her. She leaned down and kissed Randi's cheek. "Nothing to be sorry for. I'm sorry if I got a little freaked out just now."

"Are you still worried about a few extra pounds?"

"How did you know?"

Randi stroked her jawline. "I'm getting so I can read you pretty well."

"It's not you. You know that, don't you?"

"Yeah, I know. I want to tell you something, though. Do you know what really makes you beautiful?" She placed her palm on Jule's heart. "This right here." She pulled Jule in for a kiss.

Randi's clean scent made her very aware that she had too many hours' worth of grime on her own body. "Do you mind if I take a shower?"

"Not at all."

"How about I give you a shoulder massage when I get back?"

"You're spoiling me."

"I said I'd take care of you, so damn right I'm going to spoil you."

Jule grabbed the overnight bag she'd packed—just in case—and headed for the bathroom. She savored the hot stream but washed quickly, anxious to get her hands on that beautiful body.

When she returned, the light was off. She heard Randi snoring lightly. Should she wake her and give her the promised rub? After the day they'd had, she really should let her sleep. She crawled in and pulled the covers over them. She placed a kiss on Randi's cheek and whispered, "good night" before curling up behind her.

She smiled and nuzzled Randi's neck. *We still have work to do, but I think I'm going to like going steady.*

## CHAPTER THIRTY-TWO

Randi rolled down the window and reveled in the warm breeze in her hair. The beautiful weather and the two-hour drive still wasn't enough to dispel her nervousness. Despite therapy and the positive changes she'd been feeling recently, she didn't trust that it would last. Every time she thought of Carly and the trauma she would have to suffer with for the rest of her life, she felt her rage threaten to spill over. There was only one person in the world who could possibly understand what she was going through.

She pulled into the checkpoint and greeted the guard.

"Sorry. Visitation isn't till tomorrow."

Randi gave the man her ID. "Can't you make an exception?"

He studied her license and then smiled at her. "Well, what do you know. Buster Hartwell's kid. How're you doing, Officer?"

"I'll be better when you let me in to see my dad."

"I'll see what I can do."

A few phone calls later, Randi was escorted in and led to a visitors' booth. Her stomach knotted. She had no idea what kind of reception he would give her, since she'd never come to see him. She didn't have to wait long. His smile said it all the second he walked in.

He sat and they stared at each other. She'd expected him to be gray and worn down. Instead, his hair was still as dark as ever, his eyes were full of life, and he looked like he'd kept up with his regular workouts. He gestured to the phones.

"Hi, Dad."

"Miranda. My gosh, are you a sight for sore eyes. You're all grown up and you're so beautiful!"

Randi blushed despite herself. She'd had forever to prepare for this moment, and now, she was at a loss for words. *How do you make up years of lost conversation in one hour?* She resorted to what she did best—she turned on the charm.

"I take after my good-looking dad."

"Aaah, you're full of baloney. It's your mother and you know it. Is she here, too?"

"No. Just me."

He couldn't seem to wipe the smile from his face. "I'm glad you came."

She couldn't afford to waste time on small talk. She took a deep breath. Might as well just say it. "Dad, I'm not sure if you heard this from Mom or Tim, but…I got into some trouble at work. I need your help."

Her father's eyebrows furrowed. "What is it?"

"They put me into anger management counseling."

"I see." He studied his hands and rubbed them together. "Is it helping?"

"So far. But what happens if…there's a rapist on the loose. I've gotten kind of attached to one of his victims. If he's still at large when I go back on patrol…I'm afraid I might do something stupid."

He chewed his lower lip, a gesture that, despite the gravity of the situation, made her smile. She did the same thing when she was thinking.

"Like what?"

*Like kill someone,* she almost said, before remembering where she was. "I already went after him once when I was off duty."

"And you're afraid of what you might do if you catch him."

Randi sighed in relief. He understood. She knew he would. She studied his face. For the first time, she admitted to herself how much she'd missed him. It must have been torture for him to spend all this time without his daughter in his life. He'd tried. Her mother had tried. Even Aunt Sandy had tried. No one had been able to convince her to visit him. No, she'd been too angry with him for removing himself from their lives. From her life.

And yet, that's exactly what she'd done to him.

How had he done it? How had he managed to survive feeling that rejection? Maybe she'd imposed a worse sentence on him than the courts had.

"Randi, honey? You listen to me. You are not me, do you understand? You're stronger. You're smarter."

"I'm sorry, Dad." Randi's eyes filled. "I'm so sorry. I've wasted all this time."

"Oh, honey. I'm the one who's sorry. I blew it—"

"No, Dad. That's over. It happened and you've paid the price. But I made it worse." She cried harder. She wanted nothing more than to give him a big hug—impossible with that damned bulletproof glass between them. She wanted to put her fist through it to get to him.

"Hey. Come on, now. You know I can't stand to see my little girl cry."

She noticed a box of tissues by the phone. She took a moment to blow her nose and collect herself.

"Dad?"

"What, honey?"

She looked him in the eye. "I love you. And I forgive you."

His eyes grew watery, but held hers as he said, "Thank you for saying that. I love you too, honey. And I've missed you like crazy."

"I missed you, too."

They stared at each other for a few minutes, as if not sure what else to say. After making use of another tissue, Randi thought maybe she was okay to go. But they still had time left, and she didn't want to waste any of it.

"If all goes well, I'll be home soon."

Randi smiled. She'd almost forgotten. Life was about to take another turn.

"Randi?"

"Yeah, Dad?"

"Get rid of it."

Randi scrunched up her eyebrows. "Get rid of what?"

"If I'd gotten rid of mine, I wouldn't have wasted twenty years of my life in here."

*He wants me to get rid of my gun.* And give up her protection? Was he crazy?

He rubbed his eyes and let out a long sigh. "I'm going to tell you something, and I'm only going to say this once: if you keep it, then you make damn sure that if you use it, it's only because you *need* to use it—not because you *want* to, you got that?" His dark eyes bored holes through her. "You understand what I'm saying?"

"Yeah."

He slouched back in the chair and worked his jaw, as if he had more to say. "Your mother's right. You're a lot like me, you know that? Except you're better. You were always a sensitive kid. Kind. Thoughtful. I remember when you were ten or eleven you started coming home from school and wolfing down everything in sight the minute you walked in the door. Your mother thought maybe someone was bullying you and taking your lunch. She called the school to see if your teachers had noticed anything." He grinned. "Turns out you were sharing your lunch with a classmate whose family was going through a tough time. You remember that?"

*Nadine Winthrop.* Nadine never ate lunch and always sat alone. Randi felt sorry for her, so one day she sat with her. She learned that her father had been paralyzed in an accident and they were sinking every penny they had into paying medical bills and making their house wheelchair accessible. Nadine was secretly stashing her lunch money away because she wanted to contribute to the cause.

"I remember. Mom started packing an extra lunch for me to take for her."

"Your mother and I were so proud of you. We've always been proud of you, Randi."

The guard said, "Five minutes, Buster."

He pursed his lips and stared at her. "Think about what I said. Get rid of it if that's what it takes to get rid of the temptation. Either way, you need to find a healthy way to deal with your anger. And, honey, keep seeing the counselor. Make the choice to be happy."

"Thank you, Dad."

"I'm proud of you. You'll do the right thing. I know you will."

He hung up the phone and they took him away.

She rested her forehead against the window for a moment, thinking about what he'd said. *He's right. I'm so tired of being...this person.* But it wasn't her own gun she was going to give up.

It was her service pistol.

## CHAPTER THIRTY-THREE

S trike one!"
       Jule was at bat, once again trying desperately to focus on the oncoming pitch instead of the concern for Randi that had plagued her all day. They'd both been shaken up by Carly's rescue, and then Randi left early Monday morning, saying there was something very important she needed to do. That was two days ago. Jule couldn't get any more out of her than that, but the look on Randi's face told her it was serious. She hadn't heard from her, and didn't want to push, but it was driving her crazy.

She swung wildly at the next pitch, missing it by a mile. *What's the use?* She should just take herself out of the game. It was bad enough that Trish's team was hanging out on the bleachers waiting to play the next game. The glares she got from the ill-tempered shortstop weren't helping.

"Strike three!"

She dragged her bat in the dirt as she made her way to the dugout. She had filled Brenda in on everything, and now Brenda was by her side with an arm around her shoulder.

"Hey. Softball's supposed to take your mind off your troubles, not add to them."

"Thanks, Bren, but I don't think it's going to work tonight. Maybe I should sit this one out."

"And do what? Sulk on the bench?"

"I'm not helping the team. You guys are better off without me."

Brenda shook her head and got up. It was her turn to hit. "And you wonder why I stay single."

"You hate being single and you know it!" Jule called after her, but Brenda just laughed and dug into the batter's box. She drove the ball hard into a gap for a double. *Show-off.*

Jule bent over to tie a loose shoelace and then went to the bathroom. When she came out, she was relieved to see Randi's Camaro pulling into a space next to the school.

Randi got out and caught her eye briefly before looking at the ground. Jule didn't need more than that to know that she had a lot on her mind. She waited for her approach.

Except Randi didn't approach her. She headed toward the bleachers. Toward Trish. *Oh, shit.* Jule ran to Randi's side just as Randi reached Trish. She didn't say anything and returned Randi's small smile when she glanced at her. Trish turned to the two of them and stood up, along with her girlfriend at her side.

"What the fuck do you want?" Trish said.

"Just want to talk to you a minute," Randi answered calmly.

Trish glared from Randi to Jule. Her girlfriend nudged her and whispered something in her ear.

"Just talk. I promise. We can do it right here with all your friends as bodyguards. Whatever you want, Trish."

Trish hesitated for a moment before slowly stepping down off the bleachers. She crossed her arms and stood with her feet apart, ready for battle.

"I'm sorry for what happened last week." When Trish said nothing, Randi continued. "I didn't know what I was doing. I suffer from post-traumatic stress, and I had some sort of episodic reaction to something that has nothing to do with you."

"You mean like a hallucination?"

"Something like that. I'm getting help for it. I know I can't take back what happened, but I want you know how sorry I am."

Trish stared at the ground and drew lines in the dirt with her toe. She nodded and said, "Well, I'm sorry for shoving your girlfriend. I guess we both kinda lost it there."

Randi smiled. "Guess protectiveness over girlfriends is something we have in common." Randi extended her hand. "Truce?"

Trish shook Randi's hand. "Truce." They reluctantly smiled at each other.

Randi pulled an envelope from her back pocket and handed it to Trish.

"What's this?"

"Two tickets to the Passion Play show this weekend."

Trish's eyes widened. "Are you shittin' me? How did you get these? That show's sold out."

Randi winked. "I've got a friend in the band."

Trish spun around to her girlfriend. "April! Tickets to Passion Play!"

"Awesome!" April bounded down the benches to join them. "Thanks."

"Yeah, thanks."

Randi looked at Jule. "Your team's waiting for you."

Jule looked to the field. Sure enough, the ump was motioning for her to get back in the game. She ran for her glove and made it to second base just in time. She backhanded a hopper and threw out the runner with time to spare.

Yeah, she could get her head back in the game now. If she could keep her eyes off Randi, that is, who had moved her car to the outfield parking lot and was now walking around the fence to her usual spot on the center field bleachers. *I'm hopeless.*

They lost the game, but Jule didn't care. The team wrapped things up quickly and she made her way to the Camaro. There was a hot babe stretched out on the hood grinning at her. She let her bag slip off her shoulder onto the ground and joined Randi on the top of the car.

Jule said, "You are impossible, you know that?"

"What'd I do?"

"I've been worried sick about you for two days because you wouldn't tell me anything, you haven't called, and then you do something wonderful that makes you irresistible. How am I supposed to stay mad at you when you do that?"

"I didn't do it for you."

Jule laughed. "I know you didn't. That only makes you more irresistible."

Randi rolled onto her side to face her. "Don't let me off the hook so easily, Jule. I've been screwing up royally the last few months."

"You're making up for it now, though."

Jule saw something in her face she'd never seen before. There was determination, but not with the usual anger that she'd seen before. It was almost as if she was at peace with something.

She reached up and gently stroked Randi's cheek. "Tell me about it."

Randi sat up and looked out across the field. Trish and April's team had taken the field and were ready for the first batter. The lights illuminated the field, but they weren't enough to hide the night's stars. The air was still warm. It was a perfect summer night.

"Do you think it's a coincidence that my dad might be getting out of prison the week of Stevie's birthday?"

*Whoa.* Totally not what she was expecting. "No way. When's that happening?"

"Next month. Stevie was born on the Fourth."

"Stevie's birthday was—is—the Fourth of July?"

"Yeah. Fitting isn't it? He was such a stand-up guy. Patriotic. Eager to serve his community."

"It's perfect. He sounds a lot like you."

Jule sat up and Randi rested her head on Jule's shoulder.

"I saw my father today."

*Wow. Another surprise.* Jule put her arm around Randi's shoulders. "How'd that go?"

"Better than I could have ever imagined."

Jule smiled into Randi's hair. So soft. She gave Randi a tug and held her a bit closer. "Want to tell me about it?"

"I told him I forgive him. I told him I love him, too."

"And how did it feel to tell him those things?"

Randi chuckled. "You're not so bad at this shrink stuff, you know."

"Yeah, well, I wasn't very good at it a week ago."

"You're wrong about that. What you said was exactly what I needed to hear—even though it hurt like hell to hear it."

Jule brushed her cheek on Randi's hair again. "It hurt like hell to say it."

Randi lifted her head and turned to look at her. "My mom said you're a good influence on me. She's right."

Jule kissed her. "I like your mom already."

Randi grinned sheepishly. "Yeah?"

"And I really like you."

Randi kissed her cheek and then her eyes grew dark again. "There's more."

"Okay."

"I'm going to the station tomorrow to resign from the force."

"What? Are you serious?" Although she couldn't deny the relief she would feel if Randi had a safer occupation, Jule had spent her entire adult life grounded in the stability of a steady job. She couldn't imagine quitting without having something else lined up to take its place. "What will you do for income?"

"I have a few ideas. My mother offered to help me out." Randi slid off the car and extended her hand. "Let's walk. I need to stretch."

Jule followed suit and they held hands as they strolled around the outfield fence.

"I never wanted to be a cop, Jule. I did it for Stevie."

"Are you sure that's the only reason?"

"Yeah, it is. The worse thing is that I'm a cop who makes a living off my family's good name, and gets away with bending the rules— breaks the law even—because of that. That's nothing to be proud of. Think about it, Jule. A good cop wouldn't pull women over and let them out of speeding tickets for a roll in the sack."

"Well, yeah, there's that. But that's only because you haven't dealt with losing your brother. That could change if you give it time. Are you sure you want to quit?"

Randi stopped and took both hands in hers. "Yes. I want to do something that makes me happy. This job's killing me. The stuff I deal with every day is too much. The only time I'm not miserable is when I'm with you. And now that I have you, I know the difference. I don't want to be miserable anymore." Randi leaned down and kissed her tenderly. "Before you, I spent a lot of time fantasizing about… well, not killing myself, but wishing I wasn't here. I don't know if I can really explain the difference."

Jule gripped Randi's hands so tight she saw Randi flinch. She knew Randi had suffered over the awful things that had happened in her life, but until now, she hadn't fully realized the extent of it.

"Oh, Randi, baby." She pulled Randi into her arms and held on to her with all her might. "My God, you poor thing."

Randi burrowed her face into Jule's shoulder.

Jule took her face between her hands. "Promise me if you ever feel that way again, you'll tell me. You're never going to be alone again. I promise. We'll get through it together, okay?"

Randi looked into her eyes and Jule had no doubts about Randi's feelings. Randi loved her.

"Promise?"

Randi nodded.

"Say it. I want you to promise me."

"I promise."

They resumed walking, this time with arms around each other's waists. "So at the risk of sounding jealous, which one of your Passion Play girlfriends was kind enough to give you concert tickets?"

Randi grinned. "Jealous? You're jealous of Shawn?"

Jule puffed out her bottom lip. "You saw Shawn?"

"Shawn stopped by my house to show off her new car. You should see it, Jule, a brand new Camaro—yellow with black racing stripes and sport wheels. I was drooling."

"Drooling over the car or Shawn?"

Randi wiggled her eyebrows. "Both."

Jule smacked her on the arm.

"Hey, I'm kidding! You know I only drool over you now."

"You're a brat, Officer Hartwell."

"Oh no, you don't. You can't call me that anymore. I told you I'm resigning. That's why I needed to ask Shawn for LaKeisha's number."

"Who? Another girl? Just how much competition do I have anyway?"

Randi laughed. "LaKeisha's a counselor. She helped Shawn through her shit. If I resign, I can't go to the station's psychologist."

"Oh, right. Well, in that case, it's okay."

"Damn right it is."

"I'm still jealous."

"Hey, who am I with right now?"

Jule looked at her sternly and poked her in the chest. "You're with me, and don't you dare forget it."

"Not in a million years."

They were back at the car. Jule's gear was still on the ground next to it. "Guess I better put my stuff in the truck." She hefted the bag over her shoulder. "Are we staying at your place tonight or mine?"

"Don't you have to work in the morning?"

"Yeah, so. Haven't you missed me?"

"God yes."

"Then let's stop at your house for your things and come spend the night with me at mine. Deal?"

"I love it when you boss me around."

"Good, because Sirius missed you, too."

"You missed me?"

Jule pulled her down by the back of the neck and pressed their lips together. She eased her tongue inside and tasted the softness she'd been craving all night. She heard a couple of the outfielders make wolf calls at them and she kissed her even harder. She was so hungry for her. She slowly withdrew and swiped her tongue across Randi's upper lip.

"What do you think?"

"I think when I resign and turn in my gear, they might be missing a pair of handcuffs."

Jule let out a groan as her insides burst into flames. "You have to catch me first."

She spun and walked to her truck, certain that Randi wouldn't be able to take her eyes off her. She was finally feeling good about her body and she couldn't wait to get naked with her. She heard the Camaro roar to life before she even made it to her own vehicle. *Handcuffs, huh? Now that could be fun.*

## Chapter Thirty-four

R andi tapped her foot incessantly while waiting in Lieutenant Baldwin's office. Beside her on the floor was a bag full of police uniforms and other paraphernalia she carried while on duty. She thought she'd be nervous, but her mind was at ease with this decision. Her anxiety had more to do with her frustration about the rapist they hadn't caught yet, as well as the knowledge that Baldwin would probably argue for her to change her mind.

He came in with a grunt and sat heavily in his chair. "I hear you canceled your appointment this morning. Need I remind you that if you don't reschedule something this week, you'll be violating one of the terms of your agreement."

"I'm not rescheduling."

Baldwin's eyebrows drew together like a caterpillar. "Hartwell, you know I can't let you back on the force if you don't hold up—"

"I'm not coming back, Tim." She hoped using his first name, as she had called him as a kid, would resonate with him on a more personal level. She stood and dropped the bag on his desk. "I'm resigning. You already have my badge and weapon, so this should be everything."

Baldwin slid open a drawer and took out his pack of Juicy Fruit. "You want to tell me why?"

"Does it really matter? You and I both know it's the right thing to do. I'm a lousy cop."

Baldwin leaned forward on the desk. "You could be a good cop, Randi. What you're not good at is controlling your temper."

"I can't control my temper because I hate being a cop! I hate dealing with criminals. I hate seeing the ugliness in people, and the damage they do to innocent people. You've been there, Tim. You know what I'm talking about."

"Yes, I do, but don't you see? This passion you have for others is what can make you a good cop. I always know that when you're out on patrol you have the best interest of this town's citizens in mind. I know that you'd do anything to protect them. You're a better cop than half the guys on this force who are just here collecting a paycheck."

Randi paced and ran her hands through her hair. "I just can't do it anymore. I can't. I need to see something beautiful every day. I need to take pictures. That's who I am. Not this. I'm not my father. I'm not..." *Stevie.*

Baldwin picked up a pen, tapped it on the desk a few times, and then held the ends in both hands. He rolled it between his fingers. "You're right, you're not. Buster was one of the best cops I ever had the privilege to work with, and I love him like a brother. He loved being a cop, but his passion for the job had more to do with his love for the law than for people. That right there is the difference between you. I'm not saying he didn't care about them, and he wanted to do right by them. But you, you go after it like it's your mission in life."

Even if there were some truth to Tim's words, even if she were the best cop on the planet, being a cop didn't make her happy. *Make the choice to be happy.* Her father's words echoed loudly in her head.

"It was an honor working with you, Lieutenant." She shook his hand. "Now if you don't mind, I need to go see Personnel to fill out a resignation form."

She stopped at Mac's Classic Cars on her way home and asked for a job. Mac had been one of Stevie's buddies and a fellow car enthusiast. It was Mac who'd gone with Stevie to check out the Camaro and inspected it for him. Randi had gone to him for parts over the years and they'd become friendly themselves.

He was skeptical, but told her he'd look over his books to see if he could afford to take on another mechanic. He said he'd call by the end of the week.

When she got home, she went upstairs and stood outside Stevie's room. Randi turned the knob and let the door fall open. It was stupid, really, keeping a room set up for her brother as if he'd be returning to it every night. She stepped inside. Stevie had never been in this room, but she still felt his presence there every time. Most of his stuff was here, other than what their mother had at Aunt Sandy's. For whatever length of time she was in this space, she could pretend he was alive. She could picture him sprawled on his stomach on the bed reading detective novels. She could picture him sitting cross-legged on the floor with his Hot Wheels. His favorite was a police car that ran down criminals and brought them back to a police station made of Legos. She could picture him polishing his silver-plated toy gun until it shined.

"I quit, Stevie. I'm sorry. I had to." She scanned the room and stared at the manila envelope on the desk that contained Stevie's police academy application. She wished she'd never sent hers in.

She closed the door behind her. She pulled her wallet from her back pocket and thumbed a photo out of one of its sleeves. She smiled at the image: Stevie leaning back against a boulder taller than he was, his thumbs hooked in his jeans pockets, a grin on his face that could have lit up the entire Montana sky. *You won't mind if I turn your room into a darkroom, will ya, Stevie?*

*I didn't think so.*

## CHAPTER THIRTY-FIVE

Jule never thought she'd use the word "bubbly" to describe Randi, but her excitement today warranted the adjective. It was a gorgeous Saturday morning. They'd grabbed a quick breakfast after Jule picked her up, and they were now at the animal shelter. Randi couldn't stop talking about how she couldn't wait to see Carly's face when she brought her the three-year-old beagle mix named Linus.

She also learned that Randi had been volunteering at the shelter for over a decade. The size of Randi's heart never ceased to amaze her.

They followed a volunteer named Jake through an aisle of kennels. Jule tried hard not to look at the fuzzy faces that peered out at her, but it was impossible. She was afraid she'd want to take all of them home. Randi seemed to be having difficulty, too.

"Well, here we are," said Jake.

They knelt by the kennel and Randi turned to the adjacent compartment. In it was a German shepherd puppy.

"Hey," said Randi to Jake. "I know this dog. When did he come in?"

"Yesterday. The vet just released him to us. He was recovering from some injuries. He was rescued—"

"From an abuser. I know. I was one of the officers on the scene."

"Really? Good work. You'll be glad to know we helped find homes for all of them. He's the last one."

Randi put out her hand and the shepherd sniffed it. He wagged his tail and let out a whine.

Jule asked, "Can you take him out?"

"Sure. He's very sweet, but that's the first time I've seen him approach anyone. He's still timid after what he's been through."

He opened the gate and the dog went to Randi immediately, hopping up and placing his front paws on her leg. Randi's smile lit up the room. She petted him and spoke softly.

"He remembers you," said Jule.

"Yeah, I think he does. That's amazing."

Jake fitted him with a harness and retrieved a leash from a nearby hook. "Take him outside to the play area out back. What about the beagle?"

"Oh, I'm still taking the beagle. That's a done deal."

"Good to know. Take your time. I'll make sure everything's in order for Linus so he's ready to go."

They wandered around the fenced-in area and let him do his business. Other than quick sniffs, the dog showed little interest in the numerous toys strewn around—until Randi picked up a tennis ball.

"Bingo," Jule said.

Randi took off the lead and held up the ball. "You wanna play?" She tossed the ball across the yard. The dog instantly took off after it, took a few chomps on it, and trotted back to Randi. He chewed it a bit more before dropping it at Randi's feet.

"Good boy!"

They repeated this five or six more times, and then Jule took a few turns. The joy in Randi's face took Jule's breath away. Randi reattached the leash and Jule gave her a knowing look.

Jule said, "Why do I get the feeling we're leaving here with *two* dogs today."

"You're getting to know me all too well."

"You do realize you're making a commitment for about the next ten years, don't you?"

Randi seemed to mull this over for a few minutes. "That is a long time."

"This dog chose *you*, Randi. He needs you, and I think you need him, too. It wouldn't be fair to him to make this decision without thinking it through."

Randi looked away and closed her eyes. She broke into a smile when the dog scratched at her knee.

"I can do this, Jule. He needs to pass one more test."

"What is that?"

"I want to make sure he gets along with Sirius."

Jule cocked her head. "I doubt that will be a problem. What if he doesn't?"

Randi raised her eyebrows at Jule and then looked at the dog, who was staring at Randi with his ears perked as if he understood the magnitude of the answer. "I'm taking him home anyway."

"Damn right you are."

They went inside, where Randi filled out the necessary paperwork. With Linus in a carrier and the shepherd in the backseat, they headed to the pet store for supplies for one more dog.

Randi rang the bell of a small, white Colonial house. Her nerves tingled with anticipation. When Carly opened the door, she couldn't help grin. Her arm ached with the weight of the occupied pet carrier, but she lifted it to Carly anyway.

"I want you to meet someone."

Carly looked at Randi in confusion.

"Well, don't just stand there with your mouth open, you'll swallow a fly. Can we come in?"

Carly stepped back and her mother walked up behind her. "Officer Hartwell, what have you got there?" Debra asked, feigning surprise.

"Can't you see it's a dog, Mom?" Carly said, in a typical teenager "duh" tone.

"Carly, meet Linus."

Debra invited her in. Randi set the carrier on the floor and swung open its wire door. The poor dog scrunched all the way to the back end.

Randi got down on her knees about three feet from the opening and looked at him, thinking it was best that he come out on his own. Carly knelt beside her and leaned on her elbows.

"It's okay, little guy. I won't hurt you."

Randi reached into her jeans pocket. "Here, try this." She handed Carly a biscuit.

Carly held it out to Linus, and he poked his nose out and sniffed it. Instinctively, Carly pulled it away slightly, a little bit at a time, drawing him nearer to her. She repeated this until he was all the way out and right in front of her. He looked up at her and she smiled. Linus seemed to relax a little and hesitated again, unsure if it was okay to take the treat. Carly held it closer, and said, "It's okay." He gently took it from her, dropped his hindquarters onto the carpet, and crunched away. When he was finished, he stood and wagged his tail, looking at her expectantly.

"I think you've got yourself a new best friend," said her mother.

Carly held her hand out, palm down, and let him sniff. When he seemed satisfied, he dipped his head and nudged it underneath her hand so she could pet him. Carly beamed.

"I love him!"

"Good thing, since he's yours now."

"What? For real?"

"Yep. He's a beagle just like Snoopy. His name's Linus, you know, like Charlie Brown's best friend? I know you're a *Peanuts* fan, so I knew he'd be perfect for you." Randi stood. "I'll be right back. I've got the rest of your stuff in the car."

"You're serious? He's really mine to keep? Mom, can I keep him?"

Debra said, "Yes, sweetie. Officer Hartwell and I already talked about it. I signed all the papers yesterday. He's officially yours."

Carly's arms were around Randi before she knew what was happening. "Thank you, thank you, thank you!"

Randi hugged her back. "I have something else to tell you."

Carly released her and waited.

"I got a call this morning. We got him, Carly. They arrested him last night. They actually caught him trying to attack another girl, so there's no question about him going away. You're safe now."

"Oh, thank God," said Debra. She wrapped her arms around Carly, and Randi joined them and squeezed them both tight. They disentangled themselves and Debra left them alone.

Any doubts she'd had about resigning vanished. There was just one part of this nightmare she still needed to get through. She held

Carly at arm's length and took a deep breath. "I need to make you one more promise."

"What?"

"You and Jennifer will need to identify him, and possibly go to court to testify. I want you to know that I'll be by your side every step of the way."

Carly swallowed hard, fear sweeping across her face, and then her eyes hardened with determination. "I can do it."

"I know you can. You're one of the strongest people I know, Carly." She took a deep breath and let it out slowly. "When my brother died, I didn't think anyone could understand what I was going through. People tried to help me. I wouldn't let them. You probably feel that way too, sometimes. But I want you to remember something. You don't have to go through this alone. Don't push people away who love you."

Carly nodded. "Okay."

"It's okay to ask for help. Promise you'll call me or someone else if you need help?"

"Okay. I promise."

"All right then, enough of this serious stuff." Randi patted her on the shoulder. "Guess what I did?"

"What?"

"I got a dog, too. A beautiful shepherd puppy."

"That's so cool."

"Maybe we can go to the dog park sometime so they can play together."

Carly beamed. "And Sirius, too?"

"Yeah, of course."

"He's gotta be the smartest dog I ever met. I want Jule to come, too. She's pretty cool."

"She's pretty cool, all right. Almost as cool as you. *Almost.*" She winked.

Carly blushed. She shuffled her feet and looked thoughtful. "Remember when you asked me what I wanted to do after I graduate?"

"I sure do."

"I think I know."

"Yeah?"

"I want to be a dog trainer. You think I'd be good at that?"

Randi grinned as she saw the twinkle in Carly's eyes. "Are you kidding? You'd be great! I'm gonna need some help with my dog, if you want to start practicing. You interested?"

"OMG, I would love that!"

"Good. As long as it's okay with your mom."

Carly hugged her again. "You're the best, Officer Hartwell."

"Hey, that's something else I need to tell you. I'm not a cop anymore."

"You're not?"

"I resigned from the force. I decided I want to try my hand at something I think I'll like better."

Carly nodded knowingly. "Something that makes you happy, right?"

Randi's insides warmed. "Right. So you don't have to call me officer anymore, okay? We're pals. The name's Randi, got it?"

"Got it, Randi."

"Good."

While Carly took her new companion on a tour of his new home, Randi lugged in a dog bed, bowls, toys, a brush, a crate, a month's supply of food and treats—and of course, a blue blanket. Once she was satisfied that Linus felt safe, she got hugs from everyone again and was on her way.

Jule was dog sitting the other pup, and Randi was anxious to get home to see how they were getting along.

She called Jule's name as she came in through the kitchen, but heard nothing. Curious, she cautiously rounded the corner into the living room. Before her was a perfect picture: Jule was asleep on the couch with the puppy curled up beside her under one arm. The dog's front paws twitched as if he was dreaming.

She lightly stroked his head and whispered, "Looks like Jule tuckered you out already." He stirred at Randi's touch, but didn't awaken. It was probably the best nap the dog had ever had.

She quietly crept down the hall, returned with camera in hand, and snapped a few shots. She leaned over and kissed Jule's cheek.

Without opening her eyes, Jule reached up and touched Randi's face. "Hi, baby."

"Hey, angel."

Jule sleepily rubbed her eyes and scootched up. "What time is it?"

"About two."

The puppy finally woke up and looked around curiously. He seemed to remember he was in a safe place and yawned widely. He stretched his neck out toward Randi, who rewarded him with a scratch behind the ears. Happy and rested, the dog jumped down and began exploring.

Jule said, "Geez, what a lazy bum I am."

"We did have an eventful morning."

"How'd it go with Carly?"

"Great. She and Linus are bonding already."

"You did a good thing. Now do another good thing and kiss me."

Randi kissed her long and slow, and warmth filled her low in the belly. She was tempted to pick her up and take her to bed, but she heard Jule's stomach growl. They both needed food. They hadn't eaten since their breakfast on the run hours earlier, and besides, she now had a dog to take care of.

She withdrew and looked up just in time to see the dog about to lift its leg. Randi was up in a flash.

"Shit! Come on, let's go out."

Jule said that the pup was picking up Sirius's scent and was marking his territory. When they came back in, Randi ordered a pizza and then they went to work assembling the crate.

They ate and the puppy burrowed into his new bed inside the crate for another nap.

Randi said, "He sure sleeps a lot."

"He's still a baby. Jake said he's only about four months old."

"I think I'll call him Tucker."

Jule nodded. "I like it."

Randi sat on the floor and petted him. "Sweet puppy dog dreams, Tucker." She and Jule smiled at each other. "I just got him and I already love him."

"Do you have any idea what a turn-on that is to me?"

Randi got to her feet and pulled Jule off the couch into her arms. She moved within an inch of Jule's lips and whispered, "Why don't you show me?"

Jule reached under Randi's shirt and lightly ran her hands over her skin. Randi's entire body broke into gooseflesh. Jule unhooked her bra and brought her hands around to cup her breasts, their lips still not touching.

"Tell me what you want, baby." Jule whispered.

Randi's breath quickened and she leaned into Jule's touch. "I want your hands and lips all over me."

Jule ran her thumbs lightly over her nipples. "Like this?"

"Yes."

She made another swipe. "Is that it?"

"Maybe."

"You want more?"

"Yes. Kiss me."

Jule gave her a quick peck.

"Tease."

Jule smiled devilishly. "You ain't seen nothin' yet, baby." Jule stepped back and began unbuttoning her own shirt. With each button, she took another step down the hall.

Randi took one look at Tucker. Sound asleep.

"He's down for the count. But me, I'm wound up tight and I'm pretty sure you can do something about that." She disappeared into the bedroom.

Randi wasn't far behind.

# CHAPTER THIRTY-SIX

Randi grasped Jule's hand and moved it up near their faces. She opened her hand, their palms touching, and interlaced their fingers. The look in Randi's eyes was so intense that Jule couldn't look away if she wanted to.

"I need you, Jule," she whispered. "I need you so much." Randi lightly pressed her lips to hers.

Jule kissed her back, finding her tongue and caressing it lovingly. The kiss grew more passionate, and Randi wrapped an arm around her waist, pulling them closer together and then onto the bed.

Jule raised herself up and carefully rolled over on top of her. She fitted herself between Randi's legs and propped her elbows on the bed, breaking the kiss just long enough to say, "I need you, too. I'm not going anywhere."

She claimed Randi's lips again. She could never get enough of them. She felt Randi's hands on her bare back. They sat up together and lifted off each other's shirts. They shimmied out of their shorts and pressed their bodies together.

She cupped Randi's chin in her hand and their eyes met. "I'm going to take my time with you this time."

Randi placed her hand on the back of Jule's head and pulled her in for another lingering kiss. Her other hand wandered down to her backside as they fell into a slow rocking rhythm.

Jule said, "I could kiss you like this all night long."

"I won't mind if you do."

"I can't promise that I won't kiss you in other places, too."

"Don't make promises you can't keep."

"In that case, I promise to kiss you all over."

"That's more like it."

Their lips came together again. After several minutes, Jule broke away and proceeded to make good on her promise. After kissing her way up and down Randi's entire body, she settled on top of her and nuzzled her neck.

Randi whispered in her ear. "I want you to know me, Jule."

Jule froze. She looked into Randi's eyes. The combination of trust and vulnerability she saw in them made her insides turn to goo. "Baby, that is the most beautiful gift you could give me, and I cherish it. I cherish *you*." She kissed her softly. "Thank you."

Randi responded with a tender kiss that gradually increased in intensity. With each passing moment, with each touch, with each erogenous sound she elicited from Randi's throat, she grew more ravenous.

Jule peppered her neck and collarbone with kisses, and then sucked in Randi's taut nipple. Randi moaned as she teased it with her teeth and massaged it with her tongue. She felt Randi's hips lift, inviting the pressure that promised release.

"Not so fast. I have a lot more exploring to do." Jule moved on to the other breast.

Randi placed both hands on Jule's breasts and gently traced circles on her areolas until her tips were erect. She then grazed her thumbs across them over and over again.

Jule had to make a conscious effort to hold back her own climax and then, without warning, Randi's hands moved down to her ass and pulled their centers together. Jule could feel how wet they both were and knew she couldn't wait long.

She came up for air and kissed Randi hard as they continued to grind toward a building pressure.

Randi gently pushed on Jule's shoulders and broke the kiss. "I need you, Jule. Now."

Jule kissed a trail down her body and took her into her mouth. She took her time exploring, listening to Randi's moans as she responded to what pleased her, and enjoying every moment of it. She was so close herself, but she stayed focused on Randi's pleasure, not wanting to cheat herself out of what Randi had in store for her.

Randi jerked and cried out and Jule slowly withdrew. Randi pulled her back up on top of her and squeezed her tightly as she rode out the convulsions.

She placed kisses all over Randi's face. "So beautiful. Baby, you are so beautiful. I love making love to you." She rested her hand on Randi's cheek. It was wet. "Baby, are you crying?"

"No one's ever made love to me before. It's just been sex. But with you…I feel it, Jule. I feel your love. I feel your love."

Jule wrapped her arms around her and shifted so that she was on her back. Randi curled up into her. She held her close and then lifted Randi's chin so that she could look her in the eye.

"That's because I love you, Randi."

"You love me?"

"Yes. I do."

"Even after everything I've told you? Even though you know how screwed up my life has been?"

"Yes. I do. This isn't just sex to me either, you know."

Randi burrowed her head onto Jule's shoulder and draped an arm across her stomach.

"Jule?"

"Yes, baby."

"No one's ever said they love me before."

"You've never let anyone love you. You let me in. And I'm so happy that you did."

Randi changed position and kissed her deeply. She slid a hand downward and Jule tremored in anticipation. She took Randi's wrist and guided her hand, inviting her touch.

"Make love to me, Randi. I want you inside me."

Randi kissed her and slowly glided two fingers in and out repeatedly. Her touch was so soft and Jule opened up to her easily.

Jule moaned. She moved with Randi as she climbed closer and closer. Randi filled her over and over until she was about to explode. Now her thumb was on her hardened nub.

Randi lifted herself away and went down on her, caressing her with her tongue as she kissed her swollen folds.

Jule screamed and writhed at the overwhelming sensations as her orgasm crashed through her. Randi flattened her tongue against her and held her as she rode it out. As it began to subside, Randi suddenly took her again, sending her into oblivion two more times before finally releasing her and collapsing on top of her.

"Jule? Did you feel that?"

"That was amazing."

"That's because you're amazing, Jule. I never thought I could feel..."

"Feel what, baby?"

Randi held her gaze. "Love. I love you, Jule. My angel, my beautiful angel. I love you, too."

Jule kissed her. "I love you so much."

"I want to be enough for you."

The worry in Randi's eyes was too much to bear. Jule caressed her cheek. "Oh, sweetheart, you are. You're more than enough. You don't know how special you are. You're kind, and good, and compassionate. I love the way you make me laugh and call me a pain in the ass." She returned Randi's smile. "You are everything I could ever ask for, and I don't ever want to be without you."

Randi pulled Jule so tightly against her that Jule could feel their hearts beating against each other.

Jule kissed her forehead and said, "I can feel your heartbeat."

She felt Randi's warm breath against her neck as she replied, "I don't think my heart was beating until I met you. You've brought it back to life, Jule."

Jule flinched ever so slightly. She didn't mean to think of Casey. Again, an innocent comment hit home. She had never felt a connection like this with Casey, though, either emotionally or physically.

She couldn't stop the tears. She held on tighter and whispered, "I love you, Randi. This is where I belong, in your arms, right here, right now. I'm never letting you go."

Randi looked up and wiped away the tears. Randi kissed her several times on each cheek, never saying a word.

They made love well into the night. When exhaustion finally overcame them, Jule relaxed into Randi's soft snores and fell asleep in her arms.

She'd never felt more at home.

## Chapter Thirty-seven

Randi rode quietly in the passenger seat of Jule's truck. They were on their way to Aunt Sandy's house for her annual Fourth of July cookout. Aunt Sandy thought it was a good idea to maintain the tradition in honor of Stevie's birthday. Randi didn't always go. It all depended on her state of mind each year.

This year would be different from any other year. Not only because Jule was accompanying her, but also because of this year's guest of honor—her father. Buster Hartwell had served his sentence and was now a free man.

Randi carried two canvas grocery bags and Jule lugged a small cooler to the house. Randi caught herself checking her out. Now that the neighborhood was safe again, Jule had resumed her five-mile outdoor jogs, although she'd cut back to only one run a week. Jule finally seemed comfortable with how she looked, and Randi noticed that with the workouts she got playing softball twice a week, she wasn't as concerned about going to the gym as regularly. Randi had seen the transformation in her body over the last few months and damn, she looked even better than she did when they'd met—something Randi didn't think was possible. She was so incredibly beautiful. The summer sun had bronzed her skin and enhanced the golden highlights in her hair. Jule's face glowed and her eyes sparkled with a childlike happiness. It still amazed her every day that she had somehow won Jule's heart.

Randi opened the front door and let Jule go in ahead of her. Her heart was pounding. She'd spoken to her father on the phone twice since her visit. She was ecstatic to introduce Jule as her girlfriend, but nervous as hell to introduce him as her father. How do you do that? *Hey, Dad, this is Jule, the love of my life. Jule, this is my dad, who just got out of prison for killing a man.*

Aunt Sandy met them in the kitchen and took the bags from Randi after quick introductions. "Randi, honey, you go on out back. Your father's so excited to see you he's dancing around like he's got ants in his pants." Aunt Sandy winked at Jule. "Jule, set the cooler down on the floor right over there. I'll help you get the food situated."

"Go ahead, Randi," said Jule. "We got this."

Randi knew they were purposely giving her time alone with her father. She nodded in appreciation and went out the back door.

She stopped short on the porch. If they hadn't looked older, it was as if time had stood still. Her mother looked relaxed and content in a lawn chair with a glass of iced tea in her hand. Her father was behind the grill, tending sizzling burgers, grinning at his wife, and wearing the same old "Kiss the cook" apron Randi had seen him wear a hundred times when she was a kid.

The picnic table had a red and white checkered tablecloth and was ready with condiments, disposable plates, cups, plastic ware, and napkins. A nearby table was covered with food. Croquet wickets were already in place on the other end of the yard. Off to one side someone had driven horseshoe stakes into the ground. The neighborhood buzzed with laughter and the carefree sounds of family gatherings. She breathed in the smoky aromas of backyard barbecues, and a warm sea breeze tickled her face as she savored the moment.

She adjusted the settings on her camera and squeezed off several shots. Not that it was necessary. This was a scene she would never forget.

Only Stevie was missing. Yet it felt like he was here. She hadn't seen it yet, but she knew the assortment of food on the table included a birthday cake with his name on it.

Her father looked up and caught her eye. He handed the long-handled metal spatula to her mom and stepped out from behind the grill. His smile could have lit up the darkest night.

She came down the steps and walked toward him.

Unable to contain himself, he shouted, "There's my girl!" and sprinted across the lawn. He scooped her up in a bear hug and spun her around. She giggled in spite of herself.

She held on tight and burrowed her face in his meaty shoulder. Mom came over, and Dad wrapped them both into a group hug. Aunt Sandy joined them. Randi didn't mean to cry, but there was no reason to hold back anymore. Her dad was home. Her mother was stable. Her life was good. Her brother's spirit lived on in each of them. In that moment, he was there, enveloped in their embraces and love.

And she was overwhelmed with regret. Had she really wasted most of her life consumed by anger and guilt and resentment and self-loathing? What useless emotions. She couldn't change the past. She could only live in the present and hope that the choices she made today created a better future.

She looked up through waterlogged eyes and saw Jule watching from the porch with a huge smile on her face. All cried out, her family finally broke away and started laughing. Randi waved Jule over and took her by the hand.

"Dad, this is Jule. Jule, I'd like you to meet my father, Ben. But you better not call him that if you know what's good for you. Everyone calls him Buster."

"She's got that right." Her dad chuckled and gently shook her hand. "It's good to meet you, Jule."

"You, too. Thank you for having me."

Randi watched for any signs of discomfort or judgment on Jule's face and saw none. Was it possible to love her even more? *Most definitely. I'll love her more every day for the rest of my life, I think.*

"Oh, it's our pleasure," said her mother. "Make yourself at home."

Aunt Sandy said, "We're so tickled that you came. There's plenty of food, so help yourself to something to eat." She led Jule to the table and Randi laughed inwardly when her aunt added, "You need to put some meat on your bones."

*You probably just made her day, Auntie.*

It was no surprise that her family took to Jule immediately. Aunt Sandy practically asked if she could adopt her when Jule loaded her plate without hesitation and then helped herself to seconds.

"What the hell. You only live once and we have a lot to celebrate, right babe?" Jule quipped and then took a swig of Dr Pepper. "I might as well treat myself. It's not like I won't work it off in a week."

Randi shook her head and chuckled. "You're something else, you know that?" She'd never seen Jule more relaxed and her energy was contagious.

Later, Jule teamed up with her mother in a raucous two-on-two horseshoe match against Randi and her dad. Jule and her mother kicked their butts, and then celebrated by running a victory lap around the yard with their arms in the air. Dad and Aunt Sandy joined Randi in doing "the wave" as they passed by and they all laughed their heads off.

"Whew! I've never had so much fun in my whole life," said Aunt Sandy.

As the sun went down, they settled into lawn chairs and quiet conversation, followed by a toast to Stevie, and cake. Randi's heart burst with so many good feelings it was overwhelming.

Jule insisted they let her clean up as she collected everyone's plates and disappeared into the house with Aunt Sandy. Randi smiled at her parents, who were acting like honeymooners who couldn't take their eyes off each other. She knew the feeling. It was awesome.

"So, Dad, what'll you do now?"

"Well, I need to find a job. Then we need to think about getting our own place."

Her mother said, "Dear, you know we can stay here as long as we need to."

"Oh, I know. But your sister will want me out of her hair before too long."

"Whatever you do, you'd better stay close by," Randi said. She wanted to spend as much time with them as possible from now on.

"Oh, don't worry about that," said her mother. "We plan to stay in town."

Her father leaned forward and clasped his hands together. "We have a lot of catching up to do, Randi. Starting with that beautiful young lady who's captured your heart." He winked. "You'd better hold on to her."

"Believe me, I know."

"So tell me," her dad patted her knee, "how'd you two meet?"

"Well...it all started with this bumper sticker she has on the back of her truck." Randi grinned at the memory. "Did you know her German shepherd is smarter than an honor student?"

❖

Randi thought she'd be going stir-crazy after being out of work for two weeks, but she wasn't. Jule had surprised her one day with four new photo albums and urged her to dig out the shoeboxes full of photos Randi had stashed in a closet. Randi was even inspired to register for a photography class at the community college.

After filling the albums, she spent her time taking pictures. Sirius and Tucker were her favorite subjects—until Jule came home. She'd been staying at Jule's house since the cookout last week. She filled her days playing homemaker and doing minor odd jobs around the house that would help Jule with her renovations. The place was really shaping up. Once Jule could afford the kitchen remodel, it was only a matter of a few new furnishings and decorating to complete the makeover.

She would be starting a new job soon. Maybe that would be a good time to cut the strings and go home. Her stomach soured at the prospect of nights alone in the big empty house. She knew Tucker would be disappointed. Since the adoption, she and the puppy had spent more time here with Jule and Sirius than they had in their own house. He probably thought *this* was home.

Randi sat on the front porch with the dogs. She was grateful for the shade in the mid-July heat. Even in shorts and a tank, it was hot and humid, but she didn't mind. Being here when Jule got home was now a daily routine and her favorite part of the day. Sirius stretched out beside her with his ears perked and eyes glued to the driveway. Tucker sat at her feet and nuzzled her hand.

"Don't worry. She'll be home soon."

Not five minutes later, Jule pulled in. The dogs bounded down the steps to greet her. Randi stood as Jule met her at the top of the steps and they kissed as if they hadn't seen each other in months.

"How was your day, angel?"

"Not nearly as good as the last two minutes. You?"

"Every day is a gift. Especially when I'm with you."

Jule smiled at her and Randi's heart did a flip-flop. It was amazing how she still had that effect on her. They went inside. Randi poured them cold drinks while Jule went upstairs to change into shorts and a T-shirt.

"Thanks, love," said Jule, taking the chilled glass from her and sitting at the kitchen table. Things at work had improved for Jule as well. She and her friends had finally adapted to the new dynamic and were getting along much better. Jule also seemed to be embracing her increased responsibilities with more confidence.

Randi sat next to her and contemplated her next move. She folded her hands together and flexed her fingers, her knee bouncing beneath the table.

"What's on your mind, Randi?"

"Two things, actually."

"Okay. I'm all ears."

Geez, this was more nerve-wracking than she'd expected.

"Randi?"

"Yeah, right. I got a job offer today."

"Baby, that's great! Where?"

"At the Portsmouth PD."

Jule's smile disappeared. "What? You're going back? How can you—"

"Jule, wait. It's not what you think. Tim asked me if I wanted to join the K-9 Unit. As a *dog trainer*. All I have to do is take the instructional courses and pass the exams and then I'll be part of the team that trains our dogs. No fieldwork."

Jule took a moment to absorb the news. Though her expression softened, she still looked worried.

Randi squeezed her hand and looked at her earnestly. "I won't have to go back on the streets, and I'll still be helping my community. My only responsibilities will involve training the dogs and taking care of them. What do you think?"

Jule reached out and lightly stroked Randi's cheek. "I think it's perfect. But what about your photography?"

"I can still do that for fun."

"But it's your dream. Are you sure this is what you want?"

Randi smiled. "Yes, it is. For now, anyway. Besides, if I don't like it, I can always change my mind, can't I? It's my life, right?"

Jule grinned. "Right." She kissed her cheek. "You said you had two things to talk about. What's the second?"

She'd been nervous about asking this all day, but she had a feeling Jule had been thinking the same thing lately.

"Mom and Dad."

Jule furrowed her brow. "Is everything all right with them?"

"Yeah. They're great. I've been thinking about something Dad said at the cookout, though. About them moving out of Aunt Sandy's house and getting their own place." *Please let me be right about this.* "I was thinking about letting them stay at mine. It's theirs, really. Mom bought it with the money she made off the sale of the old house."

"And?"

At that moment, Tucker jumped up and placed his front paws on Jule's leg.

Randi laughed. "And Tucker wants to know if he can live here with you and Sirius."

Jule smiled and laughed. "*Tucker* wants to know? Of course he can. There is one condition."

"What would that be?"

Jule shooed Tucker off her thigh and came around the table. She took Randi's face in her hands and kissed her. "That you move in with him. Permanently, that is."

"You read my mind." Randi took Jule's hand and pressed Jule's palm to her chest. "Feel that? That's my heart, beating for you. For us. I'm finally happy."

"I'm happy, too." Jule kissed her deeply. "Are you sure you're ready for this?"

"Positive."

"I'm a pain in the ass, you know."

Randi laughed. "It's one of the things I love most about you."

Randi kissed her, tasting the sweetness she would always crave, savoring the love she would always cherish, and knowing she could never want for more. Their lips parted and she looked into Jule's eyes.

"I love you, Jule."

"I love you too, baby. This must be what heaven feels like."

Randi shook her head. "Heaven's gonna have to wait."

"And why is that?"

"Because some things are worth living for."

Jule pulled her into her arms. "I couldn't agree more."

# About the Author

Holly Stratimore has spent a lifetime expressing herself creatively. She has played guitar and written songs since the age of ten, and performed publicly at open mikes and benefit shows. She discovered a joy for writing fiction during high school when she wrote seven humorous stories that featured herself and her friends as the characters. In 2007, Holly began focusing her creative energies on writing lesbian romance. She made her debut in 2015 with *Songs Unfinished*.

A native New Englander, Holly enjoys cheering for the Boston Red Sox, attending concerts, walks on the beach, backyard barbecues, and making people laugh—and groan—with her puns and quick wit. She loves participating in author events where she can meet readers, hang out with fellow authors, and talk about writing. She and her wife reside in New Hampshire.

Holly loves connecting with fans and other authors:

Website: www.hollystratimore.com
Facebook: Holly Stratimore-Author
Twitter: @HollyStratimore

# Books Available from Bold Strokes Books

**18 Months** by Samantha Boyette. Alissa Reeves has only had two girlfriends and they've both gone missing. Now it's up to her to find out why. (978-1-62639-804-7)

**Arrested Hearts** by Holly Stratimore. A reckless cop who hates her life and a health nut who is afraid to die might be a perfect combination for love. (978-1-62639-809-2)

**Capturing Jessica** by Jane Hardee. Hyperrealist sculptor Michael tries desperately to conceal the love she holds for best friend, Jess, unaware Jess's feelings for her are changing. (978-1-62639-836-8)

**Counting to Zero** by AJ Quinn. NSA agent Emma Thorpe and computer hacker Paxton James must learn to trust each other as they work to stop a threat clock that's rapidly counting down to zero. (978-1-62639-783-5)

**Courageous Love** by KC Richardson. Two women fight a devastating disease, and their own demons, while trying to fall in love. (978-1-62639-797-2)

**One More Reason to Leave Orlando** by Missouri Vaun. Nash Wiley thought a threesome sounded exotic and exciting, but as it turns out the reality of sleeping with two women at the same time is just really complicated. (978-1-62639-703-3E)

**Pathogen** by Jessica L. Webb. Can Dr. Kate Morrison navigate a deadly virus and the threat of bioterrorism, as well as her new relationship with Sergeant Andy Wyles and her own troubled past? (978-1-62639-833-7)

**Rainbow Gap** by Lee Lynch. Jaudon Vickers and Berry Garland, polar opposites, dream and love in this tale of lesbian lives set in Central Florida against the tapestry of societal change and the Vietnam War. (978-1-62639-799-6)

**Steel and Promise** by Alexa Black. Lady Nivrai's cruel desires and modified body make most of the galaxy fear her, but courtesan Cailyn Derys soon discovers the real monsters are the ones without the claws. (978-1-62639-805-4)

**Swelter** by D. Jackson Leigh. Teal Giovanni's mistake shines an unwanted spotlight on a small Texas ranch where August Reese is secluded until she can testify against a powerful drug kingpin. (978-1-62639-795-8)

**Without Justice** by Carsen Taite. Cade Kelly and Emily Sinclair must battle each other in the pursuit of justice, but can they fight their undeniable attraction outside the walls of the courtroom? (978-1-62639-560-2)

**21 Questions** by Mason Dixon. To find love, start by asking the right questions. (978-1-62639-724-8)

**A Palette for Love** by Charlotte Greene. When newly minted Ph.D. Chloé Devereaux returns to New Orleans, she doesn't expect her new job, and her powerful employer—Amelia Winters—to be so appealing. (978-1-62639-758-3)

**By the Dark of Her Eyes** by Cameron MacElvee. When Brenna Taylor inherits a decrepit property haunted by tormented ghosts, Alejandra Santana must not only restore Brenna's house and property but also save her soul. (978-1-62639-834-4)

**Cash Braddock** by Ashley Bartlett. Cash Braddock just wants to hang with her cat, fall in love, and deal drugs. What's the problem with that? (978-1-62639-706-4)

**Death by Cocktail Straw** by Missouri Vaun. She just wanted to meet girls, but an outing at the local lesbian bar goes comically off the rails, landing Nash Wiley and her best pal in the ER. (978-1-62639-702-6)

**Gravity** by Juliann Rich. How can Ellie Engebretsen, Olympic ski jumping hopeful with her eye on the gold, soar through the air when all she feels like doing is falling hard for Kate Moreau, her greatest competitor and the girl of her dreams? (978-1-62639-483-4)

**Lone Ranger** by VK Powell. Reporter Emma Ferguson stirs up a thirty-year-old mystery that threatens Park Ranger Carter West's family and jeopardizes any hope for a relationship between the two women. (978-1-62639-767-5)

**Love on Call** by Radclyffe. Ex-Army medic Glenn Archer and recent LA transplant Mariana Mateo fight their mutual desire in the face of past losses as they work together in the Rivers Community Hospital ER. (978-1-62639-843-6)

**Never Enough** by Robyn Nyx. Can two women put aside their pasts to find love before it's too late? (978-1-62639-629-6)

**Two Souls** by Kathleen Knowles. Can love blossom in the wake of tragedy? (978-1-62639-641-8)

**Camp Rewind** by Meghan O'Brien. A summer camp for grown-ups becomes the site of an unlikely romance between a shy, introverted divorcee and one of the Internet's most infamous cultural critics—who attends undercover. (978-1-62639-793-4)

**Cross Purposes** by Gina L. Dartt. In pursuit of a lost Acadian treasure, three women must not only work out the clues, but also the complicated tangle of emotion and attraction developing between them. (978-1-62639-713-2)

**Imperfect Truth** by C.A. Popovich. Can an imperfect truth stand in the way of love? (978-1-62639-787-3)

**Life in Death** by M. Ullrich. Sometimes the devastating end is your only chance for a new beginning. (978-1-62639-773-6)

**Love on Liberty** by MJ Williamz. Hearts collide when politics clash. (978-1-62639-639-5)

**Serious Potential** by Maggie Cummings. Pro golfer Tracy Allen plans to forget her ex during a visit to Bay West, a lesbian condo community in NYC, but when she meets Dr. Jennifer Betsy, she gets more than she bargained for. (978-1-62639-633-3)

**Smoldering Desires** by C.E. Knipes. Evan McGarrity has found the man of his dreams in Sebastian Tantalos. When an old boyfriend from Sebastian's past enters the picture, Evan must fight for the man he loves. (978-1-62639-714-9)

**Taste** by Kris Bryant. Accomplished chef Taryn has walked away from her promising career in the city's top restaurant to devote her life to her five-year-old daughter and is content until Ki Blake comes along. (978-1-62639-718-7)

**The Second Wave** by Jean Copeland. Can star-crossed lovers have a second chance after decades apart, or does the love of a lifetime only happen once? (978-1-62639-830-6)

**Valley of Fire** by Missouri Vaun. Taken captive in a desert outpost after their small aircraft is hijacked, Ava and her captivating passenger discover things about each other and themselves that will change them both forever. (978-1-62639-496-4)